MERCY

BILL LITTLEFIELD

Black Rose Writing | Texas

The author grants the final approval for this literary material.

First printing

This is a work of fiction. Names, characters, businesses, places, events, and incidents are either the products of the author's imagination or used in a fictitious manner. Any resemblance to actual persons, living or dead, or actual events is purely coincidental.

ISBN: 978-1-68433-994-5
PUBLISHED BY BLACK ROSE WRITING
www.blackrosewriting.com

Printed in the United States of America
Suggested Retail Price (SRP) $20.95

Mercy is printed in Gentium Book Basic

*As a planet-friendly publisher, Black Rose Writing does its best to eliminate unnecessary waste to reduce paper usage and energy costs, while never compromising the reading experience. As a result, the final word count vs. page count may not meet common expectations.

Praise for

MERCY

"In clear prose and crisp dialogue, Littlefield deftly explores the themes of life and death, love and betrayal, family and forgiveness. We should all have mercy in our hearts and *Mercy* on our bookshelves."

–Jim Hirsch, author of
Hurricane: The Miraculous Journey of Rubin Carter

"Crackling with energy, and quick with life, *Mercy* hooks us from the start, and surprises us all the way. But its real surprise lies in its wisdom: this book has much to tell us about life and what it's really like. Written by a man who knows about a lot more than baseball, it's a wonder and a pleasure."

–Gish Jen, award-winning author of *The Resisters*

"Littlefield has long been one of America's quintessential raconteurs. With *Mercy*, that reputation grows beyond the sports narratives that he has enchanted us with for so many years, and plunges into a most human story, one that asks us to have empathy and appreciation for those who travel with us, whether as family, as friends, or just people we pass on the street."

–Amy Bass, author of *One Goal*

MERCY

BOY IN THE YARD

"What did you say?"

"What I could," I said.

Henry put down his coffee and looked at me.

"How old is he?"

"Eleven," I said.

"And how did he ask?"

"I don't remember exactly," I said. "It was something like, 'What happens when you die?' or maybe, "What happens after you're dead?' I'm not sure."

"Yikes," Henry said. Then, "Jack, maybe we should have some more coffee."

"I told him some people believe that after you die you're judged, and that judgment determines where your spirit or soul will spend eternity."

"He's eleven," Henry said.

"I had to say something," I said. "Or I thought I did. I told him some people say you go to heaven, which they think is a place where you see the people you loved while you were alive."

"He didn't ask about the other people?"

"Of course, he did. I told him the other people got punished for whatever they'd done wrong during their lives. Maybe they got to heaven later."

"How did he take that?"

"He said, 'Everything you've done wrong?' So, I told him it was maybe only the really important things."

"That can't have helped much at eleven. Taking an extra cookie, right?"

"Right," I said. "Stupid."

Henry shrugged. He is a friend.

"I also told him some people don't believe you go anywhere after you die. He thought about that for a minute, and then asked if they thought you just kind of went to sleep."

"Okay," Henry said.

"I told him I didn't think it was like that, and then I said, 'You know, there was a time before you were born. There was a time before your mother and I were born. Maybe it's like that after you die. Like the time before you were born. It's not like you're asleep. It's just like you're not. Except that people remember you. Some people.'"

"You covered a lot of ground," Henry said. "I'll give you that."

Then he looked at his watch.

"I've got to go," he said. "Ann's taking me to meet her parents."

But he didn't get up, and after a moment, he shook his head and asked, "How'd he take it? About the people remembering you after you die?"

"He said, 'Like Babe Ruth?' And I said, 'Sure. Or Walter Johnson.'"

"You remember Walter Johnson," Henry said.

"I was thinking about a story I'd read somewhere," I said. "Walter Johnson sounds like he was a good guy."

"Ah," Henry said. He still didn't get up. He is a friend.

"I suppose I could have said, 'When you die, you go to heaven.'"

"No doubt," Henry said.

"No judgment," I said.

"You think that was maybe what confused him? The part about the judgment?"

"He didn't say he was confused," I said. "He's watched a lot of baseball, you know? Enough to know that sometimes the better team loses."

"Where is he now?"

I pointed out the window. The boy was in the middle of the long, narrow backyard with a baseball and a bat. He was tossing the ball into the air and hitting it, while simultaneously narrating a game full of players only he could see. He was wearing his jersey, a St. Louis Cardinals knock-off, with the red bird perched on the yellow bat. The game wouldn't start for hours. I would drive him to the park and watch from the four-row wooden bleachers. On the way home, we'd talk about how he and his teammates had done, who'd played well, whether the umpire, a high school kid, had been any good.

Henry watched the boy for a while, and then said, "What's all the junk under the tree?"

"Tree house in progress," I said.

"Not much progress," Henry said. "But, hey, look at him out there, swinging the bat, announcing home runs. He looks happy."

"I hope so," I said.

Henry got up and nodded. "Looks like it," he said. "And that business about dead being like before you were born, that's not bad. I'm gonna try to remember that, just in case."

"Yeah," I said. "Good luck with Ann's parents. Take care of yourself."

"You, too," he said.

When I closed the door behind Henry, the boy heard the noise and looked up from his game. He waved. He was smiling.

ARTHUR BALADINO GOES HOME TO DIE

"His mistake was breathin' without the gizmo, there. That thing, whatever the hell you call it."

"The oxygen, there," Gibby said.

"Yeah. He'da kept it on, that oxygen, he'da been okay. Or jumped back on it when the guy was comin' in."

"How was he gonna know when somebody was comin' in? He's in bed. He's watchin' the TV, there, the Bruins, whatever. Even if it's the news he's got on, it's not anything on there about the guy's comin' to check on him, is it? That news is not making the cut. After the fire and the wreck on 128, whatever, they still got the dog rescued out of a drainpipe. No room left for the guy's gonna go see if Arthur Baladino's healthier than they said he was when they let him out."

"Which he wasn't, right? That's not a mistake they're gonna make. They let him out, he's down to about 80 pounds, my guess."

. . .

When he was first incarcerated, Arthur Baladino had been closer to 280. Francis had known him a little then. Worked for him, called on Gibby to help him out from time to time, and then more often after it had worked out.

After Arthur Baladino was arrested and incarcerated for the last time, Francis had kept doing what he was told to do, and beyond that he'd done what he could for Arthur Baladino for as long as anybody could do anything, maybe longer than most would have done something. When Arthur Baladino had come home after he'd been granted his release from prison because it was determined that he was about to die, Francis had come to see him.

"Not that it was business," Francis had told Gibby. "Because by then, it wasn't, which maybe you know."

"But not when he was still in," Gibby had said.

"No," Francis said. "Which you wouldn't do, either, because he was in a bed in a room full of other guys sick as he was, maybe, and none of 'em could get up outta bed. Visit somebody inside, that's not so good. I don't have to tell you about that. But in the hospital ward everybody's sick. It's worse. Smells bad, too."

"But he's out. How'd he do it?"

"He didn't do anything," Francis said. "Well, I mean, he got old and sick is what he did. Then a guy that's soft on guys like Arthur, he got him on a list where a doctor can go see him, can say he's no danger to anybody, prob'ly can't pick up a gun, somebody lays it on the bed there, and he gets to go home to die."

"The doctor goes into the ward, the infirmary, there, in the prison, and Arthur Baladino is lyin' there, and he takes him home?"

"Yeah, well, he sees 'im," Francis said. "Then there are a lotta forms he's gotta fill out, this doctor does. He has to say if it wasn't ol' Arthur, doin' the rest of his life for all what he's done, various things, he'd been in a hospice somewhere, somebody spongin' his head with cool water, rubbin' his lips with an ice cube, askin' does he wanna see a priest."

"So he was that bad off?"

"Musta been. Bad enough so when they got the forms from the doctor, he fills 'em out, they don't squawk, because Arthur's still in bed. They know that. Prob'ly on camera, too. Watch him fuckin' gaspin', ya know? They can do that."

"Jesus," Gibby said.

"Anyway, they let him out. Or they roll him out is what they do. And they're not worried about him, what he's gonna do."

"Took some time, though, I bet."

"Yeah, of course. The guy who got in touch with the doctor, this guy got some other guys out, too. Not just Arthur. And he's on the people upstairs sayin', now, get this done or it won't matter. He's gonna die where he is, they don't step on it."

"So they do."

"They do," Francis said. "It's nothin' to them where he dies, is what I think. And Arthur's good with that. I mean, as much as anybody can tell, seems like he is. The time I go see him after he's home, he's not sayin' much. Watchin' the TV, like I said."

"Same as before," Gibby said.

"'Bigger'n the one in there,' he told me. He was smilin' when he said that. So that was good."

"But he didn't die like he was supposed to."

"He did not," Francis said.

Gibby thought about it. He wondered if it had occurred to Arthur Baladino that he wasn't holding up his part of the deal. He was supposed to die with gratitude in his heart, maybe whispering the name of the guy who'd gotten him out. Made it so he could die at home in his own bed. Say "God bless 'im," or something.

"Only who knows what somebody thinks when they're about to die?" Gibby thought. "Maybe at the end, they don't think at all. Just hold on down there, somewhere below thinking."

It was occurring to Gibby that what Arthur Baladino would be thinking about—if he was thinking and not just holding on—was maybe some of the things he'd done, and Gibby would not wish that on anybody, even and maybe especially on Arthur Baladino.

"Which, about a lot of them, I don't know," Gibby was thinking. "But enough of the things, I know some, so's I'd have something to say to save my own ass if it ever came to somebody asking me about it, if it was a grand jury listening. Because some of those things, you and I did 'em, Francis. We never killed anybody for him, or for anybody else, if it comes to that, but that doesn't get us off the hook when the questions come, either of us, which they don't have to be about Arthur Baladino himself, he being dead and all. But here we are. So let's hope that does not come to pass, even if I don't have to worry about Arthur Baladino getting upset with me."

"So then," Francis was saying, "the probation guy comes to see Arthur, and he notices right away that Arthur is not dead, because there's no putting anything over on those probation guys, or at least the ones been on the job for more'n a couple days."

"Still," Gibby said, "you'd think . . ."

"There's the issue," Francis said. "You'd think. I would, too. But that's not how it goes. Ol' Arthur's sittin' up in bed, he's eatin' a fruit cup or somethin', I don't know, chocolate ice cream, and the oxygen's sittin' beside him, and it's buzzin' away, I guess, but he's not usin' it."

"He don't need it?"

"He don't need it when he's eatin' ice cream is what I think," Francis said.

Gibby nodded and Francis went on.

"But the probation guy looks at Arthur, and he thinks Arthur looks pretty good for a guy's supposed to be dyin', and he says so. So Arthur, what's he gonna do? He tells the guy to go fuck himself, which another guy might shrug off, you know, given the situation and all. But not this guy, so maybe he is new on the job at that."

"He took it personal," Gibby said.

Francis smiled and nodded.

"He did, yes," he said. "And he goes back to the office and wonders out loud if maybe Arthur Baladino is too healthy to be out of prison. Maybe if he can eat that many fruit cups or ice cream, he could pick up a gun after all, and he goes out there and shoots somebody like he was 35 again. And somebody hears what the guy says, a lotta guys prob'ly, they hear it, and pretty soon the guy that got him out—"

"The guy who's soft on guys like Arthur," Gibby said.

"Right," Francis said. "He's gotta call the doctor and say go see Arthur, so if anybody asks, he can tell 'em—that doctor can—that Arthur's still almost dead, like he was."

"Doctors are busy guys," Gibby said.

"But this guy goes, the doctor," Francis said. "And he says, 'Yeah, it's still true. Arthur's not goin' anywhere. But there was gonna be a hell of a fight, because the probation guy's no quitter, whatever else you might say about him. Or there might have been. That's what I heard."

Gibby didn't say anything for a while. He was remembering some of the stories he'd heard about Arthur Baladino. He was glad he didn't know where all the bodies were buried, but he was worried that he knew somebody who probably did, or else certainly did, and another guy who maybe did, and he was thinking about that. The second guy, who talked like he knew what he was talking about was the guy who told Gibby about the security guard Arthur Baladino had shot in the face. "Shot his face off" is what the guy had told Gibby, who thought that was probably the way it had happened.

He was thinking that had been a long time ago.

He was wondering about dying in a terrible moment of shock, when somebody shoots your face off, and then about dying at the end of a long time lying in a prison hospital, which Francis had described to him in detail, and Francis had been close enough to know.

He was thinking about dying in the middle of somebody else's argument, about where you should die and when you were going to do it.

He said, "Maybe it was a good thing he died when he did."

"Maybe it was, at that," Francis said. "Quiet, prob'ly. With the oxygen humming along, there, like it was supposed to. That would have been how it was, right? Just his wife there. Maybe some music or something. She might have put it on. The radio. Or maybe the TV still on."

Francis stopped talking. Gibby looked at him. He realized he was wondering how Francis would die. He wondered if he'd be around to talk to somebody about it after.

Then Francis was talking again about how Gibby was right that it was a good thing for Arthur Baladino.

"Because if the trip back to prison in that van didn't kill him, the smaller TV, the little black and white one in there, I think that woulda done it."

THIS IS NOT WILD COUNTRY

"A coyote, you think?"

"Selective coyote, if it was," I said.

"My sons looked all over the yard. No sign of the head."

"Weird," I said. "Maybe a zombie coyote."

"Only wanted the brains, you think?"

The headless rabbit looked full-grown. Robbie's dog had found it. The dog hadn't had to search. The corpse had been in the short grass, halfway up the slope that leads to the far border of Robbie's yard. The yard, maybe a quarter of an acre, is fenced in, but in a few places the boards have been rotted by ground water.

"The dog get at it?"

"No," Robbie said. "I was right behind him. I kicked it away from him and picked it up."

This is not wild country. Robbie Tiernan lives down the street from me and Audrey and the boy, past the Baladino house and its big yard, below it, on the downhill side. His neighbor on the other side is maybe forty feet from Robbie's fence, which is white pickets, close enough together so his little dog can just squeeze between them. A skinny, determined coyote, maybe. Or maybe the coyote got in by digging under one of the rotten boards. However it happened, funny that the rabbit couldn't have found the same way out.

Further down the hill are two big colonials under construction on a lot where one small ranch stood until last winter. The guy who'd lived in the ranch lost his business, then his house. One day when I was walking our dog, I ran into the developer who was putting up the two new houses. He told me they'd go for $1.8 million each. I wondered where the guy who'd sold him the ranch and the property was living. The developer didn't know, of course. He looked like maybe he didn't understand why I'd asked.

Robbie still had the rabbit—everything but its head—in a brown paper bag when I came down the street with Corkie. The two dogs play together in the yard all the time. When we walk by the house, if Robbie's dog isn't in the yard, Corkie sticks her nose between the slats in the fence and whimpers. Robbie's good with my letting Corkie into the yard if his dog's there, even when nobody's home. Left alone, his dog will run around in the yard, up and down the hill, until his tongue hangs out. Then he'll lie down for a few minutes, roll over, jump up, and run some more.

"Probably better not to let her in now," Robbie said.

"World's oldest puppy," I said.

I don't know if he was worried there might be another headless rabbit on the ground somewhere, or if it was just that his little dog was still jumpy.

Down the hill, the men preparing to lay the foundation for the second big house had some heavy machinery banging away at a buried rock. Robbie saw that I was looking at them.

"Starts at 7:00 AM," he said.

"I can hear it up the hill," I said. "Not like here, though. Jesus."

Neither of the dogs seemed to mind the banging, maybe because both of them had always lived in neighborhoods full of the noise of small houses coming down and big houses going up.

Everything on our street was built on a ledge. Basements sometimes filled with water. Boston was built on fill, or a lot of it was. Well south of the city, lots of the neighborhoods are full of houses with pumps in the basement. The water flows out into the street. The streets crack. Nobody gets laid off at the DPW. The bricks in backyard patios sometimes look like tides had passed under them, shifting them slightly, enough for somebody who's not paying attention to stub a toe.

None of this discourages the developers. Level it out, sweep up the loose stones, move on, and hope for the best, if you bother to think about it.

They won't be living among us.

Robbie's dog, small and brown, jumped at the bag in Robbie's hand. He lifted it up a little and said, "Forget it, Danny." Then, "I gotta get rid of this."

I pulled at Corkie's leash to get her to follow me back up the hill. She'd have been after the paper bag if she'd gotten close enough to smell the rabbit.

"I'll see you later," I said.

. . .

"Coyote," Audrey said when I told her about it.

"I guess," I said. "I don't know what else it could have been."

"We do hear them," she said.

We did sometimes. And we sometimes had deer in the yard, late at night or early in the morning. Sometimes on Corkie's first walk of a winter day, I'd see their tracks in the snow.

"It's a good thing Robbie's dog wasn't out there," Audrey said.

"I guess," I said, but I was thinking that if Danny had been out, the rabbit wouldn't have been in the yard. The coyote, if that's what it was, would have had to catch it somewhere else, and we'd have been talking about something other than a headless rabbit. Maybe it would have been what we needed to pick up at the grocery store, or whether it was worth getting the guy to spray the trees again, since it looked to me like the bugs were winning that one, no matter what he shot up into the sky with his hose, no matter how often he did it.

Or maybe we'd have been talking about what we'd BEEN talking about, off and on, since we'd learned that Arthur Baladino had died.

"She lived there all those years when he was incarcerated," Audrey would say. "Why would she leave now?"

I had no idea. I didn't know why anyone would wonder about what Arthur Baladino's widow might do next. It was her business. I'd never met her husband, of course, and I'd only exchanged the occasional nod and "good morning" with his wife. Sometimes she'd nod, too. She'd been living alone in that big house when we'd moved in next door. One of the other neighbors, since departed for retirement in North Carolina, had told us about Arthur Baladino, or told us as much as she knew, anyway, and as much as she could guess. She'd said the house was in Mrs. Baladino's name. The story she'd heard was that nobody could touch it. Arthur Baladino had been a dangerous man. He hadn't been stupid.

The house to which Arthur Baladino had returned after several decades in prison—several prisons—was solid, maybe 80 years old, built to last. Why would the woman who lived there want to move? As far as I was concerned, that was that. There were other things to wonder about.

Sometimes Audrey and I thought about moving. When we talked about selling our house, she would sometimes bring up Arthur Baladino. I didn't think his wife's being there or the fact that old Arthur had died in the house would matter.

"Nothing to it," I'd say. "Nobody buying a house cares that a notorious guy, now dead, used to live in the neighborhood. And the way we heard it, nobody laid a glove on his wife."

"What do you mean?"

"The state. The federal government, or the tax people, the I.R.S. For whatever reason, they've left her out of it. Isn't that what what's-her-name told you? The North Carolina woman and her husband. Maybe it was part of the deal the law made with Arthur when they got him. He probably had a lot to tell them about how to follow the money. Some of it, anyway."

"Okay, smartass. Maybe all that wouldn't matter to a potential buyer. Seems to me it might if he was, like, mafia," Audrey would say. "But I don't know, and neither do you, because you haven't watched any more cop shows than I have."

She was funny, and she was right, and I acknowledged it. I'd lived long enough to know I couldn't begin to understand why some people felt the way they did about the simple things, let alone something like buying a house. But if somebody'd pulled my arm around my back and told me he'd break it if I didn't guess, I'd have said I didn't think we'd have any trouble selling the place, if it came to that, and I felt the same would be true for Mrs. Baladino if she decided to get out of that big house, though I had no reason to think that was on her mind.

Hell, for some buyers, the notoriety might have been an attraction.

("What I hear is, he shot a guy in the basement. Right on those steps.")

That would have been nonsense. Mrs. Baladino didn't buy the house until her husband had been convicted, sentenced, and locked up. But it was his money she'd used to buy it, and why let the facts get in the way of a good story at a housewarming?

Selling it wouldn't have been a problem. The only house that stayed on the market for any length of time, at least since we'd moved into the neighborhood, was an odd, split-level place that looked as if it would have been more comfortable in Southern California. A woman coming out of a divorce had it built on what had been a vacant lot that sloped down to a pond stocked with trout. Years back some guys had formed a fishing club and they'd dump trout in the pond so they could pull them out later. At night, from across the pond, the enormous house, up on stilts, every light gleaming, looked like an ocean liner that had made a magical turn to rise above the water—a mirage both beautiful and ridiculous.

The woman who built the unlikely house–I never learned her name—apparently blew through her money and borrowed on the house based on what it would have been worth if it was ever finished. She lived in the place for as long as the bank would tolerate the red ink, and then she split, leaving the key under the doormat, I guess. Except for the rodents and kids who'd break in through the back door, the place was empty for a couple of years. The wooden mailbox out front was warped, and the bottom of it hung off the post until somebody probably pulled on it and then skimmed it into the pond. Grass and weeds grew up through a crack in front of the garage door.

Eventually the bank priced the place low enough so that it sold to a couple who weren't bothered by the broken glass, the graffiti, the mouse droppings, and the fact that a lot of the fixtures and plumbing had been broken by the beer-drinkers who'd made the place their clubhouse from time to time.

The new couple had a lot of the neighbors over for a big potluck dinner when they'd gotten the place back in shape. They were proud of what they'd done. The rest of us smiled and nodded at their efforts. The house, empty for so long except for when kids were breaking off pieces of it, had been a problem. I'd wondered if it should be torn down. I admired the energy of the couple who'd bought it, and their imagination. They could look at a back door hanging off its hinges and gutters full of little oak trees and they could see something terrific. They were also handy with hammers, measuring tape, and caulking guns. As a kid in junior high shop class, I'd been advised to stay away from anything with moving parts, and to look for work requiring no tool heavier than a pencil. My idea of the perfect house would be the one that was, in fact, perfect: no cracks, new roof, sliding doors that slid noiselessly. They were roll-up-your sleeves types, and that was good with the rest of us.

It was a nice evening on the night they had everybody in to see what they'd done with the place. Or almost everybody. Arthur Baladino's wife, not yet his widow, wasn't there. Nobody was surprised. She didn't have much to do with her neighbors. A lot of what she needed was delivered. She had a car—a Buick big enough to live in—but I'd rarely seen it on the road.

Neighborhoods change. In ours, which is comfortable, people stretch to buy a house where they can raise kids and feel as if they're providing them with opportunities—schools, recreation, and so on. The kids are taught by pleasant, young women who've recently gotten their master's degrees in education. Both the boys and the girls play basketball in the church league and soccer in the town league. They learn that some coaches are terrific, and that some are idiots easily ridiculed and best ignored.

The kids grow up and move away. Their parents start clunking around in the empty rooms, then they sell the houses to other couples raising kids, or thinking about raising kids. The old folks clap each other on the back for being smart and selling their houses for a lot more than they paid for them, and then they quietly worry about whether they'll have enough to pay for something else, because the two-bedroom condo in town is going for more than they'd anticipated, and then there's the long-term care for when it all begins to shut down and close in on them.

This is how it was, and how it is, and how it ever shall be, only now there are more of them, and more of us.

Arthur Baladino's wife didn't have to worry about that. Her husband had stolen a lot of money, and he had trusted people who believed him when he told them he would have them killed if they didn't do what he told them to do with it.

When the authorities came looking for Arthur Baladino's money, those people who had listened carefully to his instructions and his threats gave up a portion of that money, just like Arthur Baladino had told them to do. The authorities congratulated themselves on a job well done. The money the authorities did not get continued to beget money, so that Arthur Baladino's wife didn't have to worry about selling anything, or about the impact on the neighborhood of a silly woman who had built a house in which she couldn't afford to live, and then left it for the mice, the spiders, and the teenagers.

Meanwhile, up and down our street and on the streets to which it led, more large houses welcomed new owners after more small houses had been knocked down. The new owners would become older owners, their children, having played soccer and basketball, would leave home, and the homeowners, now old, would wonder if they really needed so much house. Or one of the two of them would die, or fall in love with somebody at the office, or lose the family money by trading stock late at night on the computer in the basement rec room, surrounded by knotty pine paneling and banners featuring team logos. He would complain—this hapless stock trader would—that his computer was too slow, at least compared to the computers people were tapping on half a world away, but the problem was not that. The problem was that the guy at the keyboard in the basement, whose name was Andy Evans, was, himself, too slow, and not just by a nose, but by several lengths. The light in his basement would be the only one on in the neighborhood, except for the flashlight under the covers in the hand of the teenager in a house down the street. She would be reading *Oliver Twist*. She would only read it after everybody in her family had gone to bed, so that nobody would know. She would not tell her friends, who would know Dickens only as the author of *Great Expectations*, an abridged edition of which they'd had to read in 8th grade, at which point they'd discovered CliffsNotes, for which they had been grateful, because who wanted to read the whole book? Who had the time? Perhaps their teacher would have cared, or maybe she'd have understood—if she had been a few years older—that only a few of the 8th graders would have gotten anything more from the novel than they'd get from the CliffsNotes, and that the ones in that small group would get what they would get and move on from there without her raised eyebrow. Without her at all.

And up and down the street you could find people certain they were just where they should be, and others restless for something else. On bad days, almost anything else, and almost anywhere else, and who, with breath in her fourteen-year-old body, especially if she's reading, wants to live in the town where she was born, and where her father knows by name not only the dry cleaner and the guys running the hardware store, but the landscaping guy, to whom he speaks in broken Spanish, which he brags about at dinner?

There were those who were committed to their marriages, and those who weren't, and those who felt awful about not being committed, and those who didn't. There were those comfortable in the present, if uncertain about the long run, and how long it might be, because their backs already hurt, and those who sometimes almost wished for a fatal accident that would reveal their treachery, great or small, and make it seem less awful than it would have seemed if they'd had to live it down.

Such was the neighborhood, and such, I suppose, were most neighborhoods, except that ours included Arthur Baladino's wife, and, for a short time, Arthur Baladino, whom nobody saw, but who came up in conversation.

Robbie Tiernan thought he must have been a pretty smart guy.

"I mean, he got caught, sure," he said. "But he didn't get caught for very long. And he sure had to know something about moving money around, the way he took care of his wife."

My own plan concerning money was to die before it ran out. I had a fantasy about how it would happen. I'd be crossing the street somewhere on my way to a ceremony at which I was to receive an award, and I'd be hit by a truck. It would be a big truck, moving fast. I'd never see it, and I wouldn't feel a thing. Afterward people might say it was sad that I hadn't gotten to accept the award, but if they did, they'd have missed the point.

The alternative was too awful to consider. I'd been in "retirement homes." Once, after visiting my grandmother in one of them, I'd been walking across the parking lot to my car, and I'd heard a terrible, shrill scream. It must have been spring or summer. The windows must have been open.

"Get me out of here!" some woman was shouting.

It was impossible to think she didn't mean it.

"Get me out of here!"

I was glad she didn't sound like my grandmother, but I was with the shouter.

It wasn't that I didn't have any good memories. It was that I didn't want to be sitting somewhere with nothing but memories and a blanket on my lap.

"It can't have been easy, you know?" Robbie was saying. "I mean, the way they can . . . you know, all the electronic stuff, the way they can track money moving from one place to another. Still must have been a lot of it they couldn't find."

"Must have been," I said, though I had no idea. I had only heard what I'd heard. But I was certain the house had cost a lot, even back when Arthur Baladino's money had bought it.

"And she's kept it up," Robbie said. "You have to give her that."

He was right. Anything less would have drawn attention to her. People in the neighborhood are people. They do what people do. Somebody lies to her husband and somebody hits his kid. Somebody's got a bottle in the garage, and somebody else looks over his shoulder while he's on the job and steals what he can. Some go to church and some don't, and they've all got secrets.

But nobody lets their lawn grow long.

Katherine Baladino was comfortable. She must have known where the money that made that possible had come from, at least in a very general way. Her husband had spent more of his life in prison than out, and she'd outlived their children. Maybe she was okay with the calculus Arthur had created. Maybe not. Maybe she didn't sleep well. In either case, she got the same hand-lettered bill each month that I did from the guy who cut the lawns—mine, and Robbie's, and a lot of the rest of them. Mr. Sanchez, whose first name I never knew because he wouldn't tell me, had gotten too old to do the work himself, but the notices still had his name on them, and they still had the little boxes with the little check marks: "trim bushes," "seed," "plow," and so on. The number at the bottom of the bill was always drawn in the same child's hand.

"Plow" was the one with which I'd had problems. A couple of years earlier, I'd seen "Plowing" painted on the side of the Sanchez Landscaping truck. One day when his guys were at work across the street, long before the house there was torn down to make room for a bigger house, I'd tried to ask one of the landscapers about plowing.

"Snow-plowing. You do it, right?"

"Warm," the man said. He looked at the blue, cloudless sky, and then back at me.

"Right," I said. "Of course. But when it DOES snow, you plow it then, right?"

He pointed at the truck.

"Yes," I said. "On the side there, where it says 'Plowing.'"

"You call," he said.

"I don't want to have to call," I said. "I always get the voicemail, and I never know if the message got through. I want you to put me on the list, so the driveway gets plowed each time it snows. Regular service, just like the lawn."

I worried then that he'd think I was asking him to plow the lawn.

He shrugged and said, "Call," and I realized he was pointing to the phone number printed on the truck, under the list of services the company provided.

When I did call, somebody answered, which surprised me. Whoever it was called out a name. A minute later I was talking to a young-sounding girl.

"Can I help you?"

"I want to get on the list to get my driveway plowed," I said.

"Okay," she said. "No problem. Name, street, and number."

I gave her the information, probably more slowly than was necessary.

"Don't worry about the snow," she said. "You're on the list."

"It sounds as if you're the official translator," I said.

"I help my grandfather," she said. "Anything else?"

"No mas," I said.

"Pardon?"

"No," I said. "That's it. Just the snow plowing. Thanks."

She was as good as her word. An hour or so after the first snow of the season, a couple of guys showed up in a truck with a plow attached to the front. It wasn't the Sanchez Landscaping truck, and I went out into the driveway to make sure the guys had the right address.

"Sanchez?" I said to the guy in the driver's seat.

"Billy Pino," he said. "How you doin'?"

"Okay," I said, "but are you in the right place? I contracted with Sanchez Landscaping."

Billy Pino looked at the house. Then he looked down at the piece of paper on the seat beside him.

"Yup," he said. "We do stuff for each other, you know? Help out with the snow, Sanchez's guys come by, help us with the leaves or gutters. I hate gutters. I got no use for ladders, ya know? It all works out."

"Are you related?"

"Yeah," Billy Pino said. "Well, sure. But don't get me started explaining how. It'd be spring and all the snow's melted, I do that."

I went back into the house on that snowy morning and told Audrey about the conversation. She was not impressed.

"It's kind of old-timey, don't you think," I said.

"It's just people helping each other out," she said.

"My point exactly," I said. "They're in it together. Where do you see that these days?"

"Family," Audrey said. Then she said she thought I was easily impressed.

We could hear the two men who'd been in the truck with Billy Pino shoveling the walk. They worked quickly, without conversation. They finished just as Billy Pino was pushing the last of the snow from the driveway into the side yard between us and Mrs. Baladino's house. A few minutes later, the truck was rumbling off down the street.

It was a neighborhood in which everybody generally had the wherewithal, so it was a surprise when somebody didn't. The woman who walked away from the house she'd had built was beyond our experience. That happened in places we'd all read about—Florida, when the real estate bubble exploded; Las Vegas, where they built those developments full of houses and nobody ever moved in. In our neighborhood, somebody walking away and leaving the key for the bank to find was news.

So was somebody having to sell her house because her husband lost her money after he'd lost his own. Then there was the house around the corner where the guy lived with his two teenage sons. This was after his wife bailed on the three of them. The guy worked a lot, and the sons had their friends over all the time. The friends used the address to receive whatever they didn't want delivered to their own houses.

And Arthur Baladino coming home to die—that was news, too.

Maybe we needed the news. The grass gets cut. The snow gets plowed. The high school kids who come into the house that's still abandoned because it's not high on the bank's list of properties to somehow address, those kids who leave their beer cans and roaches on the floor, they're not robbing anybody for drug money. They're suburban bad guys bound for college. They weren't going to get caught, and if somebody did call the police and they showed up, it would be stern warnings all around.

In another neighborhood, the abandoned house or loft or warehouse might be littered with the same debris, the same empty bottles and drug paraphernalia. When the police came, they'd find kids running out the back or the front or the windows, maybe. But those officers wouldn't know the parents of the kids too slow or drunk or stoned to get away. They'd know only approximately where the trespassers lived, in which project or development. They'd round up those kids and take them in, rather than tell them to go home and "Don't let me catch you here again." Some of the kids they brought in would find themselves in the system. They'd be incarcerated, maybe only briefly, if they were lucky. They'd face hearings. Nobody would show up to advocate for them. Somewhere over the line they'd cross, they'd learn about plea bargaining.

The houses were abandoned for the same reasons, though, and kids were kids, but the ones who didn't expect to go anywhere beyond where they were and who ran faster than the police officers wanted to run would be back the next night, or on to the next abandoned house or apartment, or out on the street. That some of them had been caught would surprise none of the others. It was what happened. They'd grown up knowing that.

None of the boys and young men piling through the broken door of the abandoned house in our neighborhood had older brothers in prison. None of them had driven to the house in stolen cars. A couple of them might have been pulled over for speeding or cited for having a six pack of beer in the back seat, but nobody had been brought to the police station. Nobody had been locked up. They'd been told to behave themselves by police officers who knew their fathers or their mothers. These boys had cell phones their parents had provided, and those parents were home when they called. They may have been tattooed—some of them—and they may have been wearing hoodies, but in a pinch "they'd clean up good." They'd also clean up effortlessly. In the closets of the rooms they had to themselves there would be several sports coats from which to choose. If everything went wrong, when they went before a judge, they'd be accompanied by attorneys provided by their fathers, rather than by the court. The attorneys would have played golf with the judge. Their wives would be in the same book club.

The boys and girls in the house with the broken back door would be playing at vandalism. They might rip down light fixtures and smash a toilet with a bat, but they wouldn't rip out the plumbing. What for? They wouldn't know where to sell it, and they wouldn't need the money.

Some of them, years down the line, or maybe only months, would have stories to tell. In dormitory rooms or fraternity houses, surrounded by other young men like themselves, they would brag and laugh.

"We were lucky!" somebody would say, and everybody would agree, because there wouldn't be anybody in the room of that fraternity house who hadn't been lucky.

This was the way it was, and the way it had always been, I guess, and maybe the way it would be. You're rich and you leave the petty crime behind when you grow up, and maybe you graduate to something more grand, like the complex math that enables you to scam a market nobody's thought of scamming. Maybe one day what you and your partner from M.I.T. have figured out how to do will be illegal, but not yet, right? Stay a step and a half ahead of the legislators who aren't partnering with you. Dinner's on you, and the airplane tickets, too. Buy a baseball team for the depreciation of the assets and the certainty that you can sell it for more than it's worth. You can do it. Sell stuff to people who've been convinced that they want it, though sometimes they'll wake at night wondering how that happened.

Some days there didn't seem to be much difference between how it had been and how it was, and on other days there seemed to be no difference at all. It was hard to believe in progress when you read about how a few people were making a lot of money simply by having it, while a lot of people were sleeping in doorways, waking up sick, with their hands out.

But it was easy not to think about it. Look up and down the street, and what you see is that almost everybody has a job to do, people counting on them to do it, kids figuring they'll get at least what the other kids get—bikes, computer games, and phones to play the games on. Look up and down the street and see the yards, all kept up, dead rabbits collected so the dog doesn't appear at the door, proud of the limp, furry corpse he wants you to see.

"Better that it didn't happen here," Audrey said. She was thinking about Michael.

"Sure," I said. "He'd have seen it up close. But maybe you're right. He saw enough to have questions. Maybe that was what started it."

"Something would have," she said. "If it hadn't been the headless rabbit, it would have been—I don't know—somebody's dog in the road. A story he heard on the school bus about a cat tearing up a bird."

"Right. Remember the bird house?"

"Sure," she said. "That time the cat was definitely the bad guy."

"He wrote, 'Welcome' on the front, and when the birds came, he said he guessed they could read."

"And when the cat jumped up and knocked the bird house off the pole, he said maybe the cat thought the 'Welcome' meant her, too, and maybe he should have written 'Welcome BIRDS!'"

"And underlined 'BIRDS.' Yeah, I remember."

"At some point, something clicks," she said. "Or after a series of points, maybe. A lot of points. I don't know. I don't remember when it dawned on me that everything dies. It must have been epic, you know?"

"Probably a defense mechanism," I said. "What child could carry on if he really got it?"

"Carry on?" she said.

"You know what I mean."

"Sometimes you sound like a professor," she said.

"Could get out of bed in the morning. Could go to sleep at night. Could look a bowl of cold cereal in the eye."

"Okay," she said. "I get it."

We looked at each other for a little while. She'd been sitting at the kitchen table, stirring honey into a mug of tea. I'd been chopping two potatoes and an onion on a board next to the sink. We'd have hash browns with barbequed chicken and sliced tomatoes. Nothing for dessert. I was trying to take some weight off my knees.

It had snowed the previous night, then warmed up, which accounted—I hoped—for the whooshing sound and then the loud thump.

"Snow," I said.

"Better be," Audrey said. "That or the bed just collapsed, and there's nobody up there, so that would be some spooky shit."

"Just snow sliding off the roof," I said. "I hope."

When you have a house you find yourself hoping all the time. I hope that stain on the bathroom ceiling has been there for years, and I'm just now noticing it, because that way the leak got fixed a couple of months ago, when the guys were on the roof. A little scraping, a little paint, and we're good. Otherwise it's a new leak and I need to hire somebody to climb up there and tell me whatever, and we wait to see if it leaks again the next time there's ice on the roof and in the gutters, and it's backing up under the shingles. Just another day of trying to keep the water out.

I walked into the living room and looked out the window. There was a pile of snow beside the house.

"I can see the snow that slid off the roof," I said.

"Excellent," Audrey said.

You hope the guys with the trucks and the earthmovers don't tear up the street too badly when they're tearing down one house so they can put up another. You hope the house "retains its value," as the real estate people put it, and that nothing's falling apart where you can't see it.

Then you catch yourself thinking like a selfish, entitled ass, worrying about whether your asset is sliding a little while people are huddled at night in sleeping bags on the heating vents outside the library.

We are who we are. The rich man, the man who is comfortable and knows he will remain comfortable, can't pretend to know what the poor man knows in his bones, what he has been taught by anxiety, if not by desperation. If he has not been taught what he knows by hunger, then he has learned it from his children who have asked him for what he cannot provide until they have learned to stop asking.

As I see it, the poor man can dream about what the rich man has, and his dreams will sometimes seem attainable, because commercials and advertisements have provided the props. They have presented the images of what the poor man may never have. They have brought those images into his home. He knows the feel of the soft sheets, the silent glide of the expensive car, the glow of the sunset over the beach cabana. He's seen it all on television. He's heard the music behind the panoramic shots. He's been in a new car, so he can smell it, too.

"Here it is!" says the woman with the soft, sexy voice. "Here's the car! Here's the beach! What are you waiting for?"

We knew, Audrey and I. We'd been there for a week. We'd sat in lounge chairs on a deck that was ours for six nights, and we'd watched the seriously wealthy climb around on their yachts anchored in the bay. I wonder if maybe we didn't understand the people on those boats any more than we understood the skinny, bruised man we'd see almost every day at the café where we ate our breakfast that week. He shuffled along on scuffed feet. He was low on teeth, and his dirty, gray shorts hung from his hips. His T-shirt, ripped along one side, said "We're Jammin'!" He stumbled around the square, talking to himself and gesturing angrily. He rubbed his head with one hand. With the other he seemed to be pointing at something only he could see. Sometimes one of the waitresses would trail after him until he'd noticed her and stopped. Then she'd give him a paper cup full of coffee and a cigarette. He never seemed surprised by this. He did not look grateful. He looked as if he expected no less. No more, maybe. But no less.

"Anyway," Audrey said, "it hasn't come up again. Not with me, anyway."

"Nope," I said.

"And the time's going to come when he's going to think he needs to act like he knew all along that we were going to die, just like everybody else."

"Are you going to get him the sneakers?"

He wanted the same sneakers his friends had. We were supposed to buy them at the same store.

"Yes," Audrey said.

"I like to think he's different," I said.

"Everybody likes to think that about their child," she said.

I didn't say anything then. I thought, "You can't BLAME everybody." If there's nobody thinking her kid or his kid is different, we're finished. Maybe we're on a treadmill, but you can't wake up every day thinking that way. Nobody pictures his kid as an adult sweating over a pile of bills on the kitchen table, reading and re-reading a letter that says the bank's about to take the house. Nobody thinks about his kid as somebody who looks over at the oven and wonders if it might be a good idea to stick his head in it.

"He's doing fine," Audrey said.

She was as right as anybody can be about that.

When a baby's born, you're just grateful the kid's got ten fingers and ten toes. Overjoyed. If the baby cries like a champ, clamps onto the breast and gets it right away—the part about needing to eat—you're ready to say it's a miracle, no matter how many thousands of years it's been going along pretty well, and pretty much the same way.

Then you've got the years when they're so small it feels as if they're in constant mortal danger: an awful, barking cough that won't stop, a cough where you can't do anything but hold on and hope the kid's catching a breath between the hacking fits. Those nights nobody sleeps. Then there's the fall off a chair. He lands on his head, and right away there's a lump the size of a ping-pong ball. Jesus! What's that all about? Is his brain swelling? Do we put ice on the lump or try to push it back in?

Later there's the cruelty of children. One day when I was eight or so, maybe nine, I was walking home from school beside a friend. Another friend ran up behind us and banged our heads together. I balled up my right hand into a fist and, without looking, turned around and swung. A lucky poke. I got the head-banger square on the nose. Suddenly there was blood everywhere. It was on him. It was on the sidewalk. It was all over me, too. The kid I'd hit ran for his house. I ran for mine. I don't know which of us was more terrified. After his mother had patched him up, the kid came across the street to our yard and started shouting at me to come out and fight. I crouched below the window in my bedroom. I was going nowhere. In an even tilt he would have killed me. Even at nine I knew that. He was fighting mad. I wasn't. I'd landed my one haymaker and then retired.

It must have been humiliating, but I don't remember the humiliation. I remember the blood.

Every kid has something like that to get through. Or bullying. Teasing. Having to go to the bathroom and the teacher won't let you go. What kind of perversity is that?

. . .

Why would an adult allow a child to squirm in his seat like that? Why would she pretend not to notice his obvious discomfort? Why would she fail to call on him, the kid raising his hand so hard for her attention that he's almost falling out of his little one-piece chair and desk?

She knew. She must have known that he'd end up letting it go, and that everybody would notice, and that she could have prevented it. She could have saved him the embarrassment he'd have to outgrow and laugh at some day.

And it might not go that way. He might not outgrow it entirely, and it might be the beginning—or the middle, because who could know what had come before it at home or at summer camp or in his friend's father's car on the way home from the playground?—but part of a retreat into fantasy, because who wanted to live in a reality where a teacher got off on refusing to let a kid go use the bathroom?

At recess, when that teacher or another one didn't know what else to do with a roomful of children who didn't know what to do with themselves, she'd line us up in front of one of the two basketball hoops in the gym. One at a time, we'd shoot. Some of us could reach the rim. Some of us couldn't. Among those who couldn't was a little girl named Alicia Lombardi. She had long, dark hair and big brown eyes, which did her no good at the foul line. She'd stopped trying. When it was her turn, she'd roll the ball underhanded in the general direction of the wall to which the backboard was attached and turn away while the ball was bouncing. Then she'd say, "The heck with it." Somebody started calling her "The Heck With It Lombardi."

How long did she carry that nickname? Maybe a long time.

Children have an excuse. They're children. But the teachers? Some of them should have found other lines of work where they couldn't take out their misery on the students.

Grim surprises arise. They are only more memorable when they ambush you as a kid.

I remember a boy named Hymen Roth. He was young when he died. He went missing from school for what must have been months, and when he came back, his head had been shaved and there was an enormously long scar across the side of his skull. They'd operated for a brain tumor, and they'd gotten some of it, but later on that year the rest of it killed him. He was a little guy, and he walked around with his teeth clenched, maybe ready to rise up with fists against anyone who said anything about his shaved head or the scar, which, as far as I know, nobody did. Maybe he was angry at being brought back to school for the remainder of what he perhaps knew would be a short life. Maybe he knew. That's how I imagined it later.

I was several inches taller than Hymen Roth. I was healthy and growing daily. My shoes pinched and my pants were too short, and

I was terrified of Hymen Roth. He seemed to draw power from his rage, his clenched teeth, and the terrible secret he seemed to be carrying. I'd never seen anyone look so pissed off.

There was a girl, too. I think her name was Margot. Like Hymen Roth, she disappeared, but that was back in grade school. It was sudden. She died of leukemia. She was okay and among us during the week until Friday, when she was absent. Then she was dead.

I don't remember asking anybody to explain that, which was, perhaps, considerate of me. What could my mother or father have said? There was no school psychologist. There was a school nurse. She had a tiny office. On one wall of the office there was a narrow cot. You could go there to lie down if you felt like you were going to throw up.

We keep at it, anyway. We know what's down the road for the kids we bring along and still we make more kids.

· · ·

Was it the winter that had me thinking like that? Remembering children who had died?

Was it the jolt of anxiety both of us felt when gravity pulled the snow off the roof and it thumped to the ground, and for at least a moment we didn't know it was only that?

Was it the shorter days, when you woke in the dark and prepared yourself for the day in the dark and then, still in the dark, went out into whatever might be waiting for you or whatever you might make?

The girl, Margot, I think, sat a couple of rows in front of me and she must have seen some bright days, enjoyed them. I think she might have ridden horses. It can't always have been winter.

That boy, Hymen, I remember especially from one encounter in a windowless corridor in the underground portion of the junior high building. I was walking to class. He came from the other direction, bearing his naked skull like a challenge. He glared at me, maybe like he glared at everybody. Neither of us said anything. He looked like he might take a step into my path and bang into me, shove my shoulder, try to start a fight. He didn't.

I kept walking to wherever I was going. Wood shop? Math? He walked the other way and died.

Was it winter then? We were in the basement. Who knows? Who knows what Hymen Roth had liked to do in the sunshine?

The rest of them grew up to assume their positions. Some of them probably delighted their parents. Some of them probably didn't, but maybe the parents joined couples groups or got therapy and were okay.

They became—those former children—accountants and bankers, lawyers, landlords, operators of grocery stores, contractors, nurses, doctors, owners of businesses large and small, architects, and teachers. One, I think, a piano tuner. Many of them became mothers or fathers of children, raising them as well as they could, except for the odd several who discovered they didn't care and that they'd have been better off without kids, and would tell you so if you asked them at the right moment, especially if you were a stranger on a plane or in a motel bar. They were more or less content again only when those children were grown and gone and not likely to come back.

"Better that way," a discouraged mother, sitting at her kitchen table, drinking black coffee, might say. "Better because what she reminds me of, my daughter, is the worst of what I find in myself. My fear, my disappointment. And that's the awful . . . I was going to say progression, but that's not it. It's the antithesis of progress, I suppose. You have a baby, a healthy baby, and she cries, of course. Sometimes she's miserable. She's hungry or she's wet. Her ass is chapped. But she's full of life. She's full of promise."

The days pass and the promise fades. Isn't that the way it happens? She learns from the older girl down the block, the heavy girl, that somebody bigger can push her over, and will do it, and will do it again if she tells anybody about it.

She learns that her father can lose his job, and that her mother can lose hers, and that if that happens to one of them, the other one can scream and shout and lay blame where it doesn't belong. Or maybe it does. That's how she learns that life isn't simple and doesn't have a moral like the stories her mother or her father has read to her, if she's fortunate. If she's not, maybe she doesn't learn to read as quickly as the other girls and boys, and somebody with a couple of letters after her name decides she's a special case, your little girl, but special not because of what she's doing, but because of what she's not doing. They begin taking her out of the classroom, where she's been quiet and well-behaved, and putting her in a room with a few other kids who can't read. Or don't. Pretty soon she's bored enough to tell the teacher going through the rote motions of sounding out words to stop. And then to shout it. And to shout it again.

"I'm sorry," says the woman on the phone. "She's been suspended."

"Why?" you ask.

"She called one of the special needs teachers a name."

When your husband comes home, he says that maybe the special needs teacher needed to be called a name. A special one. You can smile at that. But you can't smile at the road your little girl is on. It's not your road. It's not the road of which you'd had dreams when she first looked up at you with eager eyes, hungry.

Over your black coffee at the kitchen table, you too can see that the road she's on is straight as a string, and there might as well be walls on both sides. She can bounce off those walls, bounce from one to the other down the road, but that's all.

Get up out of the chair and keep traveling. That's what there is to do. She will make her way. You will make of it what you can.

Winter thoughts. Thoughts of days so short and dark it's hard to remember that they'll get longer and brighter, even in the north.

BASEBALL BOY

"He won't remember this."

That was what I thought, even as I was talking to him about the time before he was born, bringing up that there was such a time, and saying that time would go on and on without him.

But maybe what I said was enough for one day. It was enough to get him outside again, anyway, smiling and waving. A good sign, I thought.

Later, perhaps, there would be visits to a therapist. A counselor. If that wasn't sufficient, a psychiatrist. Not "perhaps." There would be tests. Who could avoid them?

If you could see what was going to happen down the line, you wouldn't do this, or that, or the other thing. You might be paralyzed entirely.

Good thing you can't see that far.

Had he been desperate on that day when he came in from the backyard for something to believe in? Was it a bad thing to offer him a story if it made him feel, well, who knows what it made him feel? It got him back out into the yard.

Someday he'd decide for himself, wouldn't he? He'd do it, and he wouldn't blame anybody. Wouldn't blame me. That would be the way it would happen.

Or he would struggle.

"How does anybody get along without that certainty?" he might ask. He might ask that at any time. He might always ask it. Would that be a bad thing? Wouldn't it all be about finding a way?

One day my father said to me that he couldn't see any meaning to life, his or anybody else's, if you didn't believe in God.

"What's the point?"

Maybe not exactly in those words. Doesn't matter, does it? That's what I took from what he said.

Almost immediately after saying it, he backed off. He said something like, "I don't mean there's no meaning."

Something like that. It was as if in saying what he'd said about God, he'd acknowledged what he'd felt was a weakness. Or maybe it was that he knew, even early on, that I didn't believe like he did, and he didn't want me to wander away thinking that as far as he was concerned my life had no meaning, since that's what he, my father, had said.

Who knew anything about anything, if not my father?

Because I was pretty young when he said it. I don't remember how young. I remember where we were when he said it, though. Or at least I think I do. I know now that we reconstruct memories, impose details on them that may not have been present—were not present—in the events we're supposed to be remembering. We may have been in the bedroom he and my mother shared in the house to which I was brought shortly after I was born. Or he may have been in the bathroom, at the sink, and I may have been sitting on the bed. He may have been shaving. I may have been looking up from a book.

"If there's no God, what's the point?"

He didn't say exactly that, but something like it. And then the retreat, and the look on his face that indicated he was afraid he'd said the wrong thing.

He'd been worried, too.

Which would have been the better thing to say to my son?

"God's there, all right. It may not always seem that way, but He's there. Trust in Him, even when you can't understand what's happening, or why. It's not for us to understand. Not beyond a certain point, anyway. That's why there's faith."

Or, "Son, each of us has to figure it out."

My father could have said that. He could have invited me to trust that I could construct something meaningful, something with shape going forward, with no resources other than the ones I could provide or discover in my fellow creatures, whom I could see and hear and touch, or about whom I could read, and within whom I could have faith or not, depending on what they did and how they did it, what they said and what I could make of that.

I had mentioned Walter Johnson to Henry. Michael was back out in the yard.

"Walter Johnson?"

"A story I heard," I told him. "He was somewhere walking with a friend. A man came up to him, excited, and told him, 'Say, it's good to see you. You don't remember me, maybe, but I went to school with your sister."

As I heard the story, Walter Johnson had nodded and smiled at the man. "That so?" he'd said. "Well, it's good to see you. How have you been?"

After a few minutes the man who'd stopped Walter Johnson on the street went on his way. Johnson's friend said, "Walter, I've known you for a long time, and I never knew you had a sister."

"I don't," Walter Johnson said.

"But that man said he'd been in school with your sister, and you let him go on about it. Why'd you do that?"

"He seemed like a nice fellow," said Walter Johnson. "Why would I want to make him unhappy?"

I guess I believed in that.

Reason says that it's a bad idea to provide religious training to children since they can't reason. The notion of an all-knowing and all-powerful being might be comforting. Or it might be terrifying. Either way, presenting the idea as fact to a child might reasonably be considered a form of abuse. Children have no defense against whatever their parents embrace as truth.

When I was maybe nine or ten—again, I'm not good at pinning down exactly when something happened—I was walking to school with my best friend, who was raised Catholic. He said to me, "It makes me sad that you're going to hell."

If I'd been old enough to be a smart-ass, and quick enough as well, maybe I'd have said, "Well, yeah. That makes me sad, too. Sucks, you know?"

But I wasn't. I don't know what I said. I don't know if I said anything. I remember only what he said, and I think he said it in the morning, as we were walking to school. I think the sun was out and the trees were green, and I think I was carrying a baseball glove, which I would have been, because we played baseball after school on every warm afternoon in those days, though, again, the mind fills in the blanks, whether or not accurately.

I was going to hell because I wasn't Catholic. My friend had apparently learned that from an especially dogmatic or uncharitable nun. Maybe he'd asked her what would happen to me, a sometime-present member of a Congregational Church, where my Sunday School class was taught by an old man named Mr. Van Vleck, from whom I learned that spending a dime for a bottle of Coca Cola, which Mr. Van Vleck dismissed contemptuously as water with a little sugar and coloring added, was foolish. Because I heard that in Sunday School class, I associated drinking Coke with waste and sloth, maybe even sin, for some time, though I continued to enjoy drinking Coke.

But that wasn't why I was going to hell.

I don't remember what I said or did about my friend's contention. I must have thought about it. Did I ask my parents if maybe we should change churches? Did I shrug off my friend's assertion? Did I think it was mean? Did I wonder whether he was secretly gloating?

Based on what I can recall, meaning what my mind has layered on to the event over the years during which I have grown much older and more sophisticated in my suspicions, there was no malice in what my friend said. I remember him as sad when he said it, unless that's just something my brain dropped in to cushion the blow.

I suppose we walked the rest of the way to school together, as if nothing had happened. I suppose we played baseball that afternoon.

But it must have felt like something. That's not great news to hear at nine or ten.

Better not to lay that kind of certainty on a child, I think. Who knows what sort of mischief he or she might get up to with that sort of knowledge.

Then there's rebellion. Bring up a child in a home with no television and that child will regard television as a delicious pleasure wherever he or she finds it. Doesn't matter what's on. He will sneak into bars and whorehouses if there's a TV set.

Tell your adolescent he or she can't associate with some character you recognize as risky, right there's the next boyfriend or girlfriend. Express doubt about the wisdom of tattooing your neck, and, if you're lucky it'll be that boyfriend or girlfriend who shows up with a swastika under each ear. If you're not, it's your kid who inks up.

Present a kid with the burning bush or the loaves and the fishes when they might swallow it whole, you may face a messy rejection at the first appearance of that pinhole through which the light of reason might seep. ("Virgin birth? Maybe Mary just found herself another carpenter, a guy with better tools.")

As parents, we do the best we can. I was older than most parents when Michael was born. I'd waited longer. We'd become certain we'd not have children. We were resigned to it, or told ourselves we were. Audrey's pregnancy came after we'd told ourselves we were ready to move along alone, together.

Right away we found that except for being slower on the stairs and stiffer on the mornings after the nights with too little sleep, we were no different from other parents. We did the best we could with the infant, and beyond. I was fine with people who brought their children up in a faith, as long as they didn't teach them to think that when they prayed, God told them what to do and assured them of the outcome. I'd even be okay with that if they didn't feel like they had to tell me about it. They look sad when they do it, as if the great mystery is not the nature of God, but why I won't buy a Ford when God tells me so plainly that it would be better than buying a Honda.

For the rest of us, "best" is what you can think of in the swirling moment going past you. Then you do it. And it comes with doubt. One day the boy could look so happy playing that imaginary baseball game in the backyard. On another day he could run to the back door, breathless, and gasp, "He's going to kill me!"

"Who?"

"Mr. Baladino."

Because he'd been listening, apparently, to somebody. He knew who'd come home next door.

"What are you talking about?"

"I broke his window," the boy said. "I didn't mean to do it. I've never hit one that far."

I opened the back door and let him in.

"I thought you were hitting a tennis ball," I said.

"Semi-hardball," he said. "The one with the rubber cover. I've never hit one that far."

"That's what you said. Don't worry. It was an accident. Besides, Mr. Baladino isn't home."

Then I remembered that he was. Just. Still, it didn't seem likely that he'd have anything to do with whatever came next. I'd heard that he'd come home to die. He hadn't killed anybody in a long time, at least as far as I knew.

"Do we have to go over there?" the boy asked.

"Of course we do, Michael."

He'd known it.

. . .

The cookies were a surprise. Out of a box, sure, but still. When Mrs. Baladino set them on the table, I was afraid the kid would ask for a glass of milk.

Before he could, Mrs. Baladino said, "I'm sorry I don't have any milk."

Mr. Baladino was nowhere to be seen. I shouldn't have been surprised. I'd imagined that maybe he'd be in a hospital bed on the first floor for the convenience of everybody involved. I was wrong.

"He's upstairs," Mrs. Baladino said, and it occurred to me that she understood how a neighborhood worked, how news traveled.

"He sleeps a lot," she said. "When he's not sleeping, he watches television. The only set is up in the bedroom. I used to fall asleep to it some nights."

So, there he was for a time, next door, a man who'd been convicted of everything but mopery, watching some old movie or back episodes of cop shows, until he could beat on his pain pump hard enough to shut out the noise and get some rest.

"Michael," I said. "What have you got to say?"

He looked at me and wiped some cookie crumbs off his face with the blue paper napkin Mrs. Baladino had put beside him when she'd offered him the cookies.

"I'm sorry," he said. "I didn't know I could hit it that far."

"He probably slept through it," she said. "I was startled for a moment. I guess I imagined a rock with a note tied to it."

She laughed then. She had a nice laugh.

"Then I saw the ball," she said. "Let me get it for you."

She left the room, and the boy said, "She's nice."

The house was quiet. If the television upstairs was on, the volume was low.

I looked around the kitchen. I knew Audrey would ask about the house.

Mrs. Baladino came back with the ball and handed it to the boy.

"Next time, aim the other way," she said.

"Yes, Ma'am," he said.

I wondered what a ball signed by Arthur Baladino would be worth. Even as the question occurred to me, I knew I'd never know. I guessed that although it wouldn't have been dangerous to ask Arthur Baladino to sign something on that afternoon, he might not have been interested. Maybe he wouldn't have been able to muster the energy, even if his wife had encouraged him.

"She's nice," Michael had said, but it might not have been that simple.

"What was she like?" Audrey wanted to know.

"An older woman looking out for her husband," I said. "But not that old, you know? Not as old as I thought."

"She told me to aim the other way next time," Michael said.

"The other way is the street," Audrey said. "Don't do that. You'll break somebody's windshield. You could cause an accident."

"You could shoot your eye out," I almost said.

"You said, 'looking out for her husband,'" Audrey said. "That's kinda weird, given, you know."

"What?" the boy said.

"Nothing," Audrey said. "Go play in the yard. Take a soccer ball, or a kite. Something you can't hit through a window."

When he'd gone outside, I said I didn't think it was so weird. "He's old," I said. "He's sick enough so she said he probably didn't stir when the ball went through the window."

"She's protecting him."

"Every man needs that," I said. "Also, every man will be released."

"The Band," Audrey said. "'I Shall Be Released.' And he was, at that, wasn't he?"

"You don't think that was a good idea?"

"I didn't say that."

"No, but the tone of your voice. You don't think they should have let him out to die?"

"I don't know," she said. "Probably a good thing it's not my call, right? I just . . . from what I know of him, why he was in prison, all that . . . I don't think mercy was something he dispensed often."

"Live by the sword, die by the sword?"

Audrey shrugged. "I know what you're going to say," she said. "I know how it goes. We have to be better than we want to be. Better than we think we can be. Mercy isn't earned. Same with grace. Both falleth as the gentle rain."

"I think we hope they do," I said.

"On my best days, I'm with you," she said. "But there are other days."

The boy kicked the ball around the yard. Sometimes he told us he wished he had a brother, somebody who could have kicked the ball back. Sometimes he was glad to be alone. He played games of his own devising. Sometimes his circumstances—the only circumstances he'd known—must have seemed natural. Sometimes he must have wondered why so many of his friends had brothers and sisters. How could he not have wondered about that sometimes?

Audrey and I felt lucky. We joked that someday in his freshmen psychology class, he would diagnose himself with all sorts of problems he'd never have experienced if he hadn't been an only child. He'd have assumed that if he'd had a sister or a brother, he'd never find himself getting out of bed to check the door he was certain he'd locked. He'd have been happier.

We only felt lucky; maybe as lucky as he'd felt when we'd gone next door and the lady whose window he'd broken had given him cookies.

I suppose Michael forgot about the broken window pretty quickly. Katherine Baladino had made it all easier than it might have been. For her, the loud crash had been alarming. She'd lept up from the chair in which she'd been reading and hurried into the room where Arthur was asleep.

She'd seen from the doorway that the crash hadn't disturbed him. She'd been grateful for that. He'd have been confused.

Later she'd swept the broken glass from the carpet. She'd been relieved to see it was a baseball that had come through the window. It had been years since Arthur Baladino had been sent to prison for the last time. Still, in the moments after the crash, Katherine had wondered if there was somebody out to make a statement with a rock.

"I can't tell you exactly what I was thinking," she told Constance Evans months later.

"Because you don't want to?"

"Because I can't," Katherine said. "Because I don't remember it clearly. It was all about fear, at least at first. I can tell you that. It was images of men with guns. It was wondering if the crash was only the beginning, and then would come the explosion. And then, almost right away, I thought, 'No. Anybody who'd do that, have something against him at this point, they'd be dead, wouldn't they?' I think it was almost right away."

"But when you heard it, the crash, you didn't dive under the table or anything?"

"I went upstairs," Katherine said. "I got to the room where Arthur was sleeping as quickly as I could. Isn't that something?"

"I think it's lovely," Constance said.

By the time they had that conversation, Arthur Baladino was gone, of course. So was the house. But from time to time, Katherine thought about the boy, Michael, who had hit the ball that crashed through her window and provoked for a terrifying moment the sort of fear she had not felt for a long time.

"Of everything, every day," she told Constance. "Or sometimes that's the way it felt."

"Of his rivals? Others doing the same things your husband was doing? Of the police?"

"There was no rest from it," Katherine said.

She hadn't talked about the fear during the time when it marked her days. Why talk about it? How? With whom? Who'd have stood for it? She could not imagine then how it would ever be different. She looked back and wondered how she had refrained from screaming. How had she made the beds each morning? Cooked meals? Driven the children to school?

"One minute at a time, I suppose."

She was talking to herself, but Constance heard her.

"Was it a relief when he died?" she asked.

"Yes," Katherine said. "And no. It was quiet by then."

"Nobody driving by," Constance said.

"Nobody left to drive by," Katherine said. "I don't know. Maybe someone. But he was a very old man."

"You must have been very young when you married him."

"I was. I didn't realize then how young I was."

Constance smiled. "Well, that's something else we have in common," she said.

"But you and your husband were BOTH young," Katherine said. "Arthur was already Arthur when we were married. You probably had a sense that you and your husband would build something together. That's how it works with young couples, isn't it? That's how it's supposed to work. I moved into something that was already built. And decorated."

"Okay," Constance said. "Which is worse? You step into a world that's dangerous and ugly, deadly, thinking you understand what you've—I don't know— signed up for? Is that too cold? Anyway, you learned, I guess—probably pretty quickly—what you were in for. Is that worse than planning to be together for a long time, that you WERE in something together, working on something together, I mean, and then comes the surprise of your life. Hello, you're married to a liar and a thief, and he's lost what you thought you were working on together, and then some. I don't mean that you knew what Arthur was mixed up in when you married him, but you must have had some sense of it, right? I mean, it can't have come as a complete surprise, the fear you're talking about."

"No," Katherine said. "I was not unacquainted with his business. My family and his family—" she shrugged.

"Okay," Constance said. "But I read somewhere that the most awful thing you can do to somebody is surprise them. What I mean is, when you find out somebody you love isn't the person you thought he was. He's not the person you love unconditionally with some, you know, flaws. Whatever. He's not that person at all.

What you thought he was, he isn't. And it turns out he never was, I guess. And there you are, all alone with nothing where you thought there was something, and you thought you knew what that something was. But you didn't. You feel like a sap. And then there's the business of putting your life back together. That's the surprise I'm talking about."

"I knew who he was," Katherine said. "Not everything, but yes. I knew."

"You had your eyes open," Constance said.

"You should give yourself more credit than that," Katherine said. "You had your eyes open, too. You married a guy who didn't gamble, and then later on, he did. It turned out he wasn't one of those guys who can start and walk away. Do something else, maybe shrug off the losses and say to himself, 'Hey, I'm not as good at this as I thought I was, I guess. Better find another hobby that's not going to wreck my life. Maybe build some furniture or something, whack together a couple of chairs, see how that works out."

"You're right," Constance said. "I couldn't have seen how it was going to go. And then when it went the way it did, it was like he was a different person. If he'd lied to me before, I didn't see it."

Katherine smiled.

"Like I said, give yourself some credit," she said. "Don't be so hard on yourself. You have plenty of company."

"And I like to think I have you," Constance said.

She leaned toward Katherine and touched her cheek with the back of her hand.

"That's nice," Katherine said. "And you do. And, yes, you can."

Loving Constance was good, and Katherine Baladino was grateful for the gift. For a long time she had not thought about loving anyone. She had made her way through the days. When Arthur had come home to die, she had been dutiful. She had hired a woman to help her with some of the physical aspects of his care, and she had sat with him for hours at a time. She had watched him sleep, a man so shrunken that even the system that had housed him for most of the second half of his life saw no reason to hold him. Sometimes she had remembered the good times and two small children.

She came to realize that she had no bitterness. She did not blame the dying man for what he had and hadn't done, what he had and hadn't been.

"Maybe it's age," she'd told herself.

Now, with Constance holding her, kissing her neck, pulling back to look at her with a smile as if to ask, "What now?" she did not think it was age. Older people could be bitter. Were too often bitter.

"No," she thought. "It's maybe knowing myself a little. It's knowing that being bitter wouldn't hurt him. It would only make it harder to love somebody. Anybody.

Later she told Constance, "It's not so hard to let it go. It's really not."

"I like to think you're right," Constance said.

"I'm speaking for myself, though," Katherine said. "I couldn't tell you what to feel."

"You could if you wanted to," Constance said. "And I would feel it."

"All right, see?" Katherine said. "You're not feeling bitter now, are you? You're not blaming him for anything."

"I'm not blaming anybody for anything," Constance said.

"And it's easy, isn't it?"

"It is."

She had her hand on Katherine's hip. She leaned down and kissed Katherine's belly.

"This is easy, too," Constance thought.

Their lovemaking was not hurried. There had been no plan. She felt no responsibility for her partner's pleasure. She knew Katherine was happy with her. She didn't have to say it. She was welcoming. Open. She was patient in a way no one Constance had loved had been. Relief was part of what Constance felt, and relief gave way to joy.

Later, as they lay beside each other, Katherine laughed.

"Never?" she said.

Constance shrugged a little.

"Now you know," Katherine said.

"Now I'm beginning to know," Constance thought.

GIBBY AND FRANCIS

"Well?" Francis said. "Not 'well.' I'd done some things for him. I knew who I was doing 'em for. But it wasn't like we were cellies."

"He have one?"

"Some of the time," Francis said. "Not when I was in."

"I wouldn't think so," Gibby said.

"Not that you'd know," Francis said.

"I'm just thinking, he was maybe better off than some guys, ya know? Until the end, I mean."

"There's degrees of bad," Francis said. "That much you got right. Inside's like other places. Some other places."

"You think it was easier for him, once he was so old?"

Francis thought about that. "So old" meant what? You don't worry anymore about what you still might have to do if you were young enough to do it? You got so old, you just waited?

"I don't know," he said.

He was thinking that maybe "so old" was a little like "so young." When you're a kid, he thought, you're just take what's right there. You got enough to eat, a place to sleep, other kids around, you're good. Then when you're old, "so old," the way Gibby had put it, you're not worried about much else then, either. Something to eat, a place to sleep, maybe some other guys around, not so many of them as there were. A lot of them are gone. It's sad, but it is what it is.

"What do you think it was like, gettin' out, goin' home to die?" Gibby asked.

"Better than stayin' in to die. That's what I think. Better than dyin' with all those other old guys, been in there forty years, whatever it is. Fifty years. Maybe some of 'em were as bad as people said. Maybe they stayed bad, never gonna come out, never try for it, tell the parole board to go fuck itself, it comes to that. Doesn't matter. They're lyin' there, messin' their sheets, too dizzy to get up on an elbow. Too sick. Nobody needs that kinda company, dyin' or not."

"I'd as soon get hit by a truck," Gibby said.

"Long as it finished the job," Francis said. "You don't want to be lyin' in the road all broken up, they haul you off, puttin' you back together with operations for the next five years, some of 'em they never tried on anybody else, but here you are, let's see what happens if we do this."

"Big truck," Gibby said. "Goin' fast around a corner. Maybe a beer truck. 'Reformed alcoholic knocked off by a truck fulla beer.' How's that for a headline?"

"Whatta you gonna do, gets you a headline?"

Gibby couldn't imagine.

"But I don't blame you," Francis said. "That's okay, what you said. I had a grandfather, healthy up 'til he was 80, ya know? But his prostate was givin' him a hard time, so they said, 'Okay, you come in the hospital, we'll fix that up for you.'"

"God's little joke," Gibby said.

"What's that? Fixin' him up?"

"The prostate," Gibby said. "Only gland that keeps growin' after the others have finished. It never finishes. Little fucker."

"What are you talkin' about?"

Gibby shrugged and scratched his nose. "I think I read that somewhere," he said. "Or saw it on TV. One of those science shows. That was probably it."

Francis sighed.

"Okay," he said. "Anyway, first night in there, before they could even go after that prostate, guy had a stroke. Lyin' there in the hospital room, quiet, clean sheets, little buzzer by his side if he wants anything. Only time he pushes the button, just the once, nurse comes in smilin'. She's happy enough to help. He's a good ol' guy, hasn't been any trouble, why wouldn't she smile? He says to her, 'I gotta terrible headache.' No, that wouldn' have been it. 'Have.' He'da said, 'I have a terrible headache.'

"'I'll get the doctor to prescribe something,' says the nurse. No more'n a night on the job to her, is it? She leaves the room, still smilin', prob'ly, comes back a few minutes later with a couple pills, little paper cuppa water, finds the old man dead as a stone."

"Some fuckin' headache," Gibby said.

"What it was, he had a hemorrhage of the brain," Francis said. "Big one. Didn't even have to get that prostate cut, did he?"

"80, you said?"

"Yeah, 80," Francis said. "And pretty good up 'til then, as I got it. Still goin' to work some days. Doin' okay, you know?"

What Gibby thought was, "I DON'T know. Also I don't wanna know."

But he didn't say anything. He wasn't thinking about Francis's grandfather and his brain hemorrhage. He was thinking about Arthur Baladino, and eventually he told Francis that.

"You think, now he's dyin' he's sorry?" Gibby said.

"Sorry he's dyin', I guess," said Francis. "Like anybody would be, right?"

"Some people are glad," Gibby said. "They got terrible pain, whatever it is. Cancer. I heard bone cancer, you get it in your back, you can't stand up, you can't lie down. Just hurts like a bastard all the time. Maybe that's when you think, 'Okay, lights out is good. Nothin' worse than this. Let's go.' But that wasn't it. I was thinkin' maybe he was sorry for the things he did. People got killed 'cause of him."

"You're inside, you got a lotta time to decide to be sorry," Francis said. "He mighta said somethin' then, he felt like it. Coulda said it to somebody, I guess. Not me."

"Is that what most decide, you think?"

"What? That they're sorry after all?"

Francis thought about it and then said, "What it is, I guess, is people are people, inside or out. Some of 'em do stuff, you know, when they're young guys, whatever. Later on they kinda can't believe they done it. Or they change. They were Mack Johnson, and then they say, 'Nah, now I'm Muhammad al Shabazz' or some damn thing—they aren't the same person. They're quiet, where they used to be all strung out and jumpy. Some of it's—you know—they slow down. Get a little older, it happens, wherever you are. But especially if you're inside. Maybe you get older faster. Anyway, they change . . ."

"But Arthur Baladino—"

"Yeah. I don't know. Like I said, we didn't talk a lot, me and him. Saw him around is all. Did some work for him, like I said, because he heard I was good at it, same as I heard it about you. I heard a lotta stories about him. Tough guy stories. Maybe they were true. Some people, you know, they don't change from what got 'em in there. Nineteen-year-old punk grows up to be a fifty-year-old punk. Makes himself something sharp out of a spoon or one of those big fuckin' paperclips. Stabs somebody. Gets himself stabbed. Whatever."

"Guys you want to stay away from, I guess," Gibby said.

"I guess," Francis said. He was suddenly thinking about the difference between stabbing somebody and being prepared to stab somebody if you thought maybe you would have to do it, get in there first. He was thinking about the time he'd been taken to solitary confinement because a search of the cell he'd been sharing had supposedly turned up two homemade blades, though Francis hadn't seen them before, during, or after the search, and rather than listen to a lot of back and forth about what belonged to whom, the guards had tossed both Francis and the other guy into solitary.

Francis had handled that, waited it out.

It had been a while back, but Francis found himself wondering what had happened to the other guy, who was called Duke. He'd called out the guards on what they'd done. He claimed the blades, if there'd been any blades, had been planted, and then he'd gone to court with his complaint. He'd been locked up long enough to have read a lot of law, and long enough to know he'd be better off before the judge in a suit and tie than he would in prison issue. The way this guy Duke told it later, he'd watched a line of "pro se" complainants, guys with no lawyers, fall on their faces because they failed to command respect. When it was his turn, Duke quoted the relevant statutes and precedents and pointed out that there was a video tape of the incident that would demonstrate the misconduct of the guard who claimed he'd found contraband and had not followed procedure. Duke maintained that nowhere on the videotape would the judge see any contraband or evidence that there had been any, assuming the judge required the guard to produce the tape, the existence of which the guard had neglected to mention.

"Meaning, your honor, that we pretty much gotta see the tape," Duke had said.

"I knew what I was doing," Duke had told Francis. "And more to the point, that judge, she knew I knew. Maybe she also knew guards sometimes plant shit in the cells of people they see as troublemakers, but she didn't even have to get to that. All she had to do was say, yeah, you know, there's tape, then we got to see it."

"So you saw it?" Francis had said.

"No, we did not, and the judge did not, and this was no surprise. What we saw was the guard talking to some guy in a suit and then saying something like, 'Your honor, forget it,' and that was the end of that charge."

"He dismissed his own case," Duke had said. "And then when we were finished, that judge asked me, did I go to law school. That pissed me off, you know? I didn't have to go to law school to learn enough to know if there's tape, we ought to look at it. But I just said,

'No, your honor. Maybe later, should the opportunity arise.' I didn't say, 'If you ever let me the fuck out, anything like that. Don't give 'em the satisfaction."

Gibby was thinking he'd appreciate a friend like that if it came to talking to a judge again some time, a guy a lot smarter than he was.

When he finished his story, Francis found he was thinking about how nobody belonged in an isolation cell, and it was too bad Duke wasn't on call all the time. He was thinking about how nobody needed to wake up alone at four in the morning in the middle of an asthma attack so bad he couldn't breathe, and nobody was gonna come when he tried to shout, which he didn't have the breath for, and what were they gonna do for him if they did come? Open a window?

"It's not something you can tell people about," he was thinking. "It's not something anybody hasn't been there would understand. I been there and damn if I understand it."

But he didn't say anything at all.

"Maybe it's like war," he thought. "You can't know it if you haven't been there."

But he was smart enough to know that both prison and war were more complicated than that, and that there was no one thing to learn about either. "Because," he thought, "I laughed sometimes. Something happens, somebody says something, it's funny. Funny, even if you're locked up. So you laugh. Must be the same in a war. Guy says something, you laugh. Somebody helps you out, prison or war, it's good. You're good with it."

"And solitary," he thought, "you got guys, they say, 'I can do thirty days standing on my head,' and they mean it. They do it. And there is a kind of person that, without shoelaces or a belt or a bed sheet, he's still gonna find a way to kill himself as soon as he's alone and it's quiet. So what are you gonna say that's true about solitary?"

"Ah, I don't know," he said to Gibby. "Maybe what it is, some guys think they belong where they are. They talk about what they're gonna do when they get out, eat a big steak, sleep 'til noon, whatever it is—they're honest, they'd just as soon stay where they are. They got it figured out. They got some guys, they're gonna be all right with them, you know. Some guys been through it, too. Maybe they been in and out enough to know it's not so easy to start up again out there. Maybe they had some money doin' whatever it was that got 'em caught. Drugs, whatever. They had the car, all that. They get out, what are they gonna do? Make minimum wage haulin' shit that's too heavy for an old guy to be haulin', maybe. Live in a halfway house somewhere, sober house, whatever it is. You seen those places, right?"

"Sure," Gibby said. "I been in and out, same as anybody."

"Like anything else," Francis said. "Good ones and bad ones."

"Bad ones and worse," Gibby said. But he was also thinking of the places in which he'd met people who weren't so bad. Sitting on an old couch somebody had donated, taping his name to the canned fruit in his corner of the refrigerator and the half bag of cookies on his half shelf in the pantry, and then finding out that somebody had eaten his stuff in the night anyway. It got old fast. Who wouldn't want out? But you'd meet somebody who could hear you. Sometimes you would. Or somebody who was really trying. Gibby remembered one place, cramped as any of them and dark in the winter, chore schedule taped to the wall in the kitchen, narrow stairs to the three small bedrooms where there were always six people, always one moving in on the same day somebody left, never a single night when you had the room to yourself. But he met a guy who'd been clean and sober for thirty years.

"Christ," Gibby had thought, "a guy puts in his time like that, crashes again, you'd think maybe he'd give it up, you know? But no. He's back in one of these little houses again. He's givin' it another go. Gotta give him all the credit for that, even if one day they go up those narrow stairs and find him dead in his bed, sheets mussed like he's been wrestlin' with somebody, blood he's coughed up on the floor. But he hasn't had a drink. Something in that. They can put it on his stone: 'Died Sober.'"

Francis could see it, the small room, the single bed with the thin blanket, the scuffed floor. He felt he'd been there, too. He could see the narrow stairs and he could hear the bumping from the other rooms across the hall, where somebody was pushing closed a drawer in the plywood dresser someone else had found at the dump, and that drawer didn't quite fit, so it complained with a squeak.

"Sad sound," Francis thought.

"So, yeah. Bad ones and worse," Gibby said.

And Francis thought, "At least you could hear something. That drawer, boots on the stairs, somebody shouting 'Goddam it! Who took my Doritos?' Sounding as mad as he'd have been if someone had stolen his car. If he'd had a car."

At least you weren't in there alone with your back against the wall and your shoes with no laces.

And Francis thought, "Maybe neither of us would know what to do with a better shake."

But he didn't believe it. He hadn't seen as much as lots of people, but enough so that he didn't believe it.

"Here's one for you," he said. "Guy's in a gang, he and three other guys, they're off to the store for beer or something, I don't know. Here come six guys from another block, six against four. 'What ya doin' here?' Alla that. Somebody shouts, 'He's got a gun!' Maybe a guy does. My guy does, anyway, and he shoots one of the six guys in the leg, gets shot at himself, shoots another guy in the chest. He's dead, that second guy, in a couple minutes. Cops pick my guy up two days later. Not much trouble in it. Lotta people talkin'."

"Known to happen," Gibby said.

"But my point," Francis said, "my point is I meet the guy, ya know, after he's been in there for—I don't know—eight, ten years, and he tells me, 'I don't consider myself a murderer.'"

"Nobody guilty in here," Gibby said.

"No, no, that's not it," Francis said. "He's defending himself, the way he sees it. Maybe he even shot first. Doesn't matter. Six against four, right? Who the hell wouldn't shoot first?"

"Okay," Gibby said.

"But the main thing, his point, this guy, he's just doing what it is he does. He's out there with his guys, that's all. He's got a gun. Of course he does. Who doesn't? It's what it is. 'Murderer?' he tells me. 'Murderer's a guy does it for money, or he hates somebody screwed him outta somethin'. He plans it, right? Like an ambush, maybe. An execution. That's not me.' That's what he says."

"He's sayin' it was like a fair contest?"

"All he's sayin', he doesn't consider himself a murderer. State does. He don't."

"Okay," Gibby said. "But then comes time for his parole hearing. It's what? Ten years? Whatever it is, and he's gonna have to say he's contrite. Isn't that it? He has to say he knows what he did was wrong, and he's acknowledging that he was at fault. The guy's dead, he did it, and he's sorry."

"Something like that," Francis said.

"You had to do that?"

"No," Francis said. "I wasn't in there for shooting anybody. I got caught up in something somebody said I did, which I did do, and my lawyer couldn't convince 'em I didn't."

"But the other guy you're talkin' about. He shot the guy."

"Two guys."

"Right. Even better. Two guys, and he's not a murderer is what he thinks. But he says that to them, they think he's an idiot."

"He says he knows he was wrong."

"And they say?"

"They say, 'Yeah, right you are there, my friend, and this is why you're gonna stay right where you are. But they don't tell him that for about six months."

"So he's wonderin' . . ."

"I don't think so," Francis said. "I think he prob'ly knew this was a dry run. Kind of a practice for the next time. He's been there long enough, knows how it works the first time for most guys, and these are guys—some of 'em—didn't shoot even one guy, and he shot two, which they're thinkin' is maybe about twice as bad, or anyway one and a half times, since the one guy is still around. He limps pretty bad, but he's around. So one and a half, anyway."

Francis turned to look out the window of the coffee shop where he and Gibby had been talking. The wind had picked up. Across the street trees along the side of the road bent south. During his brief time in prison, Francis had missed the sound of the wind in the trees. He hadn't realized he'd missed it until he'd come home and heard it again.

"What else do you remember?" Gibby asked.

"About what?"

"Any of those guys."

Francis shrugged.

"You ever see any of 'em out here?"

"Hard not to, some of 'em," Francis said. "Some, no. There's some guys who figure out how to go with something different. Maybe somebody worked with 'em when they were in, ya know? One of those groups, literacy guys, whatever. Some get out, they work with other guys who got out, work to help guys that are still in, whatever. Other guys go right back where they been. Them you might see around."

"Sure," Gibby said. "Then you see 'em again when they're back in, if you're back in, too."

"Don't want that, do we," Francis said. "Guys end up like Arthur, they're not careful. Old and tired and still inside."

"Except that's not how he ended up," Gibby said.

"No," Francis said. "But here's the thing. You want to be somebody's charity case at the end of your life? It's like when you see old people in the movies, and the younger people, the people who can't imagine they're gonna be old someday, they say, ya know,

'Oh, look at that old couple. Aren't they cute? They're going for a walk in the park, helping each other along.' And what they don't see, those goddam young people, they don't see that the old man, the first thing he does that day, he coughs like he's gonna die. And the old woman, the reason she's out there walkin' is she's outta those pants old people gotta wear so they don't stink."

"You think it was like that with Arthur?"

"I don't know what it was like with Arthur," Francis said. "What I know is, nobody knows about anything until it happens to them."

Gibby decided not to say he thought he knew something about how his own father felt at the end of his life, when the old man began to understand that his medicine and the doctor's advice and his going on about another treatment they might try was just something to say while the cancer that was killing him went about its dreary business of finishing the job. Gibby had caught on earlier. He'd watched the old man shrink in his bed, watched his life dwindle to wondering whether he'd remembered to take what he was supposed to take that morning. Or was it before bedtime?

Gibby had it figured out. He knew it didn't matter. He hadn't said anything, but he'd gotten it. He wondered how anybody could have missed it.

But he also knew that Francis was right. What do you know about anything that hasn't happened to you? And even when it has happened, or it's happening, and you've still got enough lights on in the attic that you can think about it while it's going on, how do you know it's what anybody else would have made of it when was happening to them?

"You got your people who believe they're gonna go to heaven," Gibby thought. "You got your people who don't believe in anything. How's it the same for both of them? Then you got your people that regret whatever it is they didn't do, and maybe what they did do, and your people look back on all the days and think, 'Hey, I done all right. Best that could be expected, anyway.' How they gonna compare the way they feel about things wrapping up? You got your people feel like, long as there's a priest there toward the end, a guy who can tell 'em they're okay, they relax about it. No mystery whatsoever. And then there's the guy lying there, thinking, 'What the hell was that all about?' or 'Where is everybody? How come I'm here all by myself, nobody gives a damn?' How is it the same for them?

"So maybe all you know when it happens to you is what it's like when it happens to you," Gibby thought.

He didn't say any of that to Francis.

WHERE DID THAT COME FROM?

Audrey listened quietly. She was good at it. We were sitting at the kitchen table. She'd just gotten home from work. She shook her head a little and put her hand over mine.

"Do you think I got it wrong?"

"There's no . . . it's not like that," she said. "I don't think it's like that. What's the right answer to that kind of question?'

She pulled her hand away and smiled.

"But you might have asked him where that came from. The question, I mean."

"Where it came from?" I said. "I assumed it came from that he's growing up a little, and it's something he found himself thinking about. Wondering about. Concerned about. Whatever."

"Maybe it was the squirrel," she said.

"The squirrel."

"In Robbie's yard. Or maybe, I should say, what was left of the squirrel."

"It was a rabbit. And he didn't say anything about it."

She smiled. "He said, 'What happens when you die?'"

"Something like that. Yeah."

"Based on your description that was one dead rabbit."

"Absolutely," I said.

"Maybe that was all it took. For him to ask, I mean."

We'd begun talking about what I'd said to Michael because I didn't want Audrey to say something that would further confuse him. I wanted us to be consistent. I don't know why I thought that was important.

"So," I said, "you think I should have asked him where that came from. And then he would have said?"

"Who knows?" Audrey said. "It might have been a way to let him know you were listening. Or, more than listening. That you saw there was something going on under the question, and you cared about it, whatever it was. Cared about him."

"How could he not know that?"

"I don't mean he doesn't know that," she said. "Of course he knows."

And he did know. I'm sure of that.

I tried, and he knew that, too, and if he saw that the fathers of some of his friends were better at things than I was, which he must have seen, he never said it.

I'd made teams as a child, but nothing had come easy. I'd worked hard at every sport I'd played.

I was hopeless with my hands. I'd never learned to use tools properly, partly because there hadn't been any in the house when I was growing up. My father had friends who'd helped him with projects—a shelf in the kitchen, the installation of a new hinge mechanism on the storm door, so that it would close noiselessly. He couldn't have done it himself without bloodshed. It would never have occurred to him to ask me to help.

I hadn't let my ignorance and clumsiness stop me. Not entirely. I'd built that ramshackle tree house for Michael. It hung part way up the apple tree in the backyard, and "hung" was about right. It looked as if it had been crammed into the gap between a couple of the largest branches rather than planned and cut to fit. It would have been an embarrassment if anybody had walked back there to see it. Its slanted floor, made from a palette that had been left behind by a construction crew working on the houses down the street, was just large enough for two children to sit on. I'd nailed a thin piece of beaverboard to the palette, slick side up, because I hadn't thought about it before I'd started nailing. I'd never seen another child up there with Michael, but he seemed to enjoy the tree house, unless he was only being kind to his klutz of a father.

Audrey and I sat quietly.

Maybe that time there was no argument. I was thinking about what she'd said. I wasn't arguing with her, and it wasn't as if she was telling me I'd done something wrong. When that had been the case, or when I'd felt she'd said something to Michael that I'd never have said, well, few things were worse than that. Two people bringing up children, maybe especially just one child, they're bound to have different ideas about how to handle situations. They both care. The disagreements they have are based on convictions, so there are arguments, and the arguments sometimes go in directions that seem crazy even an hour later.

"You're just like your mother!"

"You can't say no to him!"

"You worry too much!"

"With you it's always, 'What do you want to do?' He's a kid. He's not going to make the best decisions, let alone be able to plan the day. You have to take charge sometimes."

"With me it's 'ALWAYS' like that?"

"'Always' kicked it up a level. And for all that, I liked to believe that Audrey and I were less crazy than a lot of couples. I think we were. I would think about the separations and divorces just in our neighborhood. The woman who'd wandered away from the house she'd built hadn't done it until her husband had wandered away from her. The guy who'd discovered day trading as a dependable way to lose the money he'd stolen from his company, and then all his wife's money, hadn't left her with much choice about what to do next. Audrey was friendly with her and was proud that she'd become a real estate agent.

But the point was that those couples hadn't stayed together. We had. Certainly luck plays into it. But more important, I think, is making a choice. Make a choice and stay with it. Recognize it's not going to be like in the movies. Sounds simple, right? What kind of idiot believes a relationship would be like that?

But the movies and the ads and the commercials keep coming at you, and holding on to what's real isn't as easy as it should be.

Audrey got up from the table and pushed in her chair. I looked up at her.

"Of course he knows that," she said. "You're a great father."

"Better next time," I said.

"Good luck with that," she said. "Next time it'll be something else. You'll be as baffled as before, same as I'd be. Or will be. Or both of us will be, you know?"

"Part of the deal, I guess."

"Part of the fun," she said.

The trick was to keep thinking that way, I guess. Or at least to try to keep thinking that way when you'd just missed a train, or when you were in a hurry and a shoelace broke, a shoelace that could have easily quit some morning when you had all the time you'd need to hunt through a drawer full of buttons and paperclips swept off the bureau and coins from places you'd never visit again.

"There's a shoelace in there somewhere" had to become "where the goddam hell is the shoelace I saw in there?" and then the slammed drawer, the near-hopeless attempt to tie together the ends of the broken lace or to make the longer part of it somehow serve.

Why today?

On those days, it's simply no use. You're in it up to your elbows, and what you've lost can't be found.

Later you might laugh at yourself. You might turn the situation into a story that could make other people laugh.

I was standing on the platform shouting at the train. I didn't say, 'Come back!' Even while I was shouting—and I knew how crazy it was while I was doing it—I wasn't crazy enough to shout, 'Come back!' Because there is no mercy in a moving train. Not one you've missed. If you're on it, that's different. It's all good. Anyway, I don't know how the people around me kept straight faces. Maybe they were used to it. Maybe they saw it all the time, you know? Maybe there was always somebody howling at the train as it disappeared down the line. Always somebody from the U.S., right? We expect the train to be late, and then to stand still for us as we decide which car to board. Or maybe the people on the platform that day were afraid that if I caught them laughing, I'd bite off their ears or gun them down. I don't know. What did they know about Americans? How could they have known what might happen when one was provoked?

You tell some people something like that, they think you're crazy. Or maybe they just think you're funny. You can make fun of yourself. That's good, right? Healthy. Some of the people laugh, and you laugh with them. It makes a story.

Others nod. There but for fortune go they. They've missed some trains. She's left her purse in a taxi. He's left his jacket with his passport in the pocket hanging in the closet of a motel room. It could have been me.

Then there is this: what if you stepped onto the train you were supposed to be on? What if you'd been on time? Been where you were supposed to be? Understood that when the train pulled into the station, you'd better get on without delay? What would you have missed by not missing that train so that you had to take the next one?

On that next one, Audrey and I had met a couple from Scotland. They were beautiful, both of them. They'd only been married for a couple of weeks. From Nice they were going on to Greece, and then maybe somewhere else. They hadn't made any plans beyond the next week or so. Seemed to be working for them.

We said goodbye to them when we switched trains an hour after we'd met. I wished them luck.

"Dumb thing to say," Audrey told me.

"Why?"

"They need luck less than any two people I've ever known," she said.

She hadn't known them any longer than I had, but she knew. She knew. And if she was wrong, if both of us were, then neither of us would ever know it, because they were gone, those two, into the future.

Meanwhile, this time Audrey and I were on a train so full of people and baggage that we had to sit on our suitcases between two cars, never mind that we each had a ticket with a seat number.

"We'll laugh about this someday," Audrey said.

"You will," I said. "You're better at this."

We didn't laugh about it that day. When we reached the station, in a stupid attempt to get both bags off the train at the same time, I lost my balance on the steps, dropped one of the bags, and then tumbled after it onto the platform.

People stepped back. Was I drunk? Just clumsy? Was I in the kind of hurry Americans always seemed to be in? Would I writhe around on the ground clutching my knee? Would I shout about suing the railroad? Who knew what was going on with this crazy American? Nobody said anything. What if he had a gun? He is an American, don't forget.

The moment passed. Everybody moved along. Audrey and I regrouped. Nobody made off with the suitcase I'd dropped, though it had rolled, clattering, some distance from the train and come to a stop against an empty baggage cart. Nobody picked my pocket while helping me to my feet, the way it would have happened in a detective novel. This was the end of the story for everybody but me, because I was the one who'd fallen off the train. How long before I fell on another set of stairs? How long before I had to check "yes" after the question on the form in the doctor's office: "Have you fallen more than twice during the past year?"

The message is this: "You got something to do, better do it now." You think you might want to get on a train without a plan? Okay, good. Don't wait until you're likely to fall down the steps when you've reached the place where the train stops.

The other thing you learn as you go along is that you can't go back. If you try, you'll be surprised at where you find yourself. You won't recognize your surroundings. The weather will have changed. I knew that much, at least. I knew that if I sat down with the boy and asked him where his question had come from, it wouldn't have gone well.

"What question?" he'd have said.

What would I have said then? "The one about where you go after you're dead, son."

Fit in between "What kind of cereal do you want?" and "How long since you changed your socks?"

Because you can't go back. And you don't know what to say, sometimes, until later, when you can't go back and say it. You go along as well as you can, and you forgive yourself for what you haven't said, and you hope the people to whom you haven't said it will forgive you, too, if they even remember there was something that should have been said.

And if you were Audrey, you laughed about it one day. It was a gift. It truly was.

"I don't know," she said. "I just don't like to get stuck worrying about something I can't do anything about. That's all."

She was fortunate to see it that way. I was not. In my dreams, I fell off the damn train again. I stupidly tried to manage both suitcases at once, lost my balance on the step down to the platform, bounced painfully from one railing to the other, dropped the bag in my left hand, and then tumbled after it, worrying all the way down about which way my knee might bend when I hit the ground.

A man with a healthier outlook would have corrected the circumstance in his dreams. He would have asked the person behind him—his father, a beautiful woman, a dwarf with a toothy smile, whoever turned up in the dream—he'd have asked whoever was behind him to hold the suitcase for a moment while he stepped down. Having reached the platform, he'd have turned around to find that his father or the beautiful woman or the dwarf had turned into a pear tree, but he wouldn't have fallen, would he? His subconscious would have averted the pratfall. Repaired the situation with an active imagination. Knitted up the raveled sleeve of falling from the train.

Audrey would have been able to do that, but she wouldn't have had to. She'd have laughed it off in a moment, except that the moment wouldn't have occurred, because if she'd been too stiff in the knees and back to climb off a train with two bags, she'd have not only known it, she'd have acknowledged it. She'd have handed me one of the bags. She'd have asked for help. She wouldn't have packed so much stuff to begin with.

That's just one of the reasons I need her. She's got it down, this attitude. I could see it. Sometimes I could learn from it. One of the things I'd semi-learned was not to stand between the two of them. Semi-learned, because sometimes I still did it, though I knew enough to kick myself afterward.

But on my good days, I could hear them arguing, or even fighting—Audrey and the boy—and I could stay out of it. I could remember that they had worked through fights in the past with no help from me, and that when I had stepped between them, I'd fouled up the process by which they would eventually work it out.

Here's what you learn if you're fortunate: You're not as smart as you thought you were.

My father never told me that. If he had, I probably wouldn't have learned from him telling me. But he did tell me once that the first time he'd returned to the campus of the college from which he'd graduated some years earlier, he couldn't quite believe that everything there had gone on and was still going on without him. I don't remember what I thought of that acknowledgment, but I remember him saying it. It registered. It must have seemed significant. Or at least funny. In either case, it was a glimpse of a larger truth: it's only in your own mind that you're the center of everything, the most significant character on the landscape of the story. That's necessary, I guess. You're at the center of everything you experience. If you walk around the corner and witness the aftermath of a terrible accident—ambulance attendants hauling broken, screaming people from the smoking wreck of a crumpled car—it's something that happened to you. You're fine. You're not going to the hospital. You're not going to wait hours for the results of the tests that will reveal what surgery you'll need or whether you'll walk again. Your legs are working as well as they did before you turned that corner and came upon the accident. But the screaming for mercy and the smoke billowing from the wreck with the tire bent sideways and the blood on the pavement, they're all elements of the thing that happened to you, the story you have to tell. How could it be otherwise? If it were, you'd be confused about where you ended and the rest of the world began.

So, there's that, and shame on us for it, though it's not our fault we're not saints who transcend the first person singular any more than we can skip eating, drinking, and defecating.

But we can learn to shut up, sometimes. We can learn to try to remember that we don't know better than somebody else what we're looking at in the middle distance, and that it's certain we don't know better than somebody else when the somebody else is in the middle of what we're both looking at.

On my good days, I could stay out of arguments between Audrey and Michael. I could let them shout at each other. If either or both of them asked later, "Why didn't you help me out?" I could say something or nothing. It wouldn't matter.

Maybe one step toward what characterized those good days happened when my father told me the story about coming back to his college campus. He'd thought of the place as the backdrop to four years of his life, rather than a long, ongoing story in which he'd played a brief and limited part. The acknowledgment of his foolishness must have mattered to me, or I wouldn't have remembered.

What about all the things he must have said that I don't remember?

I'm glad I remember that one. We see everything through our own eyes. We're urged to walk in somebody else's shoes, to imagine what it must be like to wake up hungry with no idea where to find something to eat. We fool ourselves into thinking we can do it. We write a check. Then we go back to walking around in our own shoes and planning dinner. We've never felt the pinch of somebody else's shoes, and, having eaten a satisfactory lunch, it would be no big deal if we were called away from dinner, even if we'd said, "I'm starving" as the pots simmered. Because we wouldn't have been starving. Not even close.

Kick it up a level. The boy saw things through HIS own eyes. As time passed, I would assume a less significant role in the script he was creating day by day. I could imagine a time that would come, too soon for me and perhaps not soon enough for him, when I'd become somebody he thought of infrequently, perhaps with affection, perhaps sometimes with resentment, maybe once in a while as a fumbler who built a tree house with love and without a carpenter's eye or a carpenter's sense.

The boy would grow up like anyone else, I supposed. "Like anyone else" is a hard truth for a parent to take on. You want to believe your child will be like NOBODY else. He will be only himself. His teachers will see it. No one would be so blind as to think this young man should take a job for mere money or work "with"—never "for," that was understood—but never work with anyone who couldn't see that he was extraordinary. And they would say of him, "His father must have been wise and gentle, for the boy is certainly a wonder."

And when it doesn't happen that way, if you are lucky, you smile at how it does turn out. You welcome his bride into the family, though you can see she doesn't like you much. You applaud his promotions, though the company promoting him deals in poison. You stay out of the way.

All that is if you are fortunate enough to stay upright and mobile, keep your head while others fail to see why that should matter.

Some of the alternatives are miserable. I knew a woman whose post-partum depression had her in tears for weeks after the baby came. When she could finally talk about it, she told the doctor, "I just had this baby, and he's going to die."

The doctor didn't know what to tell her. What could he say? She was right. It might take eighty years, but it was going to happen.

They called it "depression," but the doctor had to ask himself if maybe she was seeing it all more clearly than most people. More clearly than he saw things? He wondered. Maybe so. He kept people breathing so they could see how the ballclub was going to finish the season, maybe how they'd look in the spring, too, if he got the dosage right and they did what they were told to do. They were housebound, maybe confined to their beds, or they were back and forth to the hospital often enough so that the nurses called them by their first names and had their favorite chairs ready.

There were exceptions. People kept alive long enough to say goodbye properly, in some way that brought them peace, because if they thought they had it—peace, I mean—they did. People who did something momentous with their final, dearly purchased days. That happened, too, I suppose. But how often? Mostly it seemed to be a long slide with not much at the bottom.

The woman who was inconsolable when her baby was born moved on. She didn't want to hold him. He was going to die. Then one morning she felt different. She held him, fed him, smiled into his crinkly, little face.

The next day she got out of bed and cleaned the room.

The kid motored right along, too. He went to school when it was time to do that, watched a lot of TV, like everybody else. He was astonished, like almost everyone else, by what brilliant technicians tinkering with electronics could do to enable us to send each other messages more quickly on brighter screens with more amusing graphics. It did not occur to him that each time the technicians come up with something "revolutionary," thousands and thousands of workers stop assembling what they've been assembling because nobody will want it anymore. They'll want the newer, brighter, faster thing that will also be obsolete in six months. The technicians keep tinkering, the children continue to demand the new thing that amazes them, at least for a while, and the workers keep assembling whatever they're told to assemble, until they're told to stop and start assembling something else.

Nothing they can do is as astonishing as what happened when the boy's mother began loving him despite knowing he would die.

We used to have these discussions, Audrey and I, about whether every new gizmo was necessary. We decided it wasn't, and then we bought it anyway. We held out as long as we could, but we bought the new stuff, the same as everybody else. We laughed about the old telephones, so durable you could hammer nails with the handset. But we bought the new stuff. When the boy first started to play video games, we had a desktop computer that worked well enough, until he got a new game. Then we'd get a message telling us we needed to upgrade the computer for the game to work—more memory, whatever—and, sure enough, when he tried to get those people across the dangerous land, the screen would freeze with everybody starving in the desert, halfway to Oregon, easy pickings for bears. Michael was the one who started telling us we needed "more power." So, we'd get it, update the old machine, buy a new one, and that was fine for about a week, until some genius came out with another game that everybody would be playing except for our kid, because we didn't have enough power.

That may have been when I built the tree house. Maybe I was trying to respond to the relentless message about how our lives were being made better, faster, stronger by technology. That was the out-front message. The rest of the message was nothing but a new take on an ancient refrain: you were less than adequate if you didn't have what the other guy had, and if you were on the ball, you got it before he did. Otherwise you were a loser, and what kind of father wanted his kid to think he was a loser? Maybe the same kind who'd bang together a lop-sided tree house.

Everything broke and nothing got fixed. Everything got replaced. That's where the money was. The sooner it broke, the better. Who cared? A better one was coming out, anyway.

Sometimes we bucked the tide and tried to find somebody who'd fix what we had, and sometimes we found that person, and always when we did, the boy asked why we didn't just buy a new thing, whatever it was.

"You don't just tell him 'no,'" Audrey said. "You explain."

"You having any luck with that?"

"Some," she said. "Sometimes, some."

From time to time I worried that we were creating a kid everybody would hate. His friends get new sneakers, new computer games, new phones. His friends' parents get new cars, new entertainment centers, sometimes new marriages. This is even if the old ones haven't worn out.

We explain that all the new stuff means the old stuff becomes waste, and a lot of the waste is stuff nobody knows how to handle. It goes into a landfill or the ocean or off on a barge to some place where nobody's counting anything but dollars.

"That's not good for the planet," we'd say.

If he doesn't go along with it, we're jerks, and cheap jerks at that. If he does go along with our explanation, then his friends and their parents are jerks, and one way or another, he lets them know that's what he thinks, and then he's that kid everybody hates.

"You're exaggerating," Audrey says.

"I don't know," I say. "When you were growing up, there must have been kids everybody hated. Wiseass kids. Little, weaselly kids who sneered a lot. Pathetic kids with runny noses. Kids who cringed."

"Come on," Audrey said. "Michael's not like that."

"Know-it-all kids," I said. "Kids who took the fun out of everything. Kids who showed you pictures of a bike or a toy gun or a baseball glove that was better than the one you just got. Your parents went out and did the best they could, and this kid tells you why it sucks, what they got you. It isn't as good as the one that could have been fixed."

"You must have known some really crappy kids."

"If Michael goes around telling his friends they should keep their old computers and cell phones and tablets because otherwise they'll be clogging up the system, killing the whales, burning up the planet—whatever he makes of what we try to tell him carefully and with the best intentions—he's not going to have a lot of friends. He's going to be the kid everybody avoids, because who wants to hear that he should have held on to the old computer that still worked after dad, who's got to do something, because he's moving out, bought him a bright, shiny new model that runs his games at top speed?"

I couldn't know this would happen anymore than she could know it wouldn't. That's why we have arguments, which are discussions until Audrey isn't listening to me or I'm not listening to her.

But I'm not the dad who takes off and leaves behind the new computer still in the box. She's not the mom who does that. We work it out as well as we can, knowing neither of us is going anywhere, and we watch the boy grow, and we're pretty much together in our admiration of how he's doing it. We wonder, sometimes, how much it has to do with us, and we conclude that, after a point, it won't be much.

We figure it out as it comes, together, probably pretty much the way people did when they were riding horses instead of driving cars, listening to the radio together instead of fiddling around on-line in separate rooms of the enormous houses they'd been taught to require, and, before that, way before that, in their caves or under the trees that kept off the rain.

Just people, some of them more fortunate than others, the luckiest of them, like us, paired up well and forever.

. . .

"I don't think it's about luck," Audrey said.

We were sitting at the table after dinner, waiting for the coffee to cool. Michael had gone upstairs.

"No?"

"I think we've probably had as many problems as lots of couples that haven't stayed together."

"Ah," I said. I had no idea where this was going. I didn't want to get out ahead of it.

"People decide," she said. "I mean, they make decisions. Something happens—they lose confidence in each other, whatever. And they decide, 'That's it. It's over. I'm outta here.'"

"Sounds simple."

"Sometimes it probably is," she said. "Sometimes whatever happens is just the final thing, you know? The one more indiscretion or foul-up, whatever it might be, and it pisses you off enough that you finally say, 'No more.'"

"Guy keeps saying he'll call the guy to clean out the gutters, he doesn't do it, it rains, they get water in the basement. That's that. Wife's gone," I said.

"Or he burps at the table," Audrey said. "No, that's not it. Probably not most of the time. Probably it's more complicated, more serious most of the time. But even with the serious stuff—money, arguments about what they should do about the kids—does this one need, you know, testing, therapy, some drug the doctor says he'd like to try, see if the kid can sit still. Even if it's the serious stuff, people make decisions. They decide that we can talk this through, get to a place together, even if there's some shouting along with it."

"Some slamming of doors," I said.

"That pane was loose," she said. "You know what I'm talking about. And if it doesn't happen, one of them decides, 'Nope. I'm done.'"

"Probably means that one of them has already decided there's something better elsewhere, right? Somebody. Because people don't walk away from a marriage without at least an idea that there's something to walk toward."

"You sound like you've thought about this."

"I'm going nowhere," I said. "I'm just saying that's the way it seems. People leave a relationship, a lot of the time they wind up in another one pretty quick."

It was true. Or at least it seemed that way to me. And it made me feel especially fortunate not to be among those people.

"Maybe you're just lazy," Audrey said.

"Maybe I'm just happily married," I said. "Maybe I just think we made the right choice. Maybe I value that commitment above whatever you say when I forget to call the guy about the gutters."

"Maybe that's it," she said.

"Or what I said to Michael when he asked me about what happens to you when you die," I said.

"You beat yourself up about things like that," Audrey said. "You ought to learn to let yourself off the hook."

"Easier said," I said.

"No, really," Audrey said. "Suppose you DID get it wrong. Suppose what you said, whatever it was, suppose it screwed him up. Which it didn't, we know, because you told me the next thing you know, he's out there in the yard, tossing a ball up in the air, pretending he's whoever the ballplayer of the month is, and he's not sobbing in the corner, the picture of pre-adolescent despair . . ."

"No," I said.

"But let's suppose you screwed him up," she said. "What does that make you? It doesn't make you a monster, you know? It makes you a parent. We all do it. We've all done it. Always. The only reason Jesus didn't do it was because he didn't have any kids."

"I appreciate that," I said. "The comparison, I mean."

"The least I could do," Audrey said. "Besides, it lets me off the hook, too, doesn't it? I'm like you. Like the rest. We do the best we can, and some days that's not nearly good enough. You know, you have a headache, you're worried about something else. The light's blinking on the dashboard, and you lost the manual a long time ago, you can't look up what the light means. It's not a day when you can leave the car alone to maybe figure it out for itself. You need it. And the light's still blinking, and the kid's yapping about something, and you tell him to shut the hell up. You know what? He'll get over that, too."

"I know you're right," I said.

"But you're going to beat yourself up over it anyway," she said.

"Probably," I said. "Yeah. I will."

She shrugged. "Okay," she said. "Knock yourself out."

.　.　.

Forgiveness was the secret she gave me—self-forgiveness, too, which I always needed.

"The hardest kind," Audrey said. "We think we've done something wrong, even when we haven't. Wouldn't everything have turned out okay if we hadn't lost the phone number of that woman who was so good at looking after the dog? Wouldn't that vacation have been okay if I'd planned out the days more carefully so we didn't have the kids sitting around playing computer games, and one of us yelling, 'Hey, you could do that at home,' and then we go out on that bike path where there's supposed to be an ice cream stand about every eight hundred yards and they're all closed."

"I remember that place," I said. "The path ran along the river. It was beautiful."

"And the answer is a big, fat, 'No!'" Audrey said. "Because I could have planned every minute of the week, or you could have done it, and the kids might have come down with something, or it might have rained, and the bike path might have been flooded and filled with slugs and snakes."

"So, the answer is somewhere in the middle," I said.

"No!" she said. "The answer is in cutting yourself some slack. You remember the week before that vacation? You were at work late almost every night. My mother was sick."

"I remember," I said. "And the vacation was great."

"The vacation was what it was," Audrey said. "Some of it was great. The views on the road up and down the mountain were great. Some of it was not, like Michael getting sick to his stomach from the ride up and down the mountain."

"Something to talk about when we got home," I said.

"As five days of rain would have been," Audrey said. "Or the car breaking down, or a bear on the loose so we couldn't stay in the park after all. It all would have been fine, eventually."

Audrey didn't pretend everything was fine when it wasn't, and she laughed at people who thought everything that happened was somehow for the best. But she didn't make too much of mistakes, hers or anyone else's, and she moved on. At that she was better than anyone I'd known. And she helped me to see how it worked. How she did what she did. How, on my better days, I could do it, too.

Because how much sense does it make to behave otherwise?

"Sense" isn't all there is. I know that. Sense doesn't always rule, said the man who'd stood on the railroad platform shouting out his rage at the departing train. But when you have the leisure to think about the rash with which you woke up one morning, or the stain that appeared on the ceiling above the dining room table, you don't howl at the fates that have singled you out for the itching or the paying for a new roof.

The recognition of context is part of it. Somebody else's rash is a flesh-eating virus, and he's going to lose some fingers, if not his whole hand and past his wrist to a desperate surgeon's knife. Somebody else's leak is the first sign of a tectonic shift that's going to bring the house down around her.

You've got a rash that will go away if you leave it alone. The leak? Covered by the guarantee you got from the company that replaced the roof.

I know all that. Still, I wondered how Audrey would respond to something awful, the kind of thing that drives a man to his knees and leaves him sobbing and speechless. Not waking to a rainy day on a vacation at the beach, or a birthday party canceled by poison ivy or the flu. Something much worse.

BALADINO'S SON

Whether they'd heard about it when it happened or years later, nobody who learned that Arthur Baladino's son had died of a gunshot wound would have been surprised. This is assuming they knew who Arthur Baladino was, or had been, but that was and is, perhaps, a safe assumption.

Teddy Baladino had been eating dinner early. He had no interest in crowds. That night, maybe he'd have been better off in one. The odds would have been better.

He was seated alone at a corner table when three people came into the front of the restaurant Teddy had chosen. A man in a sleeveless shirt and two women. The man was partially bald and paunchy. The sleeveless shirt was a bad idea. He looked like he might have been in his late fifties.

The older of the two women was heavily made up, a lot of black around the eyes, and she wore an extraordinary hat. The largest of the several feathers in the hat brushed the top of the doorway when she entered the restaurant. The woman grabbed at her hat.

The younger woman, who might have been the couple's daughter, wore a long red dress. She walked with difficulty on bright red, high-heeled shoes. She carried an enormous leather handbag covered with straps and zippers and pockets.

Teddy Baladino, wearing, as usual, a coat and tie, was initially surprised to see the group seated. The man's sleeveless shirt wasn't clean. Teddy wondered if the guy had just come off the beach, met the two women as they were leaving the opera, and said, "Let's get some dinner." Or maybe, "What the fuck? Let's find somewhere to eat." Because the man was loud enough for Teddy to hear him say to the maître d', "Of course I made a reservation. You prob'ly lost it!"

As the three were seated, Teddy turned his attention back to his trout. He was enjoying it. After a while, he heard the younger woman say, "That's disgusting!"

Teddy looked up. He couldn't tell what had provoked her outburst. The other two people at the table were talking at the same time, and he couldn't understand what they were saying.

Then the woman said "Disgusting!" again, and as she stood up, her chair tipped over backward. One of the waiters hustled over noiselessly to set it right. The woman turned and pushed him aside as she stumbled and then started to walk unsteadily toward the door.

Teddy heard the man say, "She's crazy."

The older woman seemed to agree. She nodded, and the feathers in her hat nodded along.

The waiters were professionals. They acted as if nothing had happened. When the younger woman was gone, the man in the sleeveless shirt beckoned to one of them and said, "Put her stuff in a box. We'll feed it to her in the car."

But it didn't work out that way. Just a few minutes after she'd left the restaurant, the woman returned, still lurching on her heels.

"Give me the fucking keys!" she shouted.

"Never gonna happen," said the man.

The older woman tried to put her hand on the younger woman's arm. The younger woman shook her off. In so doing, she knocked a glass of red wine from the table. It shattered on the marble floor.

"Get a cab," said the man in the sleeveless shirt.

Maybe he thought that's what the younger woman was going to do when she left the restaurant again. But this time she was gone for less than a minute, just long enough for her to dig a gun out of her handbag and return. She pointed the gun in the general direction of the man in the sleeveless shirt and said something Teddy couldn't hear over the roar of the first gunshot.

. . .

"Stone walls," said one of the first police officers to arrive at the restaurant. "You got your stone walls, you don't know where the bullets are gonna go."

The woman who'd done the shooting had been hustled away. Her companions were unharmed.

Teddy Baladino lay under a white tablecloth next to the table where he'd been eating trout, having avoided the crowd.

"His daughter, too," Francis said.

"His daughter what?"

"Died before he did," Francis said. "Way before."

"I didn't know he had a daughter," Gibby said.

They were sitting across from each other at a worn wooden table at Murdock's, which was a good deli for sandwiches, a favorite of theirs and lots of their associates, former and current. They were trying to decide whether to go to Arthur Baladino's memorial service, which would have been a bigger deal if he hadn't lived as long as he had.

"Sure," Francis said. "She was just a kid. Only in her 20s, I think."

"She get shot, too?"

"No, no. Nothing like that. One of those cancers that get you when you're young," Francis said. "Now they got something for it, I think, but they didn't then. And then the other one, Teddy, he wasn't exactly shot, either. Not like anybody else gets shot."

"I guess not," Gibby said. "More like a bad bounce."

"But the daughter, she died in the hospital, no more'n a couple months after they brought her in. They had, like, what do you call it, a wing, there, where they just help you die, I guess."

"Hospice," Gibby said.

"Right," Francis said. "And the last thing she said, Baladino's daughter, she said, 'I'm never gonna get old.'"

"How do you know she said that? How'd anybody know that?"

"I guess I just heard it from a guy," Francis said. "Maybe somebody knew Arthur better than I did, or knew his wife. I don't know. Because what it was, in the hospice there, she was surrounded by old people. Mostly old women, I guess. And that's what she was thinkin', right? 'I'm never gonna get old.' Course if she was still around, she might have asked her old man if gettin' old is such a wonderful thing, parole officer comin' by to see if you're still breathin', see if maybe they should cuff you to the bed."

"Well, she was his daughter," Gibby said. "She would'na asked him anything. Maybe she was a nice person."

Francis thought about that for a minute. It seemed to him a good thing that somebody was suggesting that Arthur Baladino's daughter was a nice person, even if it was just Gibby, who hadn't known her.

He wondered if anybody left after he was gone would remember him as a nice person, or remember him at all.

The matter of whether to attend the service still hung between them. Gibby was of the opinion that they owed it to Arthur Baladino, whose largesse had kept them busy and fed some of the time, and who apparently respected their work because he threw business their way when he did not require their services.

Francis, less sentimental, figured that who came to the service was one of the many things that would no longer matter to his former employer, who, as far as Francis was concerned, would soon enough decompose, unless his wife had had him cremated and was planning to release his gray ashes to whatever wind she felt was most fitting.

Either way, it was over for Arthur Baladino, and he'd not be taking names or counting the bald heads at his service.

"He don't care, one way or the other," was the way Francis put it.

"Well, sure," Gibby said. "But everybody thinks about it sometimes, right?"

"Dying?"

"That," Gibby said, "and what everybody's gonna say about you when you're gone."

"I don't think so," Francis said. "I don't think it was that way for him."

Gibby thought about it for a moment. Maybe Francis was right. Arthur Baladino might not have given much thought to what people would say about him when he was gone. Not for a long time, anyway.

"Maybe as a kid, though," he said.

"Maybe," Francis said. "But maybe then it was just, 'Hey, they'll say I was a tough guy you didn't want to cross.'"

Arthur Baladino was not a neglected child. His family was not poor. Francis knew enough about him to know that. His parents had cared for young Arthur. Once he was taken to a small museum in a city where his family was visiting friends. According to Francis, Arthur Baladino didn't know where they'd been, but he remembered the day. Maybe the idea was that even as a small child, he would absorb some feeling for the work of Cezanne or Picasso or Bosch. But the only thing young Arthur remembered, as Francis heard him tell the story, was that the museum had stairs, and that at the foot of one of the stairways, he'd seen a woman who seemed impossibly old. She was bent at the waist. She looked as if with each step she was straining to see where she should put her foot.

Arthur could see the top of the old woman's head, which was nearly bald, and he could hear her breathing, which was labored. At the old woman's arm was a much younger woman who was trying to help her along. Arthur remembered that the younger woman had looked angry, and even as a child, he wondered why somebody—the younger woman, he supposed—had thought it would be a good idea to bring such an old woman to the museum. She looked lost and miserable. A child could see that. A child did. He thought it would have been better if the older woman had stayed home. Better for everybody.

"Maybe so," Gibby said. "Maybe you're right about when he was young. He was a tough guy all the time I knew about him. Seems he was like that with you. So maybe that was it."

"What about you?" Francis asked.

"What about me?"

"You a tough guy?"

Gibby smiled. He could have said, "Try me," but he didn't. He didn't say anything right away. But he found himself thinking about a night when some people would have said he was a tough guy.

"Come on," Francis said, hitting him lightly on the shoulder once, then again. "Come on. You a tough guy?"

"One night back when I was in high school, I mighta been. Depends."

"Depends on what? You're either a tough guy or you're not."

"Do you have to remember it?" Gibby asked. "I mean, to be a tough guy, to have been one, do you have to remember it? Otherwise, it don't count? Because I don't, exactly."

"How do you forget you were a tough guy?"

"It was down the shore," Gibby said. "Somebody's house. One of those places, they'd all blow away in the wind every few years, after a hurricane, ya know?"

"Jersey?"

"Bay Head, down there somewhere. But not Bay Head. Some shit box town. It was then, anyway. Little beach houses with plyboard partitions. You could hear the guy snoring two doors down. Room just big enough for a bed and a little dresser with the little glass knobs on the drawers, fall apart if you pull too hard, slide off the track alla time. Prob'ly the whole town's gone now."

"But you were a tough guy there?"

"That night I was, a lotta high school guys on the little porch at the back of the house drinkin' malt liquor. Drinkin' it like it was beer, ya know? And I go inside after a while, fall asleep in one of those little rooms, smelled like pine. I remember that. Then sometime early in the morning, everybody's off the porch, back in the kitchen, maybe to get away from the bugs. I don't know. And here I come, wakin' up about half-way, stumbling through the kitchen, there, lookin' for the bathroom."

"You couldn't find it?"

"I don't remember, that was the problem. But one guy's there, half-again as big as me, high school football player, he's in the kitchen, drinkin' his malt liquor, and he makes a crack about 'Don't piss in the sink,' somethin' like that. And what they say, these guys told me about it, they say I told him, 'Go fuck yourself, Capelli.'"

"You don't remember?"

"No."

"But he coulda beat you to pieces, right? I mean, big guy like that, football player."

"Absolutely."

"And you told him to fuck off?"

"That's what they tell me I did, yeah. So I did, I guess. I tol' you. I don't remember."

Francis thought about that for a minute.

"What I think is, you were a tough guy that night. Or that morning. Whatever it was when you said that. Somewhere down there where you can't remember, you were. You coulda got beat up, and you said it anyway."

Gibby was smiling then.

"You like thinkin' you were a tough guy?" Francis said.

"Not that," Gibby said. "It was . . . I was just thinkin' about that next morning. I woke up sick, ya know? Terrible headache. Pukin'. Dry heaves. All I wanted was to lie there on the floor, wherever I was. I didn't even know. I think somebody musta pushed me off the bed. But there was a lotta commotion, people gettin' out like somebody might be comin' in, not too happy to find us there, so everybody was headed for the beach, they said. I got up, ya know, walked out into the sun, blasting away, prob'ly the middle of the morning by then. I remember the sand on the black road, the tar already soft in the heat, that sand stickin' to your feet. Jesus. Maybe I remember that because I couldn't look up, ya know? Too painful to do that. Raise my head up. I'm really sick, still, and we get to the beach, which kinda sucks, littered with stuff where they don't clean it up, this part of it, public beach, all the gum wrappers, cans, stuff people left behind, tin foil shining in that sun, broken goggles, ya know. For lookin' under the water. I don't know what they thought they'd find there. Other people's feet, right?

"Anyway, I lay down on a towel somebody had, wasn't me, and I thought maybe everybody leaves me alone, I could just hold my head with both hands 'til it went away, the pain, or 'til I died, which also would have been okay. Maybe they'd all go in the water, right? Leave me the hell alone. But then this girl I don't know, somebody knew her maybe, she grabs me by the arm and starts dragging me toward the water, like it was a job she had to do. I'm tellin' her, 'Fuckin' stop it, hey!' My head is throbbin', I'm worried I'm gonna throw up on her feet, on the nice nail polish she had on her toes, which I see 'cause I'm still lookin' down, musta been. Sun's still up there, beatin' down like a bastard. But she's draggin' me into the water, and then I'm in it, and it's cold as a bastard, like you wouldn't believe, and I'm gettin' knocked down in the surf, there, the little waves, but enough to knock me over. And she's laughin', this girl that dragged me in there. I remember that. She's laughin', and the next thing I realize, my head's okay. It doesn't hurt. I'm feelin' good. Tired, but good, like you can when the pain stops. Grateful."

"That's it" Francis asked.

"That's it," Gibby said. "I don't remember her name. I guess I knew it then. Maybe. She musta known me, right? Why else would she pull me up off the sand and drag me into the water, skinny guy holdin' his head? I don't remember what she looked like, either. Her toes, I guess, and her laugh. She musta been beautiful, right?"

"Sure," Francis said. "Why not?"

"And today, maybe she's dead. Lotta people from then are. But if she'd asked me—right then, that day on the beach, I'm splashin' around in the shallow water, goin' under, rollin' around—if she'd asked me to marry her right then, I'm good. 'Yeah, let's do this.' I'd have said, 'This afternoon's good for me.'"

Francis smiled and said, "Then everything might have been different, right?"

"Yeah, well, fuck it," Gibby said. "Would'na been the first guy was a sucker for bein' rescued, would I?"

"You would not be that," Francis said. "But what it was, I bet, was she was goin' as far as she was willin' to go. That day on the beach, sun beatin' down on her, same as everybody, you lyin' there like a wino or somethin', she was okay with pullin' you up and tossin' you in the drink. Like a good deed, ya know? But that was it. She done what she could, was the way she prob'ly figured it. Then you're on your own."

"Sink or swim, right?"

"Yeah. You got no headache now, pal. Figure it out."

"Maybe that was it, simple as that," Gibby said.

Outside the sun beat down on the street the way it had on the tar on that New Jersey road all those years ago, when Gibby might have agreed to anything at all. Inside Murdock's, the air-conditioning helped more than a little.

"What about when you were a little kid?" Francis asked.

"What about it?"

"Were you a tough guy then? As a kid? I mean, you join a gang, wear the colors, all that?"

"I was on the edge of it, I guess you could say."

"What's that mean?"

Gibby thought about it. They'd wanted to know the same thing the first time he was arrested.

"It means the first thing I learned when I got old enough guys started tellin' me I had to be in a gang was which alleys you could run down that there was a way out the other end."

He looked out the front window of Murdock's at the traffic in the street. His knees hurt. He was glad he didn't have to run down an alley or anywhere else.

"I think we oughta go," Francis said.

Gibby looked at him. For a moment he didn't know what Francis was talking about. Then he remembered the service.

"You change your mind?"

"Well, it's time passin', isn't it?" Francis said. "Time goin' by. Maybe it's just, I don't know—it's not good pretendin' that's not happenin'."

"I guess not," Gibby said. He was still thinking about that day on the beach. It had occurred to him that the girl's name might have been Annie. Somebody might have called to her. 'Hey, Annie! What are you doin' over there?'"

Francis was alone in thinking about Arthur Baladino, who had died more or less on schedule.

"I wonder if it made that guy happy?"

"Who's that?"

"The guy who came to see him," Francis said. "Came to see Arthur, and then he said maybe they should put him back in there, lock him up again, because, ya know, maybe he don't look so bad."

"Just meant they could close the books," Gibby said. "Made it finished for them. Neat. For those guys, neatness counts."

"Finished," Francis said. "Finished is right. That, anyway."

"So we're goin'?"

And Francis thought, yes, they would go, because that was the rest of "finished," wasn't it? However it went, that was the rest of it, except for what he would remember, and what he might tell somebody else someday over coffee, or in a car during a long ride, or maybe in bed.

"Bad, sure," he might say. "Bad as it gets, I guess. I mean, he had guys killed. He was in and out of prison right up until the end there. It's just what it was."

"Nothing he wouldn't do?"

"Not after a while, no. There was a time, I guess, when there was a thing or two, maybe he stayed away from them. Further along, I don't think so."

About that, Francis was correct. Arthur Baladino had hired people to put other people in the ground when he didn't want to do it himself, maybe because by then a lot of people were watching whatever it was he did. Listening to him talk about doing whatever it might have been. Taking pictures, too.

He had stolen what seemed to him worth stealing. He had muscled other tough guys out of the way and stayed alive under circumstances where that had seemed unlikely. He had earned the respect of those he intimidated, and he'd sometimes scared away or paid off those charged with catching him.

The choices were his, and maybe he didn't feel they were choices.

"What he said once, he could have been a cop," Gibby said.

"Where's that come from?" Francis said. "I never heard him say that."

"I read it somewhere," Gibby said. "A magazine, I think. An interview he gave."

"Oh, hell," Francis said. "Maybe they just wrote it. It's pretty hard to imagine Arthur Baladino as a cop."

"I don't know," Gibby said. "Cops beat people up, too. Shoot 'em sometimes."

. . .

"You do have to hand it to him," Evan McCauly told his wife over dinner one evening shortly after they'd heard the news about their notorious neighbor. "He died in his bed, didn't he?"

"Meaning what, exactly?" Emily asked.

"I don't mean he won," Evan said. "I mean, there's not much to admire there. But nobody hit him from behind with a shovel or snuck in and stabbed him in his cell."

"How often does that happen?

"Not often, I guess," Evan said.

"Whitey Bulger," Emily said.

"Right," Evan said. "Which just goes to show that you hear about it when it does happen. And you hear about it when somebody like Arthur Baladino dies, too, even if he dies in his own bed."

"His life is not like ours," Emily said. "That's why you hear about it. It's not like he's some kind of hero."

"No," Evan said. "He's not."

"But different," she said. "What I mean is, you hear about it and read about it because it's—"

"Exotic," her husband said.

"Right," Emily said. "Something like that, I guess."

"Only it's not," Evan said. "Or it's only exotic to somebody who wasn't born into it and has never known it. Like a crumby bar with a good juke box. You've never been there, you go in and order a beer, which is cheap and cold. You hear a lot of songs that remind you of when you were sixteen, up all night if you wanted to be, ready for more the next day. You hang around for a little while, nobody tells you 'Hey! Whatta you doin' here? Scram!' You walk away thinking it's something special. Guys in there every night, they don't see it that way."

"What happens when you go back?"

"Probably find it's closed up. Rent got too high, now it's gonna be a Starbucks when they get around to it."

"So you can hold on to your illusions?"

Evan McCauly shrugged. "I guess," he said. He didn't think his wife got it, but he didn't have the energy.

"Anyway," he said, "Arthur Baladino died in his bed. His own bed. Or the bed his wife had for him in his house. Her house. And it's a good bed, I bet. That was courtesy of the program that's about mercy, even for guys like him. Or for him, anyway. I don't know how many other guys get to do that."

"Otherwise . . ."

"Otherwise, as I understand it, he lies in a ward, which they call a hospice ward, and he's got lots of company. He's got the guy to his right who's wheezing and snorting and spitting up green and yellow. He's got the guy to his left, moaning all night, maybe he's delirious. Just guys dying, and a dying murderer sounds pretty much like a dying saint, if there are any, or a dying traffic cop. So if he's lucky, ol' Arthur's unconscious and he doesn't hear it, but that's about all luck will do for him at that point, if he's still in there. And this goes on until some morning when somebody in a uniform walks by the foot of his bed and notices that Arthur Baladino, arch-criminal and so on is no more, that he's been dead for probably a couple of hours, and he tells somebody about it, and they haul the old arch-criminal away, or the ex-arch-criminal, and there's somebody unconscious and gray in one of the cell blocks, and that guy gets the empty bed."

"Maybe he died happy," Emily McCauly said. "Or happier than he would have in there, anyway. Not happy, I guess."

"Maybe he did," her husband said.

Because Evan McCauly, who did not usually think about such things, didn't know. He did wonder, sometimes, how many people get to take stock. How many people outside of novels and plays and poems ever have the opportunity to think about how they felt about the end when it came? He'd been present at the death of his mother, but she wasn't talking. His younger brother, who'd gotten to their mother's bedside a day or so before Evan had arrived, had told him: "We've lost her voice." Evan had nodded. He'd assumed—correctly, as it turned out—that their mother hadn't said anything for a while, and that she would say no more. He was tempted to ask his brother what their mother HAD said before she'd stopped talking, but it hadn't seemed the right time. It didn't seem like the right time after she'd died, either, at least to Evan.

Who knew?

And if he had been aware of his mother's last words, what then? What if the last thing anyone had heard her say was, "Could you change the channel, please?" or "What's the weather supposed to be tomorrow?"

Sometimes when Evan thought about death, he thought about a friend he'd had in college. He and several other boys had planned a trip to New York. Evan had begged off. He couldn't remember why. On the way home, the driver had fallen asleep and the car had veered right and scraped the highway barrier. The driver woke and jerked the steering wheel to the left, taking the car into the path of a bus. Two of the boys, the two in the back seat, had escaped serious injury, as the saying goes, but the driver, Evan's friend, was trapped in the wreckage and bled to death. The fourth boy was thrown from the car and landed on his head, sustaining injuries that changed his personality so dramatically that when he tried to return to school, he frightened the people who'd known him. Where he had been studious—sometimes even solemn—now he was impulsive, moody, given to outbursts of laughter, restless, sometimes difficult to understand when he was speaking. Evan had avoided the boy, though he'd felt bad about it.

"But I still remember him," he thought. "Why's that? I remember him more clearly than I remember guys I knew better, guys I spent more time with—guys I hear about, still see sometimes."

"Is it guilt, maybe?"

That's what Emily had said on the one occasion when Evan had brought up how he sometimes thought about the damaged boy.

"You mean that I wasn't in the car?"

"I don't know," she'd said. "That you were lucky. That they weren't. That it could have been you. Sure."

Evan had thought about that. Then he thought about whether the boy KNEW he'd changed. He wondered whether, lying in bed in the dark, the boy remembered his former self, maybe even worked to get that self back, banish the reckless, scary fool he'd become.

"Maybe it WAS luck," Evan had said. "Maybe it's as simple as that. I don't even remember why I didn't go with them. Usually I'd go on those trips, you know? It wouldn't have been work. Studying,

I mean. Somebody came up with an idea to go somewhere, do something, I was there. What do you suppose made me bail on that trip?"

"I didn't know you then," Emily had said.

"No," Evan had said. "Not for a couple years. That's right."

"And a good thing," he thought. "You wouldn't have wanted to be around me if we'd met back then. I was the kind of guy who would walk away from a friend who'd been badly hurt and lost himself and changed into somebody else, and he needed a friend so badly that there was probably almost nobody who'd take on the job. Not me, certainly. I was of no use to him. Probably no use to anybody, unless I could have a good time at it. A good thing you didn't meet me for a couple years."

Evan McCauly did not tell his wife anything more about what he'd done when he was in college. If he had, she'd have surprised him. She'd have told him she'd known a lot of guys like him. She'd have said it was nothing to be ashamed of. She'd have meant it, too. Maybe she'd even have congratulated him on growing up. Maybe she'd have told him there were lots of men who'd never grown up, and that at least he could be proud of his embarrassment over what he'd done, what he'd been.

"You're a good man now," she might have said, if he'd given her the opportunity to make him feel better about his former self. But he didn't, though he could have used the encouragement, and Emily might have welcomed the opportunity to provide it, privately, when they were in bed together in the dark, or at a dinner party where other men could hear her, and each could wish he had a wife who would express the same sort of tolerance, even compassion, except for the men who STILL thought it would be funny to sit at a table with lots of other men and rate from one to ten the women who came through the door.

"You were a jerk," Emily might have said. "Who hasn't been a jerk? You came out of it all right, though. You're here now, responsible, a good provider, and, sure, I know that's nothing more than what any 1950s housewife would feel entitled to expect, but you're a better listener than you used to be, which nobody can take for granted now, and nobody ever could. You're doing all right."

Wouldn't that have been something Evan McCauly would like to have heard?

He carried around a lot of regrets, and the ones he didn't carry around—the ones he'd forgotten for a time and maybe thought he'd forgotten forever—they would surprise him. He would turn over at night and think it was his prostate that had woken him. Then, after he'd returned to bed, he'd find that wasn't it. He'd discover he was thinking about a letter he'd written to a girl he'd seen for a while when he was in college. He'd remember the words with which he'd implied that she didn't understand him, the idea being that no woman could understand the struggle in his soul.

"Jesus!" he'd think. "I was such an ass!"

He'd lie awake, wondering if he was still an ass, but an ass operating on another level, an ass who'd be incapable of understanding what an ass he still was until he got older and could look back from another plateau of wisdom, which, like the others, would turn out to be as fragile as the one he'd proudly stood upon when he'd written the stupid letter.

That would only happen if he lived long enough to look back again, lying awake in the dark with Emily snoring quietly beside him. He hoped that wouldn't happen. Then he hoped it would. Then he wondered if, when he reached the plateau on which he would die, he'd see it as the destination for which he'd striven, or as just a place to rest.

Then he'd wish he'd taken something to make it more likely that he'd sleep through the night. He'd think about taking something. He'd decide that would be a bad idea because if he took pills now, he'd be walking into walls in the morning.

Emily could wake up, or half-wake, and she'd day, "Are you okay?"

"I'm fine," he'd say. "Go back to sleep."

"You, too," she'd say, and she would curl against him and pull his arm over her, and he would be a little more inclined to forgive himself, and he, too, would sleep.

EMILY AND ANNIE

"He walks about a hundred miles a week," Emily said. "Or maybe he doesn't. Maybe he walks four blocks and sits down under a tree and falls asleep."

"Like Rip Van Winkle," Annie said.

"Sure. How would I know? It's not like I follow him."

"He's healthy," Annie said.

"I guess," Emily said. She hoped Annie wouldn't say that they both could do with more walking. She used to weigh herself each morning. Now she doesn't. She thought Annie looked like maybe she still did.

"He's happy he retired?'

"He's happy his phone isn't ringing. He's happy he doesn't have the hassles he had with the practice. Some of them. Arguments about who'd talk to the walk-in with the kid in jail, all the hiring, the office people, billing, whatever. Who's not pulling his weight. And I guess he's happy he stayed with it long enough to put away a lot of money. I am, anyway."

"Right," Annie said.

"But him, too. I'm sure."

The two women were sitting on a screened porch that looked out on the house that had stood empty for years. Emily McCauly had been one of the people who had called the town about tearing it down. For a year or so she'd been angry that nobody had paid any attention. Now she was glad they hadn't. The house looked wonderful. Its restoration had probably increased the value of her place. Who wouldn't want to live across the street from a showplace like that?

"It must be hard, though, when you've had a job like that, people depending on you and all, just to quit. What are you gonna do, right?"

"You mean—"

"I mean, besides go for walks."

"I guess we'll see," Emily said.

She didn't say that she worried that her husband had begun to fill some of his time with the business of educating her.

"What's happened is, we've screwed everything up. People, I mean."

His conversations—often they were more like lectures, Emily thought. A segment on the news about climate change could bring it on. A traffic jam during which both of them noticed that many of the vehicles stuck along with them were enormous, and that in many of them, it was only a driver. But bad weather could start a lecture, too.

"When there have been alternatives, humanity has chosen the wrong path," Evan McCauly would say. "The internal combustion engine was ugly and loud from the start. Nobody could have foreseen air travel for everybody then, okay, but why didn't the smartest minds focus on what burning gas and oil would do?"

Emily would sometimes try to work her way into the conversation. She'd say something like, "Maybe they did. Maybe nobody was listening."

By then her husband would be on to something else.

"Look at the houses right here on this street," he'd say. "This used to be an interesting neighborhood. Not exactly diverse, okay. But at least there were some smaller houses. Now they're all gone. Or going. At least most of them. Two doors down, where that ranch used to be, it's going to be a house—I heard this from a guy who poked around in there last week—the place has five and a half bathrooms. Who the hell needs five and a half bathrooms? What is it? A conference center? A damn hotel?"

Emily felt the new place, ugly as it was, would probably increase the value of their own home even more. Maybe all the building would do that. But she didn't say anything. The last thing Evan wanted to consider in the middle of one of his dark lectures was the bright side. Mentioning it would have been inviting him to sneer.

It wasn't that he was wrong, Emily thought. Like her husband, she was discouraged by stupidity and greed. Like him, each day she faced the challenge of living with her relative affluence. Like him, she sometimes wondered how to do it.

"I mean," she said to Annie, "we have homes. With heat. In the summer, they have air conditioning. Maybe it doesn't always work as well as we'd like. It's too cold. Whatever. We kick about that. But, come on. We're good, right? We're not hungry. We look at people who have a second home in the woods, or at the shore—somewhere to go to be warm in the winter—another community of like-minded friends, meaning people who have as much money as they do, and we're envious. Some of us are. But look at what we HAVE. Our kids are healthy. They get the vaccines they need. They eat fruit. They see the doctor when they need to do it. We drive them where they need to go, and they wear seatbelts. It's the law, right? We're good with that. We drive too fast and get stopped, the officer looks in the car and he says, 'Good to see everyone wearing a seatbelt.'"

"When was the last time you drove too fast?" Annie asked.

"My point is that we're taken care of," Emily said. "The lights go out, no problem. We have candles. We play games in the candlelight."

"Some of us have generators," Annie said. She and her husband had installed one after a hurricane had knocked out their power for almost two days.

"Some of us," Emily said, "and good on you, Annie. But my point, you know, the power goes out, the electric company calls and tells us when the lights will come on again. You're cold while it's out?

Check the hall closet. There's probably eight extra blankets in there. Some you haven't used in years. Forgot you had 'em. We have so much more than we need. That's my point. And so many people have nothing. A blanket would be a treasure in a refugee camp. People would fight over it. Same with the soup we throw out because it's past its sell-by date."

"You sound like my mother," Annie said. "Clean your plate. There are people starving in Armenia. Or wherever."

"She was right, though," Emily said. "She'd still be right."

"About Armenia?"

"A dozen different places," Emily said. "Two dozen. Maybe more than we can count. More than we can name, for sure. Both of us together."

She sighed, a little surprised by her own energy.

"But what I'm saying is, we go on and on, like having what we have and all those people having nothing is just the way it is. Nothing we can do about it. Evan's right about that. I do it, and you do, too. What else could we do? Go out into the street and shout about the injustice of it all?"

Annie listened. She was smart enough to know there was nothing to say.

"It's not that we're different in that regard," Emily said, "Evan and me. It's just that when he gets going, he's all by himself. And then he comes to the end of whatever has gotten him going, and then he goes to work. Or that was what he did before he retired. And maybe he hated himself, because that work he was going to, it had nothing to do with the injustice he'd been pointing out to me, all the unfairness and stupidity and greed. Nothing. He was just doing what we all do, wasn't he? He was making sure he was fed, and I was fed, and our kids were fed and dressed like everybody else's kids."

"Sneakers," Annie said under her breath. "That's what I forgot. Oh, hell."

Evan McCauly had married Emily Baker the year he graduated from law school. His plan for the years they would spend together was indistinguishable from what had happened so far. For longer than he might have thought it would take, he had studied for the bar exam. It was a lonely and tedious business, but on his third try he'd passed. At the party to celebrate, nobody had mentioned the two previous attempts.

The firm that had taken on Evan McCauly after graduation had been patient, recognizing they would earn his loyalty as well as his gratitude. And Evan McCauly did what he was asked to do. He was an agreeable associate in the office, at lunch, and on the golf course. He accepted advice from a senior partner and began having his suits tailored by a man known for how he could make extra pounds suggest solid business experience.

"What does he think about the new neighbor?" Annie asked.

"'Short-term tenant.' That's what he says."

"He probably knows."

"Not KNOWS knows," Emily said. "He never practiced criminal law. But what he told me is that they're pretty strict with the decision to let somebody out this way."

"It's not like he's going to recover," Annie said.

"No, it's not like that. Not according to Evan."

"Just another story in the neighborhood, then."

"Just that," Emily said. She filled her glass with iced tea from the pitcher on the table between them. She nodded at Annie, who said, "Sure. Thanks."

"But different, too," Emily said. "I mean, I guess there's another neighborhood in town where a house stands empty for a couple years, except for the kids who sneak in the back at night. Maybe there is. And there's another neighborhood where somebody got arrested for something. Maybe drugs or spousal abuse."

"Or embezzling," Annie said. "They got the guy who lived over on Brick Lane, the broker, you know, what's his name?"

"Evans," Emily said. "Andy Evans."

"Right," Annie said. "He's another guy who went to prison."

"Nope," Emily said.

"What do you mean 'nope?' He got caught with his hand in the cookie jar. And he'd grabbed a lot of cookies."

"Caught and charged," Emily said. "But quietly. He never went to prison. The firm didn't want the embarrassment. They worked something out to avoid a trial. No good having your clients thinking somebody's pocketed their investment money, is it?"

"He must have had a good attorney," Annie said.

"I guess," Emily said.

"The lawyer, he probably got most of the money, anyway. Or she. I hope it was a woman."

"Anyway," Emily said, "his wife left. Constance. She got her real estate license almost right away, almost like she was already thinking about it or something, and she did well for herself. That's the way I heard it. I don't know what happened to him."

"I wonder if she got to sell their house?"

"She left before that," Emily said. "There would have been some justice in it, right? Get the commission, anyway. But I think the bank got it. He really left nothing. Did the whole job."

Annie sipped her tea and looked at the house across the street. It was painted a light blue. The lawn in front of it was lush. During the years it had been unoccupied except for the teenagers, the grounds had been packed dirt and dust or mud, depending on the season and the weather.

"It must have been expensive to create a lawn there, and keep it up," Annie thought.

"But it's an investment," she said.

"What is?" Emily asked.

"Oh," Annie said, "I was just thinking out loud."

"About what?"

"Money, I guess," Annie said. "It's good that Andy Evans's wife found something she could do to support herself, right? You gotta hand it to her."

"Did you work before you were married?"

"Sure," Annie said.

"At what?"

"How much time you got? And how much iced tea?"

Emily got up. "I'll get us some more," she said.

Annie stretched her legs and thought about what she'd say. She'd been a waitress for a while after she finished college. She could take orders and flirt in three languages, but nobody she served had spoken anything but English. She'd taken the job so she could stay in Amherst, where most of her friends were still living. She had a room in a big house full of recent graduates, most of whom didn't know what they'd do next and were reluctant to leave the lives they'd made as students. Some of them were frightened of what they might become. Annie had discovered that waitresses could live pretty much like students. They could get together with their friends after work, stay up late, sleep in the next morning. They could make it on tips and the leftover food wrapped up for them by the cooks, who hoped they'd get invited to the parties they were sure the waitresses, with their long ponytails and short skirts, went to after work.

"So," Emily said, when she came back with the tea. "What did you do and where did you do it?"

"Not a big deal," Annie said. "But I worked enough so that I wasn't asking my parents for money. I was proud of that. We could still live cheap, and it was fine as long as you didn't mind that there were always people coming and going."

"It sounds like fun."

Annie looked as if she was thinking about that.

"Sometimes it was," she said. "A lot of times, I guess. But the thing you don't get then is how wide open it could have been. For a while, anyway, I mean. I could have done anything, you know? Could have devoted myself to something and gotten really good at it."

"Like what?"

"Maybe it's just the way I think about it now," Annie said. "It was a long time ago, wasn't it?"

"I guess," Emily said.

It had been before everything that was supposed to matter now had begun to matter. Before jobs significant enough for anybody to worry about whether they'd lose them. Before companions who became lovers and then became companions again, or left for somewhere else, or, in one case, killed himself, though Annie felt that had had nothing to do with her, and two therapists had agreed with her.

"I don't know what I could have gotten good at," she said.

"You're a bright girl," Emily said. "Anything you'd put your mind to, I'd think."

"I don't know what it might have been," Annie said. "Really. Or if there might have been something."

"Well, maybe . . ."

"Anyway," she said, "I gotta go. Thanks for the tea and the talk."

Annie got up and moved toward the porch steps, then turned to wave. Emily waved back, a kind of salute. A stout salute. She smiled, shook her head, and went inside.

Instead of turning toward her own house, Annie started in the other direction. It was too hot for a long walk, but once around the block would be fine, she thought.

In the heat of the afternoon, she found herself thinking of another hot day. She'd been on the beach with some friends who'd invited some of her housemates to the Jersey shore for a week. She hadn't known the people whose parents had provided the cottage at the shore, but she'd gone along. Sometimes things at the house in Amherst got tense. Whoever was supposed to be cleaning up wasn't doing it. Somebody's car was dead at the end of the driveway, and everybody had to drive on the lawn to get by it. Maybe it was something like that.

On the day before they'd piled into the Volkswagen bus that would carry them back to Massachusetts, they'd run into a group of boys, probably still in high school. They tossed a Frisbee and flirted with each other. It was safe. It would come to nothing. She and her housemates would be headed home the next morning, sun-burned and sick of the sand in their clothes. But Annie had noticed one of the boys— he was skinny, almost scrawny—curled up in the sand, moaning like he was sick.

"Short ball hitter," one of the other boys had told her.

On impulse, Annie had grabbed the moaning boy by the arm and dragged him toward the surf. He was squinting in the sun. His bathing suit looked as if he'd borrowed it from somebody bigger. He protested as she tugged at him, but without much enthusiasm. Maybe he thought it was a good idea, too.

Once in the water, she let go of his arm. The boy thrashed around and stumbled on the uneven bottom. A moment later a wave broke behind him and knocked him down. He came up spitting, pushing his dark hair off his forehead.

"Ah, Jesus," he'd said.

Annie, who had less use for religion then, couldn't help but think, "He's baptized. Baptized in something, anyway. And not in my name, because he doesn't know it."

"Christ," the boy said. Then he'd looked up at Annie and said, "My head doesn't hurt. How'd you know to do that?"

Now, looking at the hot pavement, Annie smiled. She had no idea then. She didn't know now.

Sometimes she wondered about the people she'd known when she was in school, people with whom she'd grown up, or whom she'd met in college. One woman who'd shared her waitressing shift, the first woman she'd met with a tattoo, a little tiger just below the hemline of her brown and white waitressing uniform.

"Now everybody has one," she thought. "Back then I thought that little tiger was about the raciest thing anybody'd ever done. April. That was her name. April something."

She would wonder about what happened to those people she'd not have recognized now if they'd sat down beside her on the bus, if she'd ever had reason to take a bus.

She wondered about the scrawny boy she'd pulled into the sea.

"My head doesn't hurt anymore," he'd said. Something like that. "How'd you know to do that?"

"Now I'd walk by him on that beach," Annie thought, "kids trailing after me. Now he'd have a headache all day. Or maybe somebody else would pull him into the water. Somebody else would save him. Somebody without kids."

She turned the corner, looked up, and saw her house. It didn't need painting, the gutters were straight, the lawn had been edged. The guy who took care of the grass and the bushes had swept the flagstone walk. The plastic garbage barrels lined up along the curb had tight lids.

Soon the kids would be home from day camp. Her husband would be home from work. She would prepare a meal. Before she cleared away the dishes, she and her husband would sit at the table for a while. She'd listen to him talk about his day, and he'd ask what she'd been up to. She wondered what he'd say if she told him she'd been thinking about how she had pulled a skinny, hung-over boy into the ocean at the Jersey shore on an August day as hot as today.

"Weird," she said to herself. "It wasn't that big a deal, right?"

Gibby wouldn't have recognized Annie Blake, who'd been Annie Gonzales then, any more than she'd have recognized him. She'd fared better over the years, certainly. She exercised every day. She'd attended spin classes, until she couldn't stand it anymore. She paid attention to what she ate. She took advantage of her health insurance and saw a dermatologist regularly. When they'd had too much to drink, friends would sometimes pull her aside and ask if she'd had work done.

Maybe if Gibby had seen her on the street he would have recognized her, or thought there was something in her of the slender girl who'd pulled him up off the sand and hauled him into the sea.

"I like to think so," Annie said to herself.

Annie Blake considered herself fortunate. She was not only healthy and attractive. As far as she could tell, she was also safe. She had aspired to that.

Gibby had no such aspirations. He'd always thought of himself as okay if he woke up in the morning. "Safe" meant who knows what?

"Like the manager says when the reporter asks him about the right fielder who's injured," Gibby told Francis. "He's day-to-day is what the guy says. That's me."

"That's all of us," Francis thought.

"You proud of that?" he asked.

"Not proud of it, no. What would that mean? It's just, ya know, what it is. Prob'ly the best way to think about it."

He'd seen too much to think about it any other way. He'd gone out looking for a gun when he was sixteen, and in a couple of hours he'd found one. He'd traded for it. Half a dozen hits of acid and what cash he could scrape up. That was the day after he'd been mugged by two guys from the next neighborhood over. One of them had a taser, which Gibby would learn the guy had bought from a former gang member who'd invited Christ into his life and needed to get rid of his weapons, so he'd have money for the guy who'd made the introduction, and for his church. It hadn't occurred to Gibby right away that he was lucky, since the guy who mugged him might just as easily have bought a gun.

"Hurt like a bastard," Gibby told anybody who'd never been tased, which included Francis.

"I don't doubt it," Francis said. "So your figuring was, better get a gun, right? You got to get close to use a taser on somebody. A gun, you don't have to be up in the guy's face. You CAN be, that's what you want. But you don't have to be."

"Sometimes you just have to show it," Gibby said. "Lotta times. Then people know you have it. They tell somebody else. Then maybe you don't get mugged again."

All this Francis knew, though he preferred not to carry a gun. "Everything they get you for, it's worse then," he told Gibby, who knew it as well as Francis did. "It's not good they get you for robbery, but armed robbery, that's a lot worse."

"What do you rob somebody with, you're not armed?" Gibby wanted to know.

"I'm just sayin'. An example, you know?"

"Well, it's a lousy example," Gibby said.

But then he found himself thinking about the taser, which wasn't a gun, though he supposed you could kill somebody with one if the guy was about half-ready to go with a bad heart, maybe. And then where would you be?

"Might as well have gotten a gun right off," he said to himself.

Gibby wondered what had happened to the guys who'd mugged him, whether they'd ever been arrested. If that had happened, it hadn't had anything to do with him. And then he found himself thinking that it wouldn't have had anything to do with him, even if the two guys had been arrested with his wallet and his watch, because he wouldn't have said anything. That much he'd learned a long time before he'd learned that getting tased hurt like a bastard.

"Fix it so it won't happen again."

That's what he'd learned from being mugged by the guys with the taser, and it had happened after the hot afternoon on the beach with the girl he could still remember had dragged him into the cold water. It seemed to Gibby like a long time afterward. He wasn't good at putting dates and times to things, even the important ones, but he'd been a sick, helpless kid on the beach on that hot day. How long had it been before he'd figured out he'd better have a gun?

"And so maybe that was the beginning of it," he told the counselor, because he had to tell him something. He couldn't stand the silence. The counselor could. He could sit there quietly forever. It made Gibby crazy.

"I asked him about it," he told Francis. "That's how nuts it was making me. I asked him, 'Hey, how the fuck can you sit here and not say a thing? You just look at me, your eyes look like you're tryin' to stare me down. It's creepy.' Only I didn't say 'fuck' to him, right?"

"Why not? Why's he special?"

"What he could do," Gibby said, "he could tell 'em how I'm an aggressive somethin', I don't know. I'm some counselor word, have those Department of Youth Services guys leanin' back in their chairs, thinkin', 'Okay. This one's easy. Got an authority problem, what it is. Don't even have to think about this one. Don't even have to pretend we're doin' that. Let him stay right where he is, is what we do. See what happens after a while, maybe until after I retire, then let somebody else think about it, comes to that.'"

"What did the guy say?"

"Who?"

"The counselor. When you asked him how he could sit there so long and not say anything."

"Ha!" Gibby said. "What do you think he said? He said nothin', is what he said. That's what he's good at."

"Yeah, well, you musta been pretty good at what you were doin', too," Francis said. "You got out."

"I did do that," Gibby said. "But, you know, it was only after I been in for about as long as they could keep me there. Not a big deal by the time it happened, getting out. Pretty much by the numbers, by then."

But it had been a big deal. It had been a bigger deal than Gibby let anybody know. In was in. Out was out. Anybody'd been in knew it was a big deal.

"You think that business about the guy with the taser bein' the beginning of it, or getting the gun—whatever you told the guy—you think he thought he'd helped you out, getting you to say that?"

"Francis," Gibby said, "I'm not a stupid guy. Like a lotta guys, I done some stupid things. But I'm not a stupid guy. That counselor, I told him what he wanted to hear. I told him about my family, too. I told him about the shriveled up little apples fell ona ground in the park near where we lived, and how we threw 'em at each other, hurt like hell if they hit you in the head. Like rocks. I told him about that. He was a guy prob'ly took his kids apple-picking in the fall, you know? Out in some orchard, about a million apple trees, not a shriveled apple anywhere on the place. They got guys come to work before the counselor and his kids get there, pick up all the apples aren't red and round enough, stick 'em in a big chopper, make applesauce, I guess. He never saw 'em, the counselor. Those shriveled up ones. He got the big, red ones. Him and his kids."

.   .   .

Apple-picking was something Annie understood. She and her kids, and her husband, too, maybe, on a Saturday. Her kids picked so many of them that after passing slices around for snacks for a couple of days, after making apple pies and then apple coffee cake for people in the neighborhood, she'd ended up throwing a lot of the apples away, just to get them out of the refrigerator. It was a waste, and it made her sad. Day after day the mail was full of pleas from agencies and organizations soliciting help for people who didn't have enough to eat. Some of them had lots of other problems. In the brochures, the children had bulging eyes and swollen bellies. Some of them had cleft palates, and some of them stared at nothing through eyes covered with a film that looked like plastic. There were flies on their faces, near their mouths. The mothers of these children stared into the camera. They held their starving babies with arms as thin as twigs. They were barefoot and wrapped in rags.

Apples might not have done them much good. Some of them looked like they had no teeth. Their cheeks were sunken. Their hands were claws.

"You can't save them all," her husband, Eddie, would tell her. "Pick a couple. We'll send checks. Keep track. It's deductible."

Annie looked up the charities and the non-profits and crossed off the ones that seemed to keep most of the money or spend it on colorful brochures. She tossed out the letters containing coins, figuring if the organizations that sent them were worthwhile, they'd have put the coins toward food and helping the kids with the twisted mouths and spines, rather than playing on the guilt she'd feel when she opened the letters and dumped the coins into the jar on her dressing table. They gave some money to the ones that were left.

Eddie shrugged. "I guess it doesn't do any harm," he told her. "We've got enough."

Annie had more imagination. When she wrote a check for fifty dollars, she imagined everyone in the neighborhood writing a similar check. Maybe everyone in town. Everyone in the state, except for the people whose own teeth were sticking through their lips or whose eyes were milky and useless.

"Fifty from everyone who could afford it," she'd think. "Fifty in response to each letter that came in a certain week. Christmas week, say. It might make a difference. Then throw the next month's worth of solicitations into the trash with a clear conscience, but write the checks for those that came on a certain day. An anniversary. A birthday. A kid's birthday. It might make a difference."

Pressed, she'd have acknowledged that she knew it wasn't true.

"The poor you will always have with you." Didn't Jesus say that? Or somebody? But the slightly less hungry poor—that would be an improvement, right? And a poor child whose teeth weren't poking through her lip might have a shot at something better than begging on a noisy street full of garbage.

Then there was the matter of saving oneself. She would not give until it hurt, but she would give. She would not be only for herself, but neither would she be as the lilies of the field when it came to clothes and shoes. She had not walked past the sick and pretended not to see them. Or him, at least. She had hauled him to his feet and dragged him into the sea. It had been a long time ago, but she had done that. Surely it was goodness and mercy that had motivated her, and if it was a playful sort of goodness, because it was kind of funny to hear the skinny guy protest, and then to see the look of wonder on his pale face when the pain was gone, so much the better for that. What was wrong with being playful?

"Damn," he'd said. "How'd you know to do that?"

She hadn't known. She had only done it.

And if the opportunity presented itself, would she do it again? Would she take the hand of a stranger, sick on the beach, and pull him out of his pain? Or a stranger retching on the side of the road? Would she stop and see what she could do? Or maybe just hit 911 on her cellphone and tell the operator, "There's a man on his knees in the street. Somebody should help him." And then, "You don't need my name. That's not important." Or what about the woman at the door, desperate to sell magazine subscriptions. What about a college kid with a summer job that went from house to house, soliciting money for an organization that would save the whales or the planet, assuming enough people contributed?

Would Annie Blake, who had been Annie Gonzales, do anything now like what she had done without thinking about it years ago? Or would she be careful, having been taught by experience to be suspicious? How often had she read about someone stopping on the highway to help a driver beside an apparently disabled car, only to be beaten and robbed? How many "charities" had been lining the pockets of their directors, spending most of what they raised on salaries and five-star hotel suites and first-class flights to conferences held in Las Vegas or New Orleans rather than Cleveland or Milwaukee?

Would she be too smart to stop and touch a stranger on the beach? Who knew where his hands had been?

She did not talk about these things with Emily. She'd said what she'd had to say. She did not talk about how sometimes when she and Eddie were making love, she thought about somebody else. She did not talk about her fear that she would grow to be like her mother, who'd been angry all her life. She did not talk about where she might have lived if she had not been so firmly and thoroughly anchored in the present she and her husband had made for themselves, and for each other.

Anchored or trapped. Sometimes it seemed as if it depended on the day.

Instead, she told Emily about things like apple-picking and what she had planned for the next children's birthday party—a bouncy clown castle, maybe, or a magician. Maybe both. She didn't tell Emily that she wondered sometimes if she was compensating for what she hadn't had when she was growing up. She didn't acknowledge that to herself. If she had, she'd have had no idea how to distinguish between doing something lovely and fun for her children out of the considerable goodness of her loving heart and trying to provide what had been missing when she'd reached the age when she would have found in the appearance of a magician an occasion to squeal and shriek with delight.

Annie Gonzales had solemnly excelled. As a student, she was not so much bright as dedicated. She believed in right answers and sought them with what one of her teachers labeled "near desperation." That teacher worried about her, but Annie's parents were pleased.

"She doesn't screw around," her father often said, and she didn't. She was straight-ahead and steady on the rails. She had the advantage of exotic good looks. She was disciplined enough to keep them. She had married well. She acknowledged that she wasn't unhappy.

But she never forgot that there had been a time when she might have made different choices. She might have traveled. She might have met more people. More men. She might have told Eddie Blake, no—at least the first time he asked her to marry him. She might have said, "I'm not ready," and moved on from there.

"Or maybe I WAS ready, and I just think about it differently now, because time passes and what might have happened seems more attractive than it would have been. Maybe I'd have been trekking in the mountains somewhere, high above it all. But maybe it would have rained. Hard. Or sleet, maybe. Maybe I'd have started down the mountain path and I'd have lost the trail and died up there, wherever it was, never to be heard from again. Maybe it's just as well that I'm comfortable. Better than just as well. Really good, maybe."

Therapy had taught her to embrace acceptance, to consider gratitude. Most of the time she was good at it. All she had to do was look around her home. There were photographs of family. Everyone was smiling. The furnace worked and the roof didn't leak. The car had been regularly serviced at the dealership where she'd purchased all three Camrys, one after the other.

If she was not passionate about her life, she was, she felt, at least diligent about it. She separated the trash from the recyclables. She picked up after the dog, except when the dog found her way into the tangled pachysandra. She paid attention to the news, though most of the time she felt as if there was nothing she could do. She voted. She'd read that it was possible to become a better listener by consciously limiting how much talking you did in a group, and she'd practiced that. Sometimes it seemed to her as if her friends had noticed, though nobody told her so.

She wondered, sometimes, if she would ever again do anything as spontaneous as what she had done on that hot morning on the Jersey shore, when she had grabbed a stranger by the arm and pulled him across the sand. She remembered it with pride, sometimes, and sometimes with disbelief. She wondered how she'd done it, the way she wondered about other things—how she'd held up through her father's illness. He'd died slowly, in pain, of cancer. His doctors kept saying there was something else they could try. Annie stopped believing them long before they stopped coming up with something new. But they were doctors. She was resigned to letting them continue experimenting on her father, who got smaller as the days and nights dragged on. Early one morning, lying on his back, depressed and desiccated, he asked her, "Why don't they just let me die?"

"They're helping you get better," Annie had said. It made her nauseous to say it. She didn't believe a word of it. Neither did her father.

"How'd I get through that?" Annie wondered. "How did who I know I am make it through those days?"

She shared the question with nobody. Her husband, her friends, any of them would have said the same thing: "You're stronger than you think you are."

"No," Annie thought. "I'm not."

Finally her father had died. He was unrecognizable by then, not only as her father, but as a man. He was a terrifying shadow of what he'd been, but a shadow covered with sores, a shadow made up of dark colors and sharp angles. Nearly weightless, he was a weight Annie would never be able to bear, or so she felt. She thought he'd have been better off if she'd put a pillow over his head and smothered him months earlier. She blamed herself for what had happened to him, and for what he had become. She had nodded to the doctors each time they came to her for that nod.

"God never gives you more than you can handle."

Annie had heard that from a woman in her book club. She had heard it many times, because the woman in her book club, whose name was Grace, never tired of saying it.

Annie could nod at that, too. She knew too much about starving children in refugee camps and hideous, parasite-borne diseases to believe it. She knew too much about what she had seen her father go through, and what it had done to her. But she could nod at Grace when she offered what she had to offer.

But she was always relieved when somebody in the club turned the discussion away from God and back to the book, even if she hadn't read it.

Still, sometimes Grace persisted.

Annie listened and nodded. She was grateful for what she had. She was horrified by the suffering she had seen, and the suffering she saw, and all the suffering she could imagine.

She felt as if she'd have happily thrown herself at the feet of a God capable of making it go away. A Daddy who would never weaken, never die. But Annie thought of God as—what? Changeable is how she might have put it. Capable of great compassion, but inscrutable in the face of an automobile accident that left a small child with one eye, a face hopelessly scarred by burns, and no parents.

What was that? A test. Annie preferred not to sit for the exam.

If there was only one God, which, she supposed, was the point of most religions, each claiming, albeit sometimes only quietly, to be the right one, where was He or She when everybody got cholera, dysentery, or AIDS?

What about when two armies—each full of young men, women, and children convinced they were righteously pursuing God's will— burned the land into a pocked desert—a bare, uninhabitable hell?

Was that really part of the plan?

"Some plan ya got there, Big Guy," Annie might have said, but only if she was sure nobody was listening.

As a child, she had heard the phrase "leap of faith." It was an old, white-haired chaplain who'd said it to a room full of high school students. He was a visiting speaker. He'd been the minister at a private school on the other side of town for several decades. He had grown old in the position. He had grown sure of himself, or that's the way it had seemed to Annie.

Most of her classmates regarded the students at the private school as the enemy. When the minister brought up the leap of faith, one of the boys sitting behind Annie had said, "Leap on this." If the minister heard him, he pretended that he hadn't.

"But some of them probably leapt," Annie thought. "Some of them probably did. And some of them probably died whispering prayers. Maybe it worked for them. They weren't in refugee camps. They weren't being beaten by teenage thugs in uniform. They were in beds made up with clean linen. How hard would it be to believe in a just and merciful God as long as you were being treated with justice and mercy?"

"The problem is that there is so much to get through each day," Emily said.

"Meals," Annie said.

"That and the doctors' appointments, dentists' appointments, conferences with the kids' teachers. You ever wonder why your kids can't just do what they need to do in school so the school would leave you alone?"

Annie smiled. Her teachers hadn't had to call home, except to discuss whether maybe she should skip the next grade.

"Then there's the car," Emily said. "It's always making some kind of noise it shouldn't be making. And the refrigerator. Same thing. And the bills that should have gone to the insurance company, and they didn't, and now you've got them on your desk, or worse, on the kitchen table, and they get mixed up with the magazines and the flyers and the rest of the junk. The next thing, you're digging through the trash trying to find them."

"Done that," Annie said.

"And I don't even know why," Emily said. "Because if you lose that pile of bills, you can count on them to send more. They WILL send more."

"But I get your point," Annie said. "The day-to-day stuff. That's what fills us up. No room left for anything else is how it seems sometimes. The more important stuff. The stuff that should be more important."

"And the bicycles," Emily said. "I don't know about your kids, but mine outgrow their bicycles faster than we can buy them. And they sit in the garage, or, more likely, lie out in the driveway where you back the car over them, and you get on the kids for not riding them, and they tell you they're too big for the bikes. 'You'd ride it if I got you a bigger one?' And they do for a while, and then they don't."

Annie listened. She was good company. She knew how important that was. The conversations looped around and repeated themselves. The words and gestures didn't change. Somebody got sick and you talked about that for a while. Somebody got well. Then it was appointments and paperwork, and by then the kids had outgrown the bicycles again. It didn't matter. It was connecting, wasn't it? They all understood. They all did.

GOODBYE, ARTHUR BALADINO

"Some guys, a few, I don't want to run into," Francis said.

"You owe 'em money," Gibby said.

Francis shrugged. The two had found seats toward the back of the room. Francis was slouching. If he'd had a hat, he'd have pulled it down over his eyes. Gibby figured anybody who'd care that Francis was at the service would see him all right, whether or not he was sitting up straight.

"You saw those guys out front."

"They weren't trying to hide, right?" Gibby said.

"Doin' their job, I guess," Francis said. "I hope they got my good side."

The light was low in the big room. Heavy purple drapes, sun-faded, covered the narrow windows. Organ music throbbed at a low volume.

"You think he had anything to say about how this goes?" Francis said.

"He had the time to think about it, I guess," Gibby said. "But, nah, I don't think he'd have given a damn. Far as I know, he didn't believe in anything. If he did, you'da heard about it before me, right? Besides, a lotta guys he'd known, he outlived. Who'd he have to impress?"

In the front row of folding chairs, Katherine Baladino sat dry-eyed in black. Like Gibby and Francis, she had noticed the men in suits outside the funeral home. She'd resisted the impulse to smile at the camera.

. . .

The service hadn't been her idea. She'd gotten a note saying it would happen, in case she wanted to be there.

"When someone has been ill for a long time," she was thinking, "what do you feel when it's over?"

Relief that there's no more suffering for Arthur, though toward the end, he was unconscious nearly all the time. Still, no more of that, whatever it had been.

And for herself, no more waiting for him to die. Katherine Baladino knew enough about who her husband had been to understand how unlikely it would have been that he'd die in his own bed, but he'd gotten old and sick enough to do it. She had lived for a long time without him. Without him she had mourned the death of her son, Teddy, victim of a ricochet, and her daughter, gone so quickly after her diagnosis.

"A woman marries a crook," she thought, "even a guy like Arthur, protected for a time, then not, she has to expect he goes first. That and he was an old man. But even if he wasn't, men die first. Even the good ones. Even the ones who don't carry guns and eat lots of vegetables."

But neither a mother nor a father is supposed to outlive the children, so on Arthur's day, such as it was, Katherine was thinking about the fatherless children who'd gone before him, and Arthur, locked up when they died.

Now he was gone, and she hoped he would be forgotten. The alternative might mean an ambitious congressman would begin wondering out loud if maybe there were more guys to hang now that Arthur Baladino was no longer alive to frighten somebody broke and desperate enough to talk.

"If they could have seen him at the end," Katherine Baladino thought, "they'd have known they didn't have to wait."

. . .

At some point during the service, Francis realized he was hearing the same organ music, over and over.

"It's on a loop," he said to Gibby, who had no idea what Francis was talking about, so Francis let it go. But it depressed him. "Generic solemn," he thought, and over and over the same thing. "Maybe it's all the old guy deserved," Francis thought, and then "more than most, I guess. Something, anyway, and it doesn't matter to him, so maybe it shouldn't matter to me."

But it did. It did. And sitting in his folding chair at the back of the room, Francis was sadder than he thought he'd be. He wondered if there would be any music for him.

An hour or so before they'd arrived for the service, Francis had mentioned to Gibby that though this time it was for Arthur Baladino, the fuckin' bell tolled for everybody before it was finished ringing. This thing was gonna remind them of that.

"You know something else that'll remind you about that, it's seeing a dead guy's hanged himself," Gibby said.

"You've told me about that," Francis said. "Don't tell me again."

"It wasn't like you might think," Gibby said. "It wasn't, you know, his eyes bulging and his tongue hanging out."

"Like in the cartoons," Francis had said.

"Right. It wasn't like that. It was just . . . he was a dead weight, this guy, at the end of the rope. Like a dead weight of something else."

"A sack of potatoes," Francis said.

"Sure," Gibby said.

"Or rocks."

"Yeah, or potatoes, like you said," Gibby said. "I guess I told you about that."

"Only rocks would have been easier," Francis said. "You said that was because you wouldn't be thinkin' about what the rocks might be thinkin' while you were cutting the rope and all, which you do—thinking, I mean—even if the guy is dead as rocks. Or potatoes."

"Sorry," Gibby said. "I forget who I told about it."

"Everybody," Francis said. "You've told everybody. They could all get together and tell each other the story just like you told it. With the rocks and the potatoes, and with the knife that was too dull to cut the rope, but you sawed away at it like an idiot, anyway."

"That's right," Gibby said. "I did."

. . .

Now they sat quietly, listening to the organ music that was about to start again from the beginning. Francis was thinking about how he, too, told the same stories over and over, sometimes without remembering he'd shared them with that listener, and sometimes remembering that he had, and telling the story anyway because it was easier than silence, which was sometimes uncomfortable for him, though not if the alternative was listening to Gibby's story about cutting down the guy who'd hanged himself.

Gibby was thinking about the night he'd tried to do that. And he was thinking about the part of the story he hadn't told Francis any of the times he'd told him about some of the rest of it. He was thinking about how he was supposed to have been keeping an eye on the guy, and he was supposed to have looked for the chance to bring the guy to another guy.

"And the other guy," Gibby was thinking, "that other guy was working for a guy, or he was then, anyway, and he was owed money by my guy, that I was supposed to be watching, looking for a time I could bring him to this guy, so he could get the money. Only I didn't. Stayed too far behind him is what I did, so he wouldn't see me. But it turns out he doesn't see me if I'm wearing red shoes and a wedding dress, because he wasn't looking for anybody, unless he needed somebody to give him directions to the hardware store, which he knew where it was, so he didn't, and he knew, also, that the hardware store is where you go if you need to buy some rope, which is when I should have known what he was going to do, if I'd been closer and I'd seen what he was buying there. Or that's what my guy told me when we talked the next day, which was he talked. I listened."

It had been a bad day by any measure, and Gibby felt fortunate to have gotten past it without somebody breaking his fingers or something worse, like his kneecaps.

"Maybe they felt sorry for me, what it was," he thought. "Me having to try to cut the guy down and all."

But he knew that wasn't it. The guy who'd been owed the money had the other guy, one of them, get everything Gibby'd had since he'd botched the job. That wasn't so bad, Gibby thought, because he hadn't had much. Still didn't. Then the guy, or another guy, probably, went after the wife of the guy Gibby had to try to cut down, and she didn't have much, either.

"Kid's got a paper route," she told the guy. "Might be some change in his drawer."

Arthur Baladino used to tell that part of the story sometimes. He liked the widow's courage, he said.

"Which is not to be confused with he was a good guy," Gibby thought, as the organ music began at the beginning again. "Because Arthur probably got the change. Yeah, he got it."

"I can't listen to much more of this," Francis was saying. Maybe nobody else was noticing the looped music, though that was hard for Francis to imagine.

"I don't think you want to leave in the middle," Gibby said. He had realized that he was enjoying himself. He didn't often get time to sit quietly.

"Christ," Francis said. "You think it's just the middle?"

Katherine Baladino could also have done with a shorter service. She was worried about the dog she'd left at home.

"Rest yourself," Gibby said. "You got anywhere else you gotta be?"

About that Gibby was right. By being where he was, Francis was doing what he should have been doing. His associates were around him. Arthur Baladino had built an organization, and he'd built it well enough so that it ran smoothly without him, at least for a while. It had hummed right along, never mind that Arthur Baladino had been in absentia, and no matter that he was now in absentia forevermore. His wife had been taken care of when he was incarcerated, and she'd be taken care of just as certainly now that he was dead. Up and down the line, guys like Gibby and Francis would keep doing what they'd learned to do, what they'd learned to do well, and they would adjust as they had learned to adjust. The officers outside and the news people with their cameras, they would do the same, and sometimes they'd acknowledge each other as they went about their business, which in this case, on this particular day, meant that no matter which side you were on, you knew who Arthur Baladino was and at least some of what he had done, so you showed up.

In the quiet after he got Francis to take a deep breath, Gibby found himself thinking about the end of his own life. The death he'd seen had looked final. Sometimes there had been a lot of blood. There had been screaming. When that stopped, nothing. That was how Gibby saw it. But he could not quite believe there was not some sort of reckoning.

"Not like a score-keeper, exactly," he might have said. "But something, ya know? Some way to know what was up at the end. Not where you went. Nothing like that. Just something, ya know, to give you an idea of what it meant. Had meant. I don't know how else to say it."

He didn't say that. He didn't know anybody he could have said it to, except maybe Francis, and Francis looked angry.

Outside, when the service was over, Gibby felt he'd made the right decision.

"Anyway," he said, "you didn't run into anybody you didn't want to see, right? Or you didn't want them to see you. Whatever it was."

"Not a one," said Francis. He put his hand in his pocket, as if to assure himself that his wallet was still there.

"And it wasn't so bad," Gibby said. "No open casket or anything. Because I been to some of 'em where they do that, and I'm fine if I never have to go to one of them again."

Francis stopped walking and looked at Gibby. When Gibby looked back at him, he saw Francis was smiling.

"You get spooked?" Francis asked him.

"Spooked," Gibby said. "I don't know if it's that. It's not that I'm afraid the guy's gonna jump up and grab me, anything like that. It's just, maybe . . . I don't know. I don't need to see it, ya know? Guy's dead, he's not really there anymore, is he? That . . . what's left, there, that's not him."

"Well, it's nobody else," Francis said.

"No, but you get me, right? Whether it's Arthur or anybody else, nobody or somebody, it's over, is what it is. What's left behind is just . . ."

"The wrapper?" Francis said.

"Whatever made him what he was is gone," Gibby said. "That's all I mean."

They were walking again. There was a breeze and it was pleasant enough.

"You want to eat?" Gibby said.

Francis said he thought that was a good idea, because he'd realized he was hungry, and he told Gibby so.

"That's no surprise," Gibby said.

"No?"

"No. Because what it is, you're not dead."

"Okay," Francis said. "I'm with you so far."

"You come out of a funeral and, you know, you hear the birds, hear anything, you know? The traffic in the street, whatever, and you're pretty happy you can hear it. It's good with you, right? Outside the place you been, the sun feels a little warmer maybe than when you went in. You think a cup of coffee might taste good and you get it, hot, and it does. It tastes great. Better than earlier that morning. Then you weren't thinking about coffee when you drank it. You were thinking about what you had to do, which you didn't want to do. Wasn't something you were looking at saying, 'Hey, that'll be good. Can't wait for that.' You worried about how it might go, who you might see, like you said. Like you told me. Afterward, you're good. You're not worried. You're alive, which seems pretty good. Wasn't your funeral. Not yet. You're upright and mobile. Knee's a little stiff, but not a big deal, right? Who's gonna complain about that after a funeral? Only a real asshole. So the coffee's good and maybe a sandwich, too."

"Life's grand, eh?"

"Don't get used to it," Gibby said.

"Not unless I want to go to a funeral every morning, you know, just so I got an appetite for lunch."

"Laugh all you like," Gibby said. "But that's how it works, isn't it? You're alive. The other guy's not. Good on you."

"All right," Francis said, "but what about when it's somebody that, when they're gone, you're sorry to see it happen to? A relative. A husband, maybe, and you'd still like to have him around."

"Why is it, you think, what people do when somebody dies, they bring a lot of food to the wife and kids, whoever's left? They got the casseroles, the pies, the lasagna. They got the little basket of cookies, there. Even the diabetics get the cookies. Have to give 'em to their kids, somebody. Why it is—everybody gets hungry. You might not want to say it when it happens, somebody you care about dies and all. You might not feel like you want to grill up a steak, but you're honest with yourself, you're hungry. The appetite don't mourn. Don't even slow down. Machine still needs fuel. Heat up one of those casseroles, dig in, anybody's watchin' or not."

"You're a philosopher," Francis said.

"Nah," Gibby said. "I been to some funerals is all."

Francis nodded. He could have said the same, but he didn't like to talk about the dead people he'd seen, whether they were in caskets or reduced to ashes in an urn, or whether they were dead somewhere somebody was gonna find 'em, like on the beach, he thought, gray and too big for their clothes.

"It's bad luck," he might have said, if he'd said anything then. "And they got family members can talk about 'em, they want to do it."

What he did say, after a while, was, "Damn if you're not right, though. I'm hungry."

"And no disrespect to Arthur Baladino that you are," Gibby said.

"And thirsty," Francis said.

"Another thing a funeral will do, isn't it?"

"I guess so," Francis said. "What's your philosophy say about that?"

"We'll have a beer and talk about it," Gibby said. "And we'll toast Arthur Baladino when we do that, is what we'll do. Though it won't matter to him."

It wouldn't. Unless on some level other than the one on which Gibby and Francis were talking it did. That was another thing Francis didn't talk about. Ghosts. Or not ghosts, exactly, but whatever was still around after somebody was dead. The way he figured, people still talked about that person, told stories, some of them stories they wouldn't have told, maybe, if he'd still been around to hear they'd told 'em. So how were you really gone as long as people remembered who you were, or who you'd been, whatever it was, and what you'd done, and what people said you'd done, which was the same, maybe, after a while.

It seemed that way. You were a president, a general, somebody like that. Or Shakespeare.

"What about him?" Gibby could have said. "People still goin' to see his plays, right? Even I know his name. 'To be or not to be,' right? He's got to be still around, you think about it."

"Sure. Or Clyde Barrow," he thought. "And Bonnie Parker. Or Bernie Madoff, even though nobody shot him."

"Sure," Francis might have said. "Every time somebody pulls off a big swindle, takes a lot of famous people, he knows they're greedier than they are smart, wrings 'em dry, there's Bernie Madoff's name comin' up again. In the news, on the T.V. . . . . people didn't know about him, they look him up. Guy might never die."

"And Amelia Earhart," Gibby might have said. "Never found her, did they. Still on their minds. Jesse Owens. Gotta be dead by now, but every Olympics somebody brings him up, talks about what he did back when he was a young guy."

"What you thinkin' about?" Gibby asked. He'd finished most of his beer and a ham sandwich. What he was thinking about was whether he wanted a piece of pie.

"Nothing," Francis said, but it wasn't true. He was thinking people would also remember Hitler forever, for what he did and what he tried to do, because bad or good, if what you did was big, you didn't die like almost everybody did. Or that's the way it seemed to Francis as he sipped his beer.

"Or children," he thought. "Children remember you, maybe." He remembered then that Arthur Baladino's children wouldn't be any good for that, both dead before he was.

"And now ol' Arthur himself, dead before his wife," Francis thought, and he found himself wondering, too, what she'd do, Katherine Baladino, whom he'd seen several times, but did not know, because Arthur Baladino had not been much inclined to introduce his wife to people like Francis, even when he could have done that.

But Francis had seen her.

"She was a looker," he said.

"Who?" Gibby asked. "What are you talkin' about?"

"The wife," Francis said. "Arthur's wife. You ever see her?"

"Saw her today, didn't I? Same as you did, up there in the front of the place."

"No, I mean back then. Back when she was younger. Way too young for Arthur is what I thought. Everybody thought."

"Which you did not say to Arthur, I know, because you are not dead. Instead you are finishing a sandwich and some beer. But you can say it now."

"Right," Francis said.

"But you're wrong. She is still a very good-looking woman, Francis. You have to give her that. And give Arthur that, too."

Francis thought so, too, though he didn't say it. He also thought Arthur Baladino had probably been a good-looking man, and not only in his prime, but beyond it. Francis remembered his first glimpse of the man. He'd been sitting at the bar in a restaurant that had offered a fine view of Boston Harbor. He remembered that he'd been feeling like an idiot, because for the price of the beer in front of him he could have bought two six packs and a cheeseburger somewhere else. He was hungry enough to think that way, and sober enough to know he couldn't afford to eat anything at the bar.

Arthur Baladino had been sitting at a table across the room with several other men, all of them in suits, none of them wearing ties.

Francis hadn't realized he'd been staring at them until the bartender suggested that it was a bad idea.

"They're gonna think you're a Fed," he said. "They don't have to look at you to know you're lookin' at them. They got guys to tell 'em that. Then they got guys to show up and tell you that you should'na done it."

"I can take care of myself," Francis had said, but he'd turned around on his barstool and started reading the labels on the bottles on the shelf behind the bar.

He remembered what they looked like, the men at the table, and what they didn't look like was guys who were worried about the cost of whatever they'd eat when they got around to it, which they did not seem to be in a hurry to do. That was what he'd been thinking about when he'd left the place—must be thirty years ago, he thought—and went looking for a cheeseburger.

At the time, he thought that would be all there was to his association with Arthur Baladino, and he felt quietly grateful to the bartender for warning him. But a few days later, a man Francis had never seen showed up at his apartment and asked him was he looking for work. The man said he'd been sent by a guy who maybe could use a guy who was in need of a job, and maybe could also be convinced that it was not polite to stare at people in a restaurant.

"I was between jobs at the time," Francis told Gibby. "So I listened to the guy."

"Okay," said Gibby.

"That means I did some things for him and his friends. Nothing much. And they did some things for me. Also nothing much. And then I got into the line of work I'm in now, which you know all about, because I brought you into it."

"Right," Gibby said. "I'm a grateful man. But early on, you must have done enough, you move up, and now you go to his funeral. You know about his kids, what happened to them, and not just hearing it from somebody heard it from somebody, like I did. And his wife, too. You know she's still going along pretty good, good as she can, and a pretty good-looking woman, which you also know."

"Sure," Francis said. "I kept track. From a distance. Not like staring at him or anything."

"Like you did."

"I'm a quick study," Francis said.

"So you kept track."

"Little Sir Echo," Francis said. "Yeah, I did."

"He was, like, your hero."

"No," Francis said. "Not like that." But he wondered if there was some truth to it. Arthur Baladino had been a presence. In prison, they'd talked about him. Carefully.

"He was respected," Francis said. "Even the CO's, you know? Some of them, I bet they'd get home after work, talk to their friends, tell 'em, 'We got Arthur Baladino in there, you know that? The guy ran the show for a while.' I bet it was like that. And they'd dress it up, is what I think. What he did wasn't enough, they'd pile on some more. Tell their friends who it was came to see him, the reporters. The wife, too. Tell 'em about her. Prob'ly made them feel like bigshots, talk about how they had him right in there where they worked. Punched in every day, and there he was. The boss. One of 'em, anyway. The only one they could see there in the neighborhood."

"But getting older and older, every day," Gibby said.

"Like you and me," Francis said. "All that is."

"Until the day they let him out, he got so old."

"Right," Francis said, "and now he's dead, so he'll get no older. And he's still a presence, what he is. He was what he was, no apologies, in or out."

"Watched television, slept when he could, jerked around the people who came to interview him. What else? Made friends?"

"I wouldn't know about that," Francis said.

"Anyway, he didn't get killed in there. That's interesting, don't you think? I mean, there musta been guys liked to have kicked him down the stairs, stuck him, something like that."

"I suppose so," Francis said.

"Had more guys with him than against him," Gibby said. "Musta been like that."

"Maybe it was that simple," Francis said. But he didn't think it was that simple. He thought a lot of the guys in there must have felt he was different. What they'd done, he knew, was a paragraph or two in the paper about a robbery, a carjacking that ended in a wreck after a chase, a stupid choice of customers when there was a gun needed selling—nothing that got more than a brief mention on the local news, and then where were you? Lost among all the other guys who'd done nothing anybody'd notice or remember after the video of the car chase. But Arthur Baladino . . . that was different. Here was a guy'd made a career. Here was a guy with some stories about him, and the stories got better and better, and if somebody in a suit comes in one day to ask you about one of them, you are gonna say,

"No, I didn't hear that, and I don't know anything about it." And the guy in the suit says, "Are you sure?" And you certainly are, and that's what you tell him, and you call him 'Sir' in the bargain, or maybe 'Officer,' because just because nobody stabbed Arthur Baladino or kicked him down the stairs doesn't mean somebody won't come after you, he's asked politely to do it, and maybe he drops a weight bar on your neck, so you'll never tell that story again.

"This is even if all it is, you heard the story," Francis said. "You don't know whether it happened or not. Because suppose you knew a guy who maybe was where it happened, if it did, and all he did was drive a car somewhere with something in the back seat, and it was wrapped up in brown paper, so he didn't know what it was, did he? He just drove it somewhere, and when he got there, he left the car unlocked. He went and got a cup of coffee, which there is no law against that, or leaving your car unlocked, either, it comes to that, even if somebody might wonder why you'd be stupid enough to do it. And when he comes back, the package, you can't say he lost, since it wasn't his to begin with, I guess. And it's gone, now. Somebody asks him where, he doesn't know. His eyes don't move side to side when he says that to the guy who's asking, because he doesn't know. And he says he still doesn't know what it was that was wrapped up in the brown paper, right up until they stop asking him, because he doesn't. Why would he have asked?"

"It's like the army," Gibby said. "You do what you're told."

"It's like that, and it isn't," Francis said. "Nobody telling you to get on an airplane, go to Afghanistan. Nobody shooting at you, either. Mostly not. But you do what you're told to do. Yeah."

Gibby knew. He'd done what he was told to do. He'd driven cars with all sorts of things rattling around in the trunk. He'd never asked about any of them. He remembered a time he had looked . . . pulled over on the side of a road at night and looked, and found a very nice rifle with a telescopic sight that he knew he could get rid of in about eleven minutes with a phone call, but he wrapped it up again and drove to where he was supposed to drive and threw the gun off the bridge he'd been told about, and that was that, because if he'd made that phone call, maybe it would have been somebody throwing him off that bridge, which he knew. He was better off with Francis—doing what Francis had taught him to do—than doing errands like that, which he also knew.

"Also in the army, what they do if you're no good at it, following orders and so on, they throw you out, which is not so bad," Francis said.

"Dishonorable discharge," Gibby said. "I know some guys have that. Hard to get some jobs, you have that."

"Hard to get some jobs, also, you want to walk somewhere, you need two canes."

"I know a guy like that," Gibby said. "Young guy. He was, anyway. Played some football. Had an older brother did some things for some guys, and he said—the young guy, the football player—said he could help out with it. So he ran around with some stuff, left it where he was supposed to leave it, until one day he took it home instead, and the next time he came running around the block to take something somewhere, a guy with a bat chopped him across both kneecaps, and that was that. For football, I mean. I don't know about two canes. Maybe, though."

"I wonder if that had anything to do with Arthur Baladino?" Francis said.

"I don't remember anybody's name," Gibby said. "Not even the kid."

"That's the idea," Francis said. "The more you don't remember, the better. The only thing better than that, you never heard the story at all."

Gibby nodded. "Yeah," he said. "I don't think I did."

.   .   .

Late that night, lying awake in his single bed, Gibby listened to the traffic in the street below his apartment. A public works crew had been working outside his window for most of the day. They'd left an enormous steel plate over the hole they'd made in the street. A car going over the plate wasn't too bad, but when a truck hit it, Gibby thought he could feel the building shake. He knew how some people who grew up in the city got so accustomed to the noise that they couldn't sleep when they went anywhere else. Chattering squirrels or rippling streams drove them nuts.

They needed the sirens, the shattering bottles, the kid upstairs telling his father to fuck off.

It had never been that way with Gibby. He'd wake at the squeal of a taxicab's brakes. Sleep through a helicopter overhead? Forget it.

Now he could hear the biggest trucks rumbling along blocks before they'd hit the steel plate, and he'd tense a little and wait for the bang-slam of the plate on the street as the tires left it to fall. Between trucks he thought about some of the stories he'd forgotten, or never heard. Then he thought about a time when, assuming he lived long enough, he would have forgotten lots of other things.

"Like how to brush my teeth," he said to himself.

He thought about Arthur Baladino, old enough to be let out of prison, never mind what he'd done. He thought about what Francis had told him about Arthur Baladino's children, one dead of some disease that killed you quickly, the other the victim of a crazy accident, neither of them likely to be remembered, unless somebody wrote a song or a long poem about Arthur Baladino, dead and gone.

"Stranger things have happened," Gibby thought. He fell asleep for a few minutes, and then another truck, an eighteen-wheeler, he thought, caught the steel plate just right. The building shook, or seemed to, and Gibby wished he had somewhere else to be, and he found he was still thinking about Arthur Baladino and his dead children.

"It could happen," he thought, because he remembered a song about Joey Gallo and how it made the gangster out a hero because he said he wouldn't carry a gun, because he was around too many children. Then there was Pretty Boy Floyd, the outlaw Oklahoma knew well. Gibby couldn't remember Floyd's last name, but he remembered that Floyd was said to have provided Christmas dinners for families on the dole. He remembered that somewhere in the same song there had been something about men who robbed you with a six gun, and some with a fountain pen. Gibby considered himself fortunate. Nobody'd robbed him with either one, though he'd been threatened by men with guns, or men who led him to believe they had guns in such a way that he did not doubt them when they were telling him what he should do next.

Then he remembered that when he'd once mentioned to Francis that he'd escaped both forms of robbery, Francis had called him an idiot.

"The guys in that song with the fountain pens, they've moved on," Francis had said. "They got computers now. They got all sorts of ways to rob you, you don't even know it."

Gibby often deferred to Francis on matters more complicated than where to have lunch, and, lying on his back, waiting for the next truck to rock the steel plate back and forth, he concluded that Francis was probably right. He'd probably been robbed lots of times without knowing it had happened.

That might explain the single bed and the noise outside.

"Bang-boom!" went the next truck, maybe a fair-sized panel truck by the sound of it.

"Some people sleep somewhere it's quiet," Gibby thought. "Must be nice. But most people hear the noise like that, pretty much like me, I guess."

The thought was at once discouraging and a comfort.

"Most people just get along," Gibby thought. "Get up in the morning and do their job, whatever it is, or have a cup of coffee and wait for the phone to ring, or somebody comes to the door with something you gotta do for somebody heard you were good at it. You could do it without a fuss. You done it enough for that."

Though it was still dark, Gibby didn't think he'd go back to sleep. He sat up in bed and looked out the window. Against the early morning sky he saw the lights of an airplane moving among the stationary stars. He remembered seeing the planes at night when he was a kid, and wondering where they were going, and wishing he was on one, wherever it was going to land.

"Maybe not so different from lots of kids," he thought. "When you're a kid, hey, what kid wants to stay where he is? Part of growing up is getting sick of where you are, I guess."

And then he thought, "But I haven't been anywhere. All the trips I took, soon as I was done with what I was there to do, I came back. Somebody asked me, I couldn't tell 'em what I'd seen, just that I'd done what I was there to do. And nobody asked."

Gibby scanned the sky for another plane. Somewhere in the building somebody turned on the hot water or turned up the heat. The pipes rattled. Gibby ran a hand over his jaw and decided that he would have to shave.

No more planes appeared.

He sat up and swung his legs over the side of the bed. He rubbed the spot on the lower part of his back that hurt each morning but almost always felt better once he started to move around.

"Maybe just as well I don't have to catch a flight," he thought. "Back would probably hurt worse if I had to sit in one of those airplane seats all day."

In an hour or so he would meet Francis, whom, he figured, was still asleep.

"Prob'ly dreaming of winning the lottery," Gibby thought. "Or maybe he dreams about airplanes, too. Maybe he'd like to go somewhere, same as me."

He knew Francis was a good sleeper. He'd sat beside him in the car, both of them supposed to be watching for someone, Francis snoring.

"You could sleep through a hurricane," Gibby had told him more than once.

"A hurricane?" Francis would say, "I hope so. We get a hurricane, what good am I gonna do anybody bein' awake? Help count the trees comin' down?"

"You don't worry," Gibby would say.

"Sure I do," Francis would say. "I just don't worry about the same things that get you down. Things I can't do anything about, I don't worry about that. Something I can do, I tell a guy, 'Yeah, I'll do it.' That's so he doesn't worry about it, and then he doesn't, and then he calls me again the next time, he's so happy he didn't have to worry about it."

It made sense to Gibby, for somebody else.

Francis was happy enough to let it go at that. He was fine with Gibby telling him all sorts of things about himself. He enjoyed some of the stories, though not the one about how Gibby had tried to cut down the guy he was supposed to bring to another guy, but the guy had hanged himself. He wasn't likely to forget the story about Gibby on the beach with the girl who must have been beautiful, hauling him into the waves. Francis thought about that one sometimes; sometimes the girl was blond and sometimes she was a redhead. She had a great laugh. The laugh was always there. And she was strong for her size, right? She had to be to get Gibby, all hungover, off the sand and down to the water. He couldn't have been much but dead weight, sick as he'd been.

"I probably ought to tell him more of MY stories," Francis thought sometimes. "That's something I probably should do."

CHARACTER WITNESS

"That's what she says," Patrolman Jackson told his sergeant.

"She hasn't been . . . She doesn't need a character witness, yet," Emerson Black said. He was sitting at his desk, leaning forward on his elbows. Now he pushed himself out of his swivel chair. "Tell her to go away," he said. "Tell her somebody will call her when they need her. When WE need her. Tell her that. Say 'we.'"

"I told her," Patrolman Jackson said.

"So now she's . . ."

"Right outside, there, waiting to talk to my superior. Today that's you."

"Every day," the sergeant muttered. "All day, every day, even when I'm not here. Even when you're not here."

He walked around the desk. Halfway across the room, he turned back to the patrolman. "All right," he said. "Don't worry about it. Let's see if she'll go away when I ask her to go away."

In the newer part of the building, which was connected to the room the sergeant was about to enter by way of a short, tiled corridor, there were half a dozen cells. They weren't as bad as the three cells in the older part of the building. Two of them had been turned into storage closets. The other one had become the second evidence locker. Nobody liked that arrangement because the cell with the leftover evidence in it had no room for a man to sit comfortably among the disorderly piles of paper and cardboard boxes, and protocol said there should be somebody there, or at least near enough to the evidence room so that if somebody tried to steal something, they'd have a challenge. "Near" meant somewhere in the damp hallway that ran the length of the row of former cells. It was the safe duty nobody wanted.

Su-Su Evinrude sat alone in one of the new cells. She thought she knew what would happen next.

She didn't.

She was calm now that there was nobody to shoot and nothing with which to shoot him. Her father had told the police officers who'd come to the restaurant that he was washing his hands of her. He'd made elaborate hand-washing gestures when he'd said it. The woman with him had said, "Lady Macbeth," but in the din of the work of the EMT boys and the bustling of waiters and the arrival of a fire engine with, for some reason, a blaring siren, nobody had heard her.

If he'd heard her, Su-Su Evinrude's father would have said, "Jesus. She's crazy, too."

The sergeant entered the room where the woman who'd identified herself as a character witness sat up straight on a bench of blond wood. The sergeant's initial impression was that she was younger than he'd imagined. He hadn't expected her to look as if she could walk away from their conversation and get a job as a model for an exclusive fitness club.

The woman started to stand when Emerson Black came toward her and he made a patting motion with his right hand.

"Please, don't get up," he said.

He sat heavily beside her on the bench and said, "What can we do for you?"

The woman recognized that as a polite way of saying, "What are you doing here?"

"I know Ms. Evinrude," she said. "I've known her for some time."

She wondered if the officer would take out a notebook and a pen.

"She's been through some terrible things," the woman said. "He tried to kill her, for one."

"Who's that?" Black asked.

"Her father," the woman said.

"The man she was trying to kill," Black said.

"I don't know that she was trying to kill anybody," the woman said.

"The way it's come to us, ma'am, she left the restaurant and came back with a gun, which she fired several times. This suggests intent to inflict great bodily harm, at the very least. To me, anyway, that is what it suggests."

"Maybe it was self-defense."

Despite his intention to advise the woman to go away until she was needed, probably by whoever would defend Su-Su Evinrude rather than by Black or anybody else on the police force, Emerson Black was curious, and the woman's eyes were luminous.

"Self-defense," he said.

"You've read Carl Rogers," the woman said.

The sergeant shrugged. "Tell me about self-defense," he said.

"He tried to kill her when she was a child. He held her head under water in the bathtub."

"He . . ."

"Her father. She told me about it," the woman said. "He was bathing her. She splashed him. You know, kids. But he pushed her head under water. She might have drowned. Probably would have. But she grabbed on to the shower curtain and pulled hard enough so that the bar came down. Pulled it right out of the wall. It made a lot of noise, and Su-Su's mother came in and caught him trying to drown their child. She grabbed a glass bottle of mouthwash off the basin and hit him on the side of the head with it. There was blood everywhere."

"She remembered all that?"

"Wouldn't anybody?"

"She was . . . He was bathing her, you said. How old would she have been?"

"What if she had been a he?"

"I don't follow you."

"If a young man told you his father had tried to kill him when he was a child—"

"Nah," the sergeant said. "I think I'd still wonder how somebody would remember all that. I mean, the shower curtain, I guess. But that the bottle was mouthwash? Did the mother maybe tell the kid the story? Maybe a lot of times?"

Esther Vain—for that was the name of Su-Su Evinrude's character witness— understood. The sergeant was bound to be skeptical. He knew what he knew, which was that the woman whose childhood they were discussing had fired several shots at the man with whom she had very recently had a loud and very public argument. There would have been even more witnesses to the argument and the assault, except that one of the people close enough to see everything and hear most of it, Teddy Baladino, was dead as a consequence of one of the shots Su-Su Evinrude had fired in the direction of her father.

"Here's the thing you need to understand," Esther Vain said. "She's not, like, crazy. I mean, criminal crazy."

It was not the first time Esther had tried to convince somebody of that. She said the same thing to the man who'd run the basement office from which she and Su-Su Evinrude had tried to sell insurance to people who hadn't asked for it.

"She was listening," Esther said. "We weren't supposed to do that. We were just supposed to talk. When Mr. Moyer overheard her one day, he said, 'Goddam it! You're telling people not to buy the stuff! I'm an old man! I don't need this shit!'"

"She couldn't—what he called it—Mr. Moyer—she couldn't 'close the deal.' She'd, like, double check to see if the person she was talking to really wanted the insurance."

"Sounds like a good way to lose a job," Black said.

"I tried to talk to her," Esther Vain said. "I tried to explain that the only way she was going to make the money she needed was to sell the stuff, whether the people wanted it or not. You know, talk to them, help them decide."

"'Decide' is a funny word for it," Black said.

"I couldn't convince her," Esther said. "What happened was, she convinced me. We both left."

"Poor Mr. Moyer," Black said.

"The seats weren't empty for long, I bet," Esther Vain said. "It was a job, you know?"

Emerson Black had entered the room intending to get Esther Vain out of the police station as quickly as he could. A few minutes into their conversation, he'd looked at her left hand to see if she was wearing a ring, and he'd seen that she wasn't.

"You tried to save her job," he said.

"It wasn't a job worth saving, was it? She showed me that. She was ahead of me in her way. We'd both have been out of there before long, I guess. There was a lot of turnover."

"No doubt," Black said.

"We used to talk about it," Esther said. "Su-Su got a guy one night who told her he had all the life insurance he needed. We were supposed to ask about it, then tell the customer about a better deal we could give him . . . say it was better than whatever he had. This guy said his life insurance was being handled by Smith and Wesson."

"Hard one to beat," Black said.

"Right. He was going to shoot himself when he felt the time was right. It took Su-Su a little while to understand what he was saying, but then she kept him on the phone most of the night, trying to convince him not to think that way. But she didn't try to sell him anything."

"Lost hours," Black said.

"That's the way Mr. Moyer saw it," Esther said. "It wasn't too long after that we were gone."

"Together?"

"No," Esther said. "I lost track of her after that. Then I read about the shooting."

"And you figured she could use some help," Black said to himself. "And she surely could, but what can you do?"

"I read about what happened," Esther said. "I couldn't imagine there would be anyone who'd stand up for Su-Su. I mean, knowing what she'd told me about her family. Everybody would think she was crazy, right? Who'd help her?"

Throughout his career, Emerson Black had encountered a lot of people who'd been called crazy. Sometimes there was an official diagnosis—post-traumatic stress or something having to do with impulse control. Some of the people Black had known were crazy only in the presence of their estranged or philandering husbands or their wayward wives. Others turned to craziness out of boredom, and some of them just got beaten down by time and bad luck. As far as Black was concerned, what Esther Vain said about her friend applied to most of the people he'd seen labeled as crazy. What they had in common was that nobody came forward to help them.

"So, that's what you're doing," he said.

Esther nodded. "I wanted to try," she said.

"All any of us can do, isn't it?" Black said. But he was thinking, "Who is it she reminds me of?"

"A little thing," Esther said. "Coming here, I mean. A little thing, but it's what I could do."

"Not such a little thing," Black said. "A lot of people, they wouldn't come to a police station for anything. For anybody."

Esther Vain smiled and shook her head a little, as if to dismiss what she was doing, and Black knew who it was.

"And it shouldn't be," he thought, "because they don't look anything like each other. Esther Vain is a brunette, and she looks like she pays a lot of attention to how she looks."

Emily Nickerson had been blond, and all day her shag had looked tousled, as if she'd just gotten out of bed, which Emerson Black, age fourteen, thought was about as sexy as anything could be. She'd sat behind him in Latin class, which was all Black remembered about Latin class, except that the teacher, a short, stooped old fellow with dandruff on his checkered sport coat used to beg his students to ask their fathers if they had a summer job for him, and then say he was only kidding, though even at fourteen, Black knew he wasn't. Everyone knew it.

In those days, Black had worn shirts with button-down collars. They had a button on the back, and one day he'd been sitting in that class, failing to remember what it was he was supposed to remember about Gaul or wars or farmers, and he'd felt fingers at the back of his neck. He knew who was back there, so he hadn't moved or said anything, and eventually Emily Nickerson said, "There."

Then Black turned and found her smiling at him. Her tousled hair seemed to promise everything.

"I did up your button," Emily said.

"Thanks," Black croaked. He hadn't known what else to say. He'd barely been able to say anything. Emily Nickerson had giggled.

Latin class must have gone on. Maybe the stooped old man had called on Emerson. Maybe in response he'd read to the class about some battle in which Caesar had triumphed, at least according to Caesar.

From that day on, each day before Latin class, Black made sure the button at the back of his collar was undone. On days when Emily Nickerson wasn't in school, it never got buttoned.

Black wouldn't have called it flirting. "Flirting" was a lightweight word. What Emily did for him was not lightweight. Not for him. She and her attention to the button gave him hope. Someday, perhaps, a beautiful girl would unbutton the front of his shirt, and he would unbutton the front of her shirt, and his life would change.

"She didn't have anybody else," Esther Vain was saying.

Black had been looking at his hands. Now he looked up. For a moment he was surprised to see that the woman talking to him was not Emily Nickerson.

"I don't know what to tell you," he said. "Time might come when you can help her."

He knew it wouldn't be up to him.

"Tell you what," he said. "You leave me your number, your address, whatever you like, and I can get in touch with you, if, you know, there's something you can do to help your friend."

Esther Vain looked at him then, grateful. She felt he was taking her seriously, though she could see that he felt there might be nothing she could do for her friend.

Emerson Black was still remembering Emily.

They got up together and Black saw her to the door of the police station.

"Thank you," she said.

Emerson Black smiled and touched her elbow. "Take care of yourself," he said. It was something he said often, out of habit. But he meant it. Who else was going to take care of you? Nobody, he thought. You were on your own, so take care of yourself.

"You, too," Esther Vain said. "And please don't forget to let me know if there's anything I can do for Su-Su. She's really not a bad person."

Black nodded. He watched from the door as Esther Vain walked away. He thought about some of the people who weren't really bad. Then he thought about some of the bad things some of those people had done. Years earlier, a probation officer who'd been on the job for a while had shrugged and told Black, a young man at the time, "Good people sometimes do bad things."

Black and the officer were talking in the waiting room of a state prison, a large section of which had been closed, in part because a strike by inmates had convinced a handful of state legislators that although crowded cells might not constitute cruel and unusual punishment in and of themselves, crowded cells with no heat probably did. Or at least there might be a judge who felt that way. The prison, portions of which had been built in 1909, had been deemed impossible to heat, which the men living there had known for several winters. The probation officer had been referring to a couple of the inmates who had led the strike. Previously they had done bad things. They had done those things while wearing gang colors, and they had been arrested, tried, convicted, and sentenced to a lot of time in prison. There, years later, they had impressed the probation officer, the legislators, and the judge with their organizational skills and their determination to keep the focus on the crucial issue, which was that the men living in much of the prison were very cold.

"There were guys who wanted to lump in a lot of other issues, include them in the strike demands, right? And they were perfectly good issues. No bullshit. You got the food out there, which was not your balanced diet, even by the old ketchup-is-a-vegetable Ronald Reagan standards, ya know? And you got guys getting tossed into solitary for nothing, or nothing much. Some of my guys, they used to tell me when they'd get out of the hole, a guard would come by and say, 'Hey, I know you didn't do anything. Shit deal. What can I say? Sorry, man.' But they'd say it quietly, and they'd say it just to the guy, and they'd say, you don't tell anybody else, 'cause I'll swear I never said it. You made it up, right?"

Black, too, had been impressed. The leaders of the strike had kept the other complaints off the table, and they'd managed to keep in line the men who wanted to bring up everything else. "Later with the food," they'd said. "And don't bring up the guards. They don't like standing around in the cold any more than we do. You see 'em with the down vests under their uniforms, right? Two pairs of socks. Wool caps. People start asking questions, those guards are gonna say, 'Yeah, it's cold all right. Bet your ass.' Can't hurt us, right? Maybe it helps."

They were good organizers. And because he'd gotten to know several of them, Black knew that at 40 or 45, they were not the same people they'd been when they were wearing gang colors.

And he knew there was nothing much he could do about it.

"What if somebody had been taking notes on me when I was a kid, before I enlisted?" he thought.

Because he hadn't had to think about what to do when he was wearing the uniform. He'd done what he'd been told to do. For a time, it hadn't seemed a bad way to go. Then, when he was sick of it, he got out and found that he'd made some decisions he hadn't known he was making.

"Probably not so different for a lot of those guys inside," he thought. "Had some decisions made for 'em. Found out what they meant later on. Only thing was, they didn't get sick of running around in a gang, trying to prove themselves to somebody, didn't get sick of it soon enough. Maybe that was it."

Although Emerson Black had not made a career in the military, he was smart enough to work his service for what it had provided. He went back to school. His record was solid. Every city had a police department. He could have worked for any of them. He presented well. He didn't advertise his doubts, which grew over time.

In the early evening, Emerson Black left the station. He drove without purpose for a while. Out of habit, he noticed what was going on in the street. On the corners he passed, men stood in small groups, talking, sometimes laughing. Neon signs in the windows of the neighborhood stores advertised cigarettes or beer. In front, on the basement entrance to a church, a sign read: "Clothes Drive."

Black's thoughts turned to Esther Vain and her impulse to help Su-Su Evinrude, who certainly would need help.

"Crazy," Black muttered to himself. He felt it was probably the only thing Su-Su Evinrude had going for her. Do something so crazy that nobody could see a plan in it, maybe you'd get put away for treatment for a while and get out after they'd found the drugs that could calm you down and provoke you to say, "Yeah, that was pretty crazy, what I did." They'd send you on your way to whatever free lunch place or shelter might have a slot. Pick up something out of the bin at that Clothes Drive. Thank the lady working there. Pull your Clothes Drive coat tight around your shoulders and go wherever it was you could go until lunch or dinner time or check-in time somewhere you could sleep, with your coat still wrapped around you, because who wouldn't want a warm coat like that?

Black felt Esther Vain's impulse to help was real. He didn't think it would matter.

"What's she gonna do for that crazy lady?" he thought. "And what's anybody gonna do for the poor sap got hit with the ricochet and then died? Man, there's bad luck, and then there's you shoot at somebody like a crazy person, and you might get away with it because you're crazy, but you kill somebody by mistake. Musta made his old man crazy, too, when he heard about it."

Arthur Baladino HAD heard about it as quickly as the news could travel from the authorities outside the prison to those who were inside, more quickly than he'd have learned about it if he'd been watching the small TV in his cell. His son had never visited him. They "had never known each other well" was the way Arthur Baladino might have put it, if he'd ever mentioned his son. Maybe he saw some irony in the way Teddy Baladino died.

Black stopped at a light. A slender man with a bucket, a sponge, and a squeegee came striding toward his car. The man wore a dark sweatshirt. Black noted the absence of a hood. He also noted that the dress pants the man was wearing had been part of somebody's expensive suit. Black pulled his wallet out of his back pocket and let his window down half-way.

"I'll give you two dollars to leave the windshield alone," he said.

"Just clean it up for you, chief," the man said. He shook his sponge and smiled.

"Four bucks, but that's it."

The man with the bucket saluted with the squeegee and stepped away from the car. Black let the window down the rest of the way and handed him four singles.

"You should have held out for five," he said. "I'd have gone to five."

"Just don't tell me, 'Don't spend it all in one place,'" the man said. "I hate when they say that. I heard it a lotta times."

"Your money now," Black said.

"God bless," said the man.

"Take care of yourself," Black said. He remembered that he'd said the same thing to Esther Vain.

"Ain' nobody else gonna do it, right?" the man said. He saluted again with the squeegee and turned toward the curb.

Black smiled and drove on. "Ain' nobody else gonna do it," he thought. "Right. But how fine it is that they sometimes try."

"Because," he thought, "there's dropping a few dollars on the guy with the bucket full of dirty water and the squeegee, and then there's walking into a police station and saying, "Hello. I'm here to help a friend.""

Maybe she could keep in touch with Su-Su Evinrude, Black thought. Maybe that's what he could tell her. Most of the people who get locked up don't have too many people doing that, at least not after a while. Or you could put some money in her account, so she won't be short of toothpaste, soap, and candy bars. Put in enough, she can buy herself some clothes better than the ones she's issued. Buy herself a warm sweatshirt.

But this was assuming Su-Su Evinrude was found competent to stand trial and be held responsible for her actions, which had included shooting somebody dead, albeit not the person she'd apparently intended to shoot.

"Murder by bad luck," Black thought. "But attempted murder of her father, certainly, unless they found her to be nuts, which maybe happens, since the father gets overheard saying she's crazy, and the woman shooting up the restaurant doesn't seem much like the friend Esther describes, so maybe this Su-Su's got a handful of personalities, only one of them armed."

Black wondered if he should call Esther Vain and tell her he'd been thinking about how she said she wanted to help Ms. Evinrude. He was thinking he might say, "If you say anything to her, tell her not to talk to anybody. Tell her, let the lawyer get everybody thinking she's not competent to go to trial. Probably the best bet now."

He knew he'd be better off not telling Esther Vain anything. He'd be better off if he left it alone. He knew that. He did.

"Just thinking about what you said," he said when he called her.

"Which?" Esther Vain said.

"About wanting to help your friend," Black said. "It was a nice thing to want to do. I wish I could think of something."

"Maybe you will."

"What I mean is, I don't see it too often. Not often at all. Somebody who wants to help."

Esther had been about to go to bed when the phone rang. It was late to be calling, she thought, and then, maybe just late for her. She'd been surprised to hear Emerson Black's voice, and then not so surprised.

"Maybe you don't get out enough," she said.

"How's that?'

"That you don't hear people saying they want to help."

"Ah," Black said. "Sure. Could be that, or it could be my line of work, I guess."

He could hear her listening. After a moment, he said, "It's late. I hope I didn't disturb you."

"No," Esther said. "No problem."

After another moment of silence, Black said goodbye and hung up the phone.

Esther Vain returned to the bench in front of the mirror opposite her bed, where she'd been brushing her hair when the phone rang. She was smiling. She looked at her reflection and wondered how it had occurred to her to say, "Maybe you don't get out enough." She decided she was glad she'd said it.

Black had heard the invitation in what she had said. Or what he assumed was an invitation. He would call back some evening. He would say he'd been thinking about what she'd said.

"What was that?" she would ask.

"About my not getting out enough," he would say.

"Oh, that," she would say. "I hope you didn't think I meant anything by it."

"I was hoping you did," Black would say. "Why don't you help me out with that? Meet me for dinner somewhere. Anywhere you like, because I don't get out enough to know where to go."

She would laugh. She would find him charming. They would meet somewhere and perhaps after the first few minutes, the subject of Su-Su Evinrude wouldn't come up again.

Whether it did or not, Black assumed things would go badly for the woman who'd shot at her father, missed, and killed Teddy Baladino.

"A family dispute, alcohol, and a gun," Black would have told Esther Vain, if Su-Su Evinrude's future had been what they were talking about. "Nothing good's gonna come of that, ever."

"You make it sound like she's a statistic," Esther would have said. "She's not. She's a person, like you or me."

"Not like you," Black would have said. "You don't strike me as a woman who drinks too much, and I'd bet you don't own a gun. And not like me. I've got a gun, but it stays strapped in a holster. I've been a police officer for some years now and I've never shot anything but a paper target."

It would have been a conversation by which Esther Vain and Emerson Black would have gotten to know each other better, which was why Black was imagining it. He'd had a lot of practice.

Esther Vain also had an imagination. When she had first thought about trying to do something to help her allegedly felonious friend, she had imagined all the things that could go wrong. She might make a fool of herself. She probably would. She could get caught up again in the life of a woman who was deranged, or at least seriously disturbed. She knew that about Su-Su Evinrude. She'd seen her elated and she'd seen her depressed. She wasn't sure which was worse. She'd watched her in action, sabotaging her opportunities with admirable motives and manic energy. Su-Su Evinrude was, by anyone's measure, volatile and potentially dangerous. Her history was rife with disaster and disappointment. Abuse not only couldn't be discounted, the evidence suggested it had to be assumed. That's what Esther had seen, and she couldn't leave it at that, move on to rescuing a dog in a shelter.

When she'd thought about her previous relationship with Su-Su Evinrude, Esther had bounced from regret to resignation and back, over and over.

Still, she'd stepped up.

"That's it," Emerson Black would have said if he and Esther had been having the conversation he'd lately been imagining. "That's what attracted me to you. Or that's part of it, anyway." Here he'd have smiled, rather than saying outright that he thought she was gorgeous. He'd have left it for her to guess whether he was referring to her beautiful brown eyes or the way she shook her head a little when she smiled.

"What I mean is," Black could imagine himself saying, "is that you've got courage. More courage than sense in this case, maybe, because I don't know if there's anything you can do to help this woman. Maybe you'll get the chance to say she seemed crazy some days and not others, I don't know. But the courage is there. You could have walked away. It didn't need to be your concern."

"No," Esther would have said.

"It's terrific," Black would have said. He'd have smiled when he said it. She'd have been encouraged by that. She'd have been less uncertain. Maybe she'd have felt as if she'd done the right thing.

"Sometimes doing the right thing doesn't change what's going to happen," Black would have said.

She'd have looked down, then. He'd have had the opportunity to notice the curve of her neck and the tiny diamond stud in her ear. He'd have wanted her to look up so he could see her eyes again.

. . .

The next morning, Emerson Black woke up wishing there was something to solve in the shooting death of Teddy Baladino.

"If I had questions, I could ask them," he said to himself. "I could ask her."

But he had no questions. Su-Su Evinrude had discharged a weapon several times in a restaurant. As a result, Teddy Baladino, son of Arthur Baladino and otherwise undistinguished, was dead. Teddy had no record. All Black had been able to find out about him was that he had probably been an unhappy, lonely man, and that his connection with his once-illustrious father had been minimal, if that. If he'd lived long enough to look Su-Su Evinrude in the eye while he was dying, he might have said "Thanks."

"Maybe she was doing him a favor," Black thought. "Son of a crime boss and all. Maybe he felt guilty."

Black's father had been a police officer. He'd come to the job after a decade as a corrections officer. As a small child, Black had thought it was cool that his dad went to work in a prison each day, but his father had taken the job because it was all he could find, and he'd learned gradually what the work could do to a man. At the dinner table one night, he'd said, "Sometimes it seems like the only difference between them and me is that I get to go home at night. But I still got to go back in the cage in the morning."

"Sure it is," Black's mother had said. "And that's except for the nights when they call you back in."

Black remembered the conversation. Looking back, he thought maybe that had been the night his father decided to study for the police exam.

After that had worked out, he could tell his son stories about kids he'd encouraged to stay in school and men and women he'd warned away from stupid decisions they might have been about to make.

"You're on the street," he'd say, "you see things, hear things. You might stop something before it gets started. Maybe not, but maybe, you know? Help somebody avoid something that mighta been worse. Maybe a lot worse. Even jus' bein' around. Let 'em know you're payin' attention. Maybe they get that you don't want 'em to screw up. You're rootin' for 'em."

Emerson Black was proud of his father. When some of his classmates gave him a hard time because he was the son of a cop, he called them out for their ignorance, but it didn't happen often. Most of them knew Emerson's father by sight, and a lot of them had family members he'd helped in one way or another. The more he learned about what his father did, the prouder Emerson became, and the more relieved he was that the man had escaped work in the prisons. Corrections officers died young. That's what the statistics said. Black looked them up. He learned that a lot of the men who worked in the prisons killed themselves. And he learned from his father that a police officer on the street could invite people in the neighborhood to call him by his first name, and that he could get to know the names of their children, and that sometimes, long after he was off the clock and back in his civilian clothes, that police officer might visit some of those people in their apartments, just to see how they were getting along.

"All that and the Marines," Black might have said to anybody who'd asked him why he'd decided to join the force. But the checking on people, that thing his dad had done, that was maybe what made Emerson Black think it might be worthwhile to look in on Su-Su Evinrude. He wasn't going to stop something from happening. Too late for that. But he could let a prisoner know that somebody was concerned. If nothing else, he could tell her she hadn't been forgotten. He could tell her Esther Vain had come to him to see if she could help.

"Because I am a man," Black said to himself, "but I am not a brave man when it comes to picking up the telephone. I am not the kind of man who could just call without having something to report."

.   .   .

"Have you come to get me out of here?"

Black wasn't surprised at the first thing Su-Su Evinrude asked. Or the next thing.

"Has somebody bailed me out?"

"I'm afraid not," Black said. "I wanted to see how you were doing, that's all. And to tell you Esther Vain has been asking about you. She wants to know if you need anything while you're here. If there's anything she can do."

"She's here?"

"She came to see me," Black said. "She saw on the news what had happened. She wants to help."

"Not likely, is it."

Black smiled at her. Sitting on the bunk in her cell she looked small. She didn't look dangerous.

"Not right now," Black said.

Su-Su smiled, as if she suddenly understood. "You want to fuck her," she said.

"She is crazy," Black thought. "Because who says that to a cop?"

"What you're gonna do, you're gonna call her now and tell her you've seen me. She'll ask about me. You'll tell her . . . I don't know. Whatever. Doesn't matter. You'll have your reason to call her. I don't blame you. She's hot. Tits like they're built for Hollywood."

"Crazy," Black thought.

"Don't mention them," Su-Su said. "She's had 'em since she was fourteen. She's self-conscious. Boys used to bump into her accidently on purpose. Assholes."

"I'll call her," Black said. "I will do that. I'll tell her I've seen you. If she asks, I'll tell her what happens next, if I can find out. I don't know if I can right now. Not exactly a straight-forward circumstance we're got here, is it?"

"It was an accident," Su-Su said. "Anyway, I'm not guilty by reason of insanity. Ask my father. Or ask his girlfriend. Ask both."

. . .

"I saw her," Black said.

"Is she okay?"

"I wouldn't say that."

"What did she say?"

"She said she was crazy, and if I didn't believe her, I should ask her father."

"That's all?"

"She said she thought I'd come to see her so I'd have a reason to call you," Black said.

Esther Vain didn't say anything. Black listened to the silence for as long as he could stand it.

"Are you okay?" he finally said.

"Do you have plans for this evening?" Esther said. "We could meet somewhere for dinner."

"That would be nice," Black said. "I'd like that."

.   .   .

When they'd been seated at the barbeque spot he'd recommended, Black looked across the table at Esther. She'd dressed for a date—a black silk blouse and tailored jeans. Clean running shoes. In the same slacks and jacket he'd been wearing at work, Emerson Black felt old and slow in her company, but not as old and slow as he'd worried he might.

"I thought about visiting her," Esther said.

"Well . . ."

"I'm not gonna do it. I don't think I'd be . . . it would be strange, seeing her in a cell."

"Nobody in there's at their best," Black said. "It's like they say, 'No such thing as a flattering mug shot.'"

Even as he said it, he wondered if it was a stupid thing to say, but Esther smiled at him. Then she shook her head.

"It must be—I don't know—discouraging to see that," she said. "I mean, people at their worst."

"Sometimes it is," Black said. "She's a funny one though, your friend. She seemed like she wasn't so unhappy where she was. She asked me if I'd come to get her out, but she didn't sound like that would have been, maybe, such a good thing."

"Maybe because being in the company of her father would have been worse," Esther said. "You probably were good with your father, right? She hasn't had that."

"Why do you say that?"

"I told you," Esther said. "I know her a little. She talked about her family sometimes, when we worked together."

"Not that," Black said. "About me, I mean. What makes you think I was good with my father?"

Esther shrugged. "I don't know," she said. "Stability. Something. Am I wrong?"

"No," Black said. "He was a police officer, too. A good guy. He worked with kids, you know, in the neighborhood and around. A guy he knew, a retired cop, started a kind of club for kids. He had a little basement room he fixed up as a gym, mats on the floor for exercise, couple pairs of boxing gloves. He had a little lot on the side where he put up a basketball hoop. He got the kids T-shirts, you know, different colors. Made up teams. He had this book, a scorebook, where he'd keep track of who won, all that. Foul shot contests, races around the block. My father would work with him when he could, bring kids by so they'd have somewhere to go."

Dinner arrived on platter-sized plates.

"I should have warned you," Black said. "They're generous with the portions. Some people order a half, you know?"

Esther Vain looked across the table and smiled. She had a forkful of pot roast halfway to her mouth.

"I'm good," she said.

Black watched her attack her dinner. He thought, "no more conversation for a while, I guess." If somebody'd asked him right then if that's when he knew he was falling in love, he'd perhaps have said, "Yeah, maybe. Yeah. Then."

.　.　.

That night, after he'd seen Esther Vain home, Black sat on the edge of his bed and thought about the last time he'd felt the way he was feeling.

"The girl in the club where they had that band," he said to himself. "Played covers. She was sitting up near the front, same as I was, hanging on the words of that Bob Dylan song, 'Tangled Up In Blue.' I watched her. She knew the words of even the old stuff, 'Blind Willie McTell,' stuff like that. Stuff I cared about. Unbelievable. Cheryl, her name was. Beautiful. We sat there together after the singer packed up, talked about the music. I walked her out to the parking lot when the place was closing, got in the front seat with her. It was a sweet promise."

He had not pushed then, either. "There'll be tomorrow," he'd said. "Lots of days and nights."

He remembered that she'd looked surprised at the way he put it. And there were some tomorrows, and some tomorrow nights, too, but it hadn't worked out like he'd hoped.

A couple of weeks later, she'd told Black that when she'd met him at the club where she knew all the words, her boyfriend of a couple of years had told her he was going to join the army. He'd decided it was his duty, now that the nation was at war.

"It's always at war," she had said, but she hadn't been able to convince the boyfriend. He'd kissed her goodbye and said that as soon as he got some things straightened out, he was going to enlist. "And then he didn't," she said. "I don't know what he was doing those couple of weeks, but he never enlisted. Maybe somebody talked him out of it. Then maybe he was too embarrassed to come along and tell me he'd changed his mind. But he did that, finally, this morning. So, we're back together."

Emerson Black was a young man then. He felt older after he got the news. He'd thought he and Cheryl had something more than shared tastes in music. He'd learned that he was alone in thinking that.

At the time, he thought about arguing that she could do better than to go with a guy who couldn't make up his mind, and then who had to wait weeks to tell her that he'd changed it. He thought about arguing that the boyfriend had chickened out on service to his country. He didn't say any of that. Something told him that even if she agreed with him, it wouldn't matter.

"Well, shit," he said.

"Yeah," she said. "I'm sorry. You're a good guy."

No poetry there. But for those few weeks, it had been something he'd never known. He woke up with a smile. He loved finding Cheryl next to him. On the nights they hadn't spent together, he loved knowing he'd see her later that day, coming around a corner or standing at his door when he came home. He was overwhelmed by how easy it was to be close to her, to feel the closeness even when they weren't together, to anticipate her return to his apartment, where some of her clothes were already hanging in the closet, and a pair of her shoes, a little muddy, had been forgotten by the door.

Now he could imagine that maybe it was going to be like that again. He was older, but not so old, right? Lots of guys his age . . .

"She came in looking for a way to help her friend," he thought. "Only less than a friend. Just a woman she'd worked with at some point, a woman she knew was going to need more than she was going to get from a system that didn't know what to do with her, so it locked her up. Esther thought she could explain. She thought somebody would listen. Me, as it happened."

But what could one police officer—even a sympathetic police officer who'd fallen in love with the woman who was trying to help her friend—what could such a police officer do? Slip the woman a key to her cell and look the other way? Not even in the movies, right?

And then there was whatever Su-Su Evinrude might do if she got out by less dramatic means—bail, under the care of a therapist, on her own shaky recognizance, whatever. She'd killed a guy. On some level, she might understand that her life was unlikely to settle again into whatever unholy groove it had been traveling in, never mind that she didn't know the guy she'd shot.

What if, after Black had vouched for her, she bought a blond wig, hacked into her father's bank account, and fled?

"You have to hope sense will temper compassion," Black thought. "I have to hope that we'll move on from whatever I can't do, move on from what it was that led her to find me, something bigger, for us."

"Because," he thought, "there was Emily Nickerson and me in Latin class, when she was fiddling with the button on the back of my shirt, and there was Cheryl, whose last name I can't remember. There were girls at dances, and girls I sat with at basketball games, and a girl I put my arm around at a concert where I hoped the music might say something I didn't know how to say, and after the music stopped, she went home with friends. Next day I called the number she'd given me, and I got a delicatessen. I hadn't thought about her in a long time, and I bet she hasn't thought about me. But now there's this."

.   .   .

"You're one love-sick puppy," Su-Su Evinrude said to him when he next visited her cell.

Emerson Black shrugged.

"I'm glad you didn't deny it," Su-Su said. "It's out there, man. The way you walk in here. All over your face, too."

"Is there anything I can get you?" Black asked.

Su-Su looked at him and smiled. She shook her head. "I don't think so," she said. "Not unless you can get me a clock that I can turn back a few decades, maybe. Maybe all the way back to zero. Zero for me, I mean."

Black had inquired into her case, but he hadn't learned much about what was likely to happen to her. She was facing a gun charge in a state where that was no minor concern. Teddy Baladino was dead. Her family had not been forthcoming when questioned, and nobody who'd spoken with her father felt he'd be of much use to Su-Su or to anybody else, including himself, come to that.

"He's a fuckin' idiot," is how one social worker had put it when she'd talked with Black. "If you could find something for which you could put him in jail, you'd be doing everybody a favor. Guy's a creep. His girlfriend's just as bad."

Black had resisted the temptation to say he couldn't arrest somebody for being a creep. He'd just asked about other family.

"None I've found," the social worker told him.

"Maybe none to be found," Black thought. It made him consider how fortunate he'd been to have a solid family while he was growing up. He'd outlived them all, but they'd been there for him when he was younger. On occasion, he could still hear his father's voice.

"Not perfect," Black would tell anyone who'd asked about his childhood. "Not perfect, but solid. My dad was there for me. My mother yelled at him sometimes, if she thought he was taking chances he didn't have to take. It's not easy being married to a cop. She didn't want to be one of those women on the TV news, standing beside a hole in the ground while somebody plays a bugle over the father of your children, and then some old guy in a blue uniform comes over and hands you a flag, all folded up, like that's going to help."

"Me," he'd have said, "I was proud of him. Proud of my mother, too, for what she did herself and how she brought us up. I got the speech when I was a kid, probably before I could understand all of it, but I got it. 'Policeman stops you some time, you put your hands where he tells you to put them, you look him in the eye, and you call him "Sir."' Didn't matter that my father was an officer, too. Both of them, my mother and my father, knew how things worked. Both of them had made their ways through it and come up okay. Making it to some place that felt pretty good didn't mean they didn't understand what could happen to their child—any of their children—at any time."

"We have to understand what we're getting into," Emerson Black told Esther Vain sometime later.

"What's to understand," she'd said. "You're black. I'm white. We'd have bi-racial children. Lots of them around."

"Yes," Black said. "Lots of them. And for some people, the more of them the more threatened they feel."

"We would love them all the more for that," Esther said.

"And they would need every bit of it," Black said. "Or they will, I should say. Because we're going to do this, aren't we?"

"We are," Esther said. "We are. And with joy, my love."

Afterward, sometimes Emerson Black wondered sleepily if Su-Su Evinrude had been put on the earth to connect him to Esther Vain.

Asleep beside him, Esther was dreaming that she was sailing on a boat across a quiet lake.

"People have lived and died to lesser purpose," Black thought. Then he caught himself up, acknowledging that he had no idea what he was talking about or where the thought had come from, and that death was a pretty far-fetched notion with regard to Su-Su Evinrude's immediate future. She was young and reasonably healthy, and she wasn't going to die for what she had done.

. . .

She didn't even stay long in prison. After a short hearing, she was transferred to a state facility where she could be more thoroughly evaluated. The judge who'd made the decision to send her there didn't know what else to do. Certainly somebody who'd been discharging a gun in a restaurant shouldn't be let off with nothing but a warning to refrain from doing it again.

"You can't have people running around the city with guns," the judge had said to herself. Then she realized how ridiculous she'd have sounded if she'd said that to anyone out loud.

"I wouldn't have been a judge for much longer," she said to herself. "Not around here. Not today."

Still, there was a distinction between somebody who waved a gun around in a restaurant and eventually shot Teddy Baladino while apparently meaning to shoot her father, and somebody who carried a gun around for some other reason. That was why Judge

Midge Milway had ruled that somebody ought to examine Su-Su Evinrude's head for at least thirty days, thereby determining if she was likely to shoot anybody else, whether on purpose or by mistake.

Once she'd thought about the judge's decision, Su-Su was all right with it. She liked to talk, and for at least thirty days, she'd have a captive listener.

And she'd been in worse places. Her father's house was poisonous. It had been for years. He was a foul-mouthed, ignorant man who'd been born into enough wealth so that he hadn't had to work, which he regarded as just about right. On his most charitable days, he considered his daughter an obligation.

Whenever living in her father's house had become intolerable, Su-Su had moved in with a friend or an acquaintance who'd been a friend.

After she'd driven the friend or acquaintance to throw what Su-Su had brought with her into the hall and slam the door, she'd lived on the street, where she had depended on the free lunch places and overnight shelters. She knew when to line up for the places where nobody was likely to steal her shoes.

Being sent some place for observation felt okay. Better than okay. She'd have a place to sleep without having to stand in line to get it, and she was sure her father wouldn't be allowed to visit her, even if, for some reason, he were to try. There would be some stipulation against it.

She would be fed regularly. There would be coffee, and it would be hot, and she could scream and shout if it wasn't, and maybe somebody would make it hotter. Or she could ask politely. She knew how to do that, too.

She'd have the company of lots of people, some of them probably no crazier than she was. Who knew? Maybe she'd make a friend. There had to be people there as desperate as she was for human connection.

It would be a temporary friendship, built on temporary circumstances they were sharing.

How often was it otherwise?

As it happened, the room she shared with the woman who never talked had a window that looked out on the highway. Su-Su found the constant hum of traffic soothing. She liked the idea that everybody out there had somewhere to go. It encouraged her to believe that someday she might have a destination.

Several times she asked the woman who never talked if she felt the same way about the traffic, but her roommate kept her thoughts and feelings to herself. Su-Su didn't envy the staff member assigned to her roommate, though the staff member didn't mind. She felt as if she'd been listening to nonsense and self-serving lies and witless fantasies, some of them terrifying, for most of her professional life. She was tired. Silence was okay with her. When it was time to write her report, she'd draw whatever conclusions she could from body language and the slender case study she'd been given before the first interview with the woman who never talked.

Each time a session ended, she'd be tempted to write that maybe the woman just had nothing to say and was wise enough to know it. Instead, she'd write something about trauma and resistance, and she'd offer a suggestion about what somebody else should do next.

She'd understand—or at least intuit—that nothing she said to the woman or wrote about her was likely to change anything. But she would stay with the woman through the designated forty minutes of their appointment and beyond. She would sit and be company for her client for as long as her client chose to remain in the chair. If the woman reached toward her, she would take the woman's hand. If something seemed to frighten or upset the woman, she would say something like, "I'm here," or "I'm with you." She wouldn't say, "Don't worry," because she knew the woman had every reason to worry, and that worry had been with her for a long time, and that it probably wasn't going anywhere.

She was not unkind. She would not look at her watch.

Su-Su Evinrude did not know what happened when her roommate left the room for her sessions with her therapist. She did know that the woman was as quiet with the social worker and in the group sessions as she was in their room.

Sometimes, lying in bed, waiting for the thirty days to pass and wondering where she would lie in a bed when those days were up, she thought about another woman who had been silent. A woman Su-Su had known years earlier, when she was still in school and had become involved with a Buddhist sect that recommended retreats during which those in residence did not speak. The woman Su-Su had known, whose name was Denise, remained on retreat for a year. On the day she left the retreat and came home, her husband, who'd waited patiently for her, asked her if there was something she'd missed, something she particularly wanted, now that she was back in the noisy world.

The woman asked him to get her a cheeseburger.

Lying in the dark, Su-Su thought of that and laughed.

From the bed across the room, her roommate asked, "What's so funny?"

She didn't say anything else during their time together.

CHILD AT THE WINDOW

Early on the first morning after the heat broke in the neighborhood that summer, a little girl peeked through the blinds of her bedroom window. She was called Libby, short for Elizabeth.

For the first time in several days the window was open and the blinds rattled a little in the breeze. During the night, when the temperature had dropped after the rain, her mother had padded into the hallway and switched off the air conditioning. Then she'd gone into Libby's room and opened her window.

The little girl hadn't stirred.

Now she was the first one awake in the big house that had been built on another of the lots where there had been a small house. The change, characteristic of lots of neighborhoods, but especially evident here, was something for people who'd lived there a long time to talk about. The people who'd moved into the big houses didn't talk about it. They'd only known what they'd been looking for, and they'd been looking for a big house.

The little girl looked over the green lawn, still wet in the early sunlight. Across the street, an older man walked a dog named Corkie. Libby had met the dog on several occasions. At first Corkie shied away from her, and the man had explained that she was skittish. The little girl nodded. Later she asked her mother what "skittish" meant.

"Frightened," her mother told her, and Libby wondered how anybody or anything could be frightened of her.

Eventually, when the man who always walked the dog explained how to approach Corkie, the little girl learned to stand still with her hand by her side so the dog would walk up to her, sniff her hand, and lick it. Then she would allow herself to be patted.

Now, peeking through the blinds, Libby said, "Hi, Corkie." She said it softly. The dog kept sniffing at the wet grass. Maybe it smelled a rabbit or a chipmunk. The man walking the dog didn't look up. When the dog had finished investigating the lawn in front of the little girl's house, she trotted on to the next yard, pulling the man along behind her.

Across the street there was a house that had been empty for a few weeks. Until the previous evening, there had been a sign in the yard reading "Sale Pending." Libby had heard her parents talking about it. They wondered who would move into the house, now that it had been sold.

"Hello, house," Libby said. She hoped the family moving in would have children, and maybe a dog.

Libby's mother often walked around on the lawn in front of their house talking on the telephone. If somebody had asked her whether she intended for people to hear what she was saying, she'd have pretended to be surprised. She'd have said, "Of course not."

"Why can't I have a dog?" Libby had asked her mother.

"Because I'd be the one who'd have to take care of it," her mother had said.

The little girl wasn't sure if that was true. Her mother was sure.

The neighborhood Libby was watching was quiet. When the older man and his dog had walked around the corner and out of sight, there was nobody to see from the window. There was nothing to hear but the birds.

A little later, the men who took care of the lawns would arrive, and there would be the whining of shrill motors and fragments of chatter in a language Libby couldn't understand.

"If I had a dog," Libby said to herself, "I could tell her how blue the sky looks today, because dogs can't see colors, and she wouldn't know. I could ask her if she was ready for breakfast. I could tell her that later we would walk down the street and around the block, and maybe she could play with Corkie."

If Libby's mother could have heard that, maybe she'd have been more likely to believe Libby would have taken responsibility for the dog, even though she'd still have been right about having to do a lot of the work herself.

Who would save Libby from a mother who walked around the yard talking on the telephone? What could the little girl imagine were she free of the people who were no longer amazed by the world into which they'd brought her? Maybe there would be a selective tornado, a hurricane, an impossibly unlikely weather event of some unknown variety that would change everything for her.

Libby stayed at the window, looking out at the still-quiet, still-cool day. She counted the houses she could see along the street that ran perpendicular to her own.

"One, two, three, and sort of three-and-a-half," she said. "Because I can't see the whole front of that house because of the trees. So, three and a half."

Behind the trees shading the house the little girl could only partly see were the two front windows of the room in which Arthur Baladino lay dying, but not dying quickly enough to suit the officer who'd visited him, whom Arthur Baladino had told to go fuck himself.

Arthur Baladino had also once wanted a dog. He'd never said so. He knew as certainly as any child knows anything that he'd never be allowed to have one. By the time he left home at sixteen, he'd almost forgotten that he'd wanted one.

"It's a good place for a dog," the little girl was saying to herself. "Right out the front door there are three directions the dog could go. She could pick. She wouldn't get bored. Or she could go down the hill through the woods and walk around the pond. She could learn to swim."

Libby had seen dogs swim. At that pond down the hill, she'd seen a golden retriever paddle after a dirty tennis ball. She was delighted when the dog captured the ball in its teeth without going under water, then somewhat clumsily turned and paddled back to the muddy shore. The dog scrambled up the bank. She shook herself, spraying everybody near her with pond water. Then she dropped the ball at her owner's feet and looked up at him, ready to chase it back into the water. She looked as if she'd happily repeat the process until somebody said, "Let's go home."

"If I had a dog," Libby said to herself, "I'd put her in my life jacket before we went to the pond. The one I have to wear when we go on a boat. Just in case. She might get tired of swimming when she was out in the middle of the pond, and I'd go in and get her, and I'd pull her to shore in her life jacket, and she'd lick my face."

Now she could hear noises in another part of the big house. Her parents were awake, or at least one of them was. She heard a door close softly, the bathroom connected to her parents' bedroom. Soon whichever one of them was up—her father, she guessed—would pad down the stairs and make coffee. If he'd remembered to grind the coffee beans the previous night, she would only hear the running water and the "clunk" or "clink" that the carafe made when her father set it down. If not, she'd hear him grinding the beans, and she would smell them.

She turned again to the window, hoping somebody else would walk by with a dog.

"Not the mean one," she whispered.

The mean one was noisy and brown. She or he—the little girl didn't know—would bark and growl when another dog came along. The man who walked Corkie would pull her toward the other side of the street when the mean dog appeared from around the corner.

"My dog wouldn't growl at other dogs," Libby said to herself. "She'd be friends with all of them. They'd play together, and I'd teach them to share."

The little girl's room was painted pale blue. On the wall opposite her bed was a framed print of a line of ducks. Six little ones marched behind their mother. Libby had always assumed they were happy.

Except for the ducks, Teddy Baladino could have matched the room in which he'd spent his childhood against Libby's. Like her, he hadn't had a dog, but like her, he'd had birthday parties. His mother had seen to that, even when his father was not available, which was often the case. For various reasons, most of them less obvious than his father's absence, it was tough being the son of Arthur Baladino.

It might have been less tough once Teddy left home for boarding school, where he fell in love with his history teacher, a young, exceptionally clean-cut scholar named Richards Warren.

"Love" wasn't the way Teddy would have put it. He wanted to BE Richards Warren, with his short haircut and his dark, tweed jacket and his chino pants with the sharp crease, and his easy grace. He wanted to be married to somebody like Richards Warren's wife, with her warm smile and the chocolate chip cookies she made and distributed to the fortunate boys who lived in the dormitory where her husband was the housemaster. He wanted to be the father of Richards Warren's children, though one of them, the little boy, was overweight and noisy. He wanted to feel as if he could remain at the school, teaching history while his wife baked and distributed chocolate chip cookies, until their children grew up and moved away and, eventually, Richards Warren himself died and was celebrated during a chapel service as a wonderful teacher and a great friend to generations of boys like Teddy Baladino, all of whom, Teddy imagined, must have wanted to be Richards Warren.

If, on one of her good days, Su-Su Evinrude had been told about the life of Teddy Baladino, she might have patted herself on the back for cutting it short. From wherever he was, Teddy might have patted her on the back, too. Su-Su hadn't done it on purpose, and she had not been able to think straight any more than she'd been able to shoot straight. If she'd been able to shoot straight, she'd have killed her father and perhaps seriously wounded his girlfriend, all of which Teddy Baladino would have witnessed, and from which he would have walked away.

. . .

Anybody who got even a glimpse of the little girl at the window on that morning when she watched the older man walking his dog and then, when they were gone around the corner, counted the houses she could see until she got to three and a half, would have figured her for a better life than the one Su-Su Evinrude, only fifteen years Libby's senior, had known. The little girl's father loved her. Nobody would have said otherwise. Su-Su Evinrude's father, bald, scrawny, pot-bellied and pale as a cadaver, was embarrassed by his daughter on the good days. On the bad days, she terrified him, which was why on that day in the restaurant, where Teddy Baladino was killed by a ricocheting bullet, Su-Su Evinrude's father had told his girlfriend that his daughter was insane. "Crazy," was what he'd said.

He'd said this even before Su-Su had come back into the restaurant with the gun. He'd said it when she'd made what would have been a scene in the restaurant if the waiters hadn't been too polite to acknowledge what was going on. They let her screech and swear and demand "the fucking keys" from her father as if that sort of thing went on all the time and was okay with them. The same waiters had been too polite to tell Su-Su Evinrude's father that he was not appropriately dressed when he arrived at the restaurant, claiming to have made a reservation that nobody could discover, because he had not made it.

Things would have been different for Teddy Baladino if the waiters hadn't been so polite, or so professional. One of them, down on sleep and about full-up with sloppy, self-important, rude men and their ridiculously flamboyant companions might have popped Su-Su Evinrude's father in the nose instead of bowing to him and ushering him to a table, despite his sleeveless T-shirt and his fat, dirty toes overlapping each other in his ugly tan sandals. Maurice

Evinrude, party of three, would have had to find somewhere else to eat, or maybe they'd have skipped the meal and gone to find an attorney who'd go along with suing the waiter for assault, or at least threatening to do it, which might have changed everything for the waiter. Maybe he'd have walked away from the restaurant, changed his name, and found a job driving a cab.

In any case, Teddy Baladino would have finished his solitary meal in peace, if not happily. His life would have gone on. Odds are he would have outlived his father, though Arthur Baladino grew to be very old, as well as very ill, by the time he was taken in an ambulance from the prison in which he had spent about all the time he could without dying.

But it hadn't gone that way, and when Richards Warren, now an old man himself, had learned about Teddy Baladino's death by ricochet, his customary, slightly crooked smile had straightened out for a moment, and he'd said to his wife, "Maybe you remember him. Kind of a sad case. His father was sent to prison—or sent back, I guess—while he was here. Teddy."

"Oh," Richards Warren's wife had said. "Right."

She hadn't exactly remembered Teddy Baladino, but she remembered that there had been a boy whose father had gone to prison, and that it hadn't been the first time he'd been sent there, and that some of the people at the school were proud of themselves for keeping Teddy on, though nobody asked Teddy.

And nobody, least of all Richards Warren or his wife, could have imagined that if somebody HAD asked Teddy what he'd like to do, he'd have said he'd like to be adopted by Richards Warren and his wife, so that he could change his last name to Warren, and it would still be okay, he guessed, for people to call him Teddy.

When Warren himself grew older, nobody noticed, at least not at first. Hadn't there always been a little gray in his close-cropped dark hair? And hadn't he always walked with a little bit of a limp, maybe from an injury he'd picked up playing weekend hockey with various chums? Or, more likely, lacrosse?

Young or old, Richards Warren couldn't have imagined Teddy Baladino's life any more than Teddy could have imagined a world in which he didn't think everybody was talking about him behind his back.

Had he lived longer, and had he been inclined to associate with his former classmates, and had they remembered him well enough to associate with Teddy, he would have learned that things at the school hadn't been so wonderful for a lot of them. Teddy had been a lost soul, but a lot of the other souls passing him in the halls and pushing him around on the athletic fields had been, if not lost, at least temporarily mislaid. Most of those souls would be found when the bodies in which they lived had grown up and accepted themselves for what they were, whether they were Nobel Prize-winning scientists or real estate developers with multiple bank accounts, some of them identifiable only by numbers. As boys, many of Teddy's contemporaries were worried about themselves. They had no energy left over for worrying about Teddy, or even, in many cases, to notice him, even the boys whom Teddy imagined were comfortable in their apparent triumphs. The best hockey player at the place had been frequently kicked out of the room he shared with a guy who'd met a fearless girl, who would sneak into the room a couple nights a week, hoping the hockey player's roommate, whom she was certain came from a wealthy family, would be careless enough to get her pregnant. Marrying him would rescue her from her stepfather's fumbling fingers.

Numbers of Teddy's classmates felt they'd only be able to compete academically by studying all night. They took whatever they could find to stay awake, and they were half sick much of the time from the stimulants and lack of sleep. Some of the most anxious and frightened of them hallucinated. Some of them did it loudly. A few of them did it when they were wide awake. Most of them recovered after they'd graduated.

But Teddy'd had as little to do with the place as possible while he was there, and nothing to do with it once he'd left. He regarded it as best forgotten, though he couldn't forget it. He sometimes had nightmares in which he wandered the halls of the old, wooden, two-story classroom building in which he'd taken math quizzes, one every Friday afternoon. In his dreams, he could smell the floor wax and the new, black rubber tread on the old stairs. Outside the tall windows, daylight was fading. It was just as Teddy remembered, a dream too real. When the math class ended, he would walk alone across the now-dark quadrangle to the dining hall with his hands over his ears so he wouldn't hear his classmates comparing quiz answers. At one of the long, heavy wood tables, he would eat boiled potatoes. There must have been more on his plate, but he remembered the potatoes. In the dreams, the master charged with teaching him algebra, an unusually tall man with an enormous head, loomed over him, waving his quiz papers, smiling at his mistakes. His classmates howled with delight and relief. Teddy would always take the brunt of the mockery, so his classmates were glad he was among them.

In that land, sarcasm was the coin of the realm, and Teddy was an easy target. He came to know his place.

Years later, the school, like lots of similar places, would come under scrutiny for various crimes and embarrassments. Some teachers and former teachers would be singled out as criminal abusers of children, though most of them would be too far gone to face the consequences, and some of them would be dead.

As for the habits of sarcasm and ridicule, they would be sarcastically ridiculed and regarded as quaint, rather than abusive, especially compared to the sexual battery and statutory rape. The old system would feel like the detritus of the supercilious and smug academies of the previous century, recreated by stern white men with too little imagination to do anything but follow in the footsteps of the governors and headmasters who'd gone before them and died certain of the righteousness of their mission. Then and much later the portraits of these champions of learning and probity would remain on the walls of the old buildings, some of which bore their names.

Teddy had never gone back to a reunion, never felt the pull of the place, never been even vaguely inclined to wander the paths between the hallowed halls or the corridors of the old, brick buildings, some of them covered in ivy, and the new ones, the construction of which some of his own classmates had underwritten. Had he visited, he'd have seen their names on discreet brass plaques affixed to the bright bricks.

"Immortality," he might have thought in the presence of those plaques. "Immortality for Hamilton and Brewster, for Moss and Healey and Simmons. Immortality for Koch, as well, and for Cartwright and Sauvage and Adams the Greater and Adams the Lesser, whoever they all may have been."

"Baladino" was affixed to no plaque, though it might have been if Teddy's father had thought that way. Or if he'd had a sense of humor. After he'd been arrested for the final time and incarcerated again, the school might have felt obligated to take the plaque off whatever science laboratory or library addition or weight room Arthur Baladino might have funded. But maybe there'd have been a fight about it in the boardroom. Maybe some philosopher able to take a broad view of things would have argued that taking down the plaque and returning the Baladino money wouldn't have been of any use to the people Arthur Baladino had ordered buried in shallow graves or tossed into a quarry with cinder blocks chained to their ankles. Maybe this philosopher would have pointed out that money was money, after all, and it would have been hypocritical to accept what the proprietors of various financial institutions and hedge funds had stolen under the law, not to mention what various union-busting magnates and slave-owning statesmen had realized from the sweat of countless dark brows, while turning away the loot Teddy's father had provided, just because the Baladino money came from shopkeepers who knew they'd be robbed if they didn't rent Arthur's promise that they wouldn't be.

"How do we turn down what he made selling whatever he sold 'em?" the philosopher might ask. "We've got money from guys who ran automobile companies where they calculated how much damage the lawsuits could do before deciding to keep right on making cars that would keep right on exploding when somebody rear-ended them. We've got a whole family made their money in asbestos, then sucked the resources into offshore accounts and declared bankruptcy about ten minutes before the courts got hold of them. On some of those buildings—the newer ones—we've got the names of lawyers who built their firms busting unions full of coal miners who cursed them with their last, wheezing breaths. And the family that owned that pharmaceutical company that made all those pills, hired the doctors to say they weren't addictive, sold by the boxcar, pharmacists shrugging, 'Hell, you got a prescription, I guess it's okay.' How many people did they kill, all told? I don't want to think about the ghosts in the bright hallways of those places, the sterile labs, the depots where the trucks loaded up the crates full of dope and headed for the little towns where nobody was working and everybody was in pain. And you want to give Arthur Baladino his money back?"

It might have happened. It didn't, but it might have, had Teddy Baladino been less miserable at the academy, or had Arthur been interested in having his name on a brass plaque.

Instead, he lived to control and build the enterprise he'd run until he forgot there was anything else to do, if he'd ever thought there was, and when he was eventually prevented from doing that, he read crime novels in his bunk and gave interviews from time to time. The people who came to interview him hoped they could get some insight into why Arthur Baladino had done what he'd done with his life.

"Where I grew up, it's what you did," he told them. "Or you could become a cop. Some of my friends did that. One of 'em told me one day when I was out, 'I coulda been you, and you coulda been me.'"

"Why do you suppose he said that?" the hopeful interviewer would ask.

"Why don't you ask HIM, you lazy little shit?"

Arthur Baladino sometimes said things like that if he was tired of the interview and saw no glimmer of intelligence in the eye of his interrogator, only ambition.

"I should help you out?" he would think. "Fuck that."

But if the interviewer had sense enough to hold off the questions and wait for the next thing Arthur Baladino might say without provocation, the old crime boss might offer something like, "What he figured was, I wasn't so dumb, and he wasn't so smart. Or maybe it was the other way around, since I had the house with the eight-foot fence around the big yard and the rest, and it was mine, 100%, and he was still paying off some shitbox that had started falling apart, the kitchen counter pulling off the wall, water comin' in all over the paint, and nobody could find the leak because he bought what an honest cop could buy. Maybe I was the smart one. Anyway, wasn't any difference between us but he went one way and I went another, maybe both of us signing up for the family business. Little bit of that, I guess, what he was saying."

The people who read the interviews might have told themselves they'd learned something about the criminal mind, or at least something about what it was like to be living out a long prison sentence. They didn't understand that the days when Arthur Baladino was talking to someone who had a notebook and a pencil meant a break for him, nothing more. He didn't give a damn whether what he said was printed, or distorted, bent into something he wouldn't recognize. When he'd been asked by the few other inmates he talked to why he put up with the people who came to ask him questions, and then profit from the publication of whatever he said, he told them "space."

"You walk to the visitors' room, never mind there's a guard alongside. You sit down at a table across from some guy, or sometimes it's a woman, right? That's all right. And you stretch your legs. You want to, you can walk from one end of the room to the other, look out the window at the yard. Some of the guards, you can do that."

It wouldn't seem like much to somebody who didn't have a cell where he had to slide his feet under the bunk each time he needed to sit on the toilet.

But Arthur Baladino didn't talk about that when he was being interviewed, so it wasn't in any of the stories, how he had to maneuver in his cell. He talked about former associates who were dead, if that's what the reporter wanted. He talked about the excellent food in the places where those associates, now dead, once met. On a couple of occasions, he talked about his children, now dead, his daughter of cancer, his son of a bullet that bounced around the stone walls of a restaurant until it found the back of Teddy Baladino's head.

"Woman killed him didn't know who he was," Arthur Baladino told one reporter. "I never killed anybody I didn't know who it was. You can write that, you want to."

And they would. They would write down anything Arthur Baladino said. They felt his words counted. People who couldn't imagine what it was like to live as he had lived were curious, just as they were curious about what it might be like to live with the knowledge that you might get shot or stabbed by the brother or lover or the nutball cousin of somebody you'd cheated or threatened or beaten with a bat, which the much younger Arthur Baladino would sometimes do if he thought it necessary.

"It's different, a day when I talk to one of 'em," Arthur Baladino would say. "Sometimes that's good. My call, you know? How long they stay, how many questions they get, when they come in here. All that. I don't like 'em, I get up and leave. Something on the TV I want to see, I don't talk. They come in then, they can wait, come back later, whatever. Write about somebody else."

Nobody would ever write the whole story, but the men and women who came into the prison to ask Arthur Baladino questions often left satisfied. Those who'd never been in a prison were proud of the courage they'd demonstrated in taking the assignment. Didn't people get stabbed in prison? Didn't prisoners sometimes take hostages and hold razor blades or sharpened spoons at their throats while they demanded to talk to the governor or the mayor or Oprah? By going through all the doors that clanged or clattered or buzzed behind them, they'd established something. Cred? Something. Whatever they got from Arthur Baladino was gravy after that.

"It's a funny damn thing," Baladino told his wife when he came home to die. "They're excited, you know? Sometimes they're surprised that it's not like on TV, with bars all around and everybody dressed the same. In orange, probably, right? Where I saw most of 'em, it was just a little room inside the place, you know? There might be a guard, a guy who stayed there in the hall while we talked, and there might not. What was an old guy like me gonna do? But they're excited. They're talking to a guy who did a lot of things, they never knew anybody else who did 'em. I don't know. More things than I did, but that doesn't matter to them. I'm surprised some of 'em aren't here, too."

"Here?"

"Sneakin' around the house, knockin' on the door," he said.

And she thought, it wasn't that he wanted it that way. He didn't need the attention. He knew he was dying. Of course, he knew that. But he got talking, and he thought about how some of those magazine writers had looked at him when he told them the little bit he felt like telling them. He played them, maybe because there was nothing else to do. It was a way to amuse himself in a place where there weren't many ways.

"You'll have 'em comin' around after I'm gone," he said.

But he was wrong. Katherine Baladino was never bothered by a reporter after her husband died. There had been flowers after her son had died. There had been flowers after her daughter had died in hospice. But nobody bothered her after her husband died. She wondered if it was something in her bearing. She was a tall, proud woman who walked with purpose. Her natural expression offered those who saw her no reason to doubt that she was fine.

If she'd been familiar with words such as "bearing," that's what the little girl at the window might have thought on the day she saw Katherine Baladino walking away from the Baladino house—the half-house, Libby called it—and then disappearing around the corner.

It was early, the little girl's favorite time.

"Maybe nobody else sees her," Libby thought. "Maybe that's why this is when she walks."

There was no traffic. She could hear the birds. The morning seemed clear of everything but potential, a promise, though Libby couldn't have said what it was.

As she saw Katherine Baladino turn the corner, Libby thought that maybe the woman walking away was sad, though even at her age, Libby knew that "sad" and "alone" weren't the same.

"Still," she thought, "it would be nice if she had somebody to walk with. Somebody to listen to the birds with her."

When Katherine Baladino had disappeared around the corner, Libby found herself imagining that if she tried hard, she could make somebody else come out of one of the houses. Or somebody would open a window, or let a dog out, or push the button that would raise a garage door, just because Libby was thinking that it might happen.

When none of these things did happen, she decided it was because she didn't need anything but the singing birds and the soft feel of the early morning air on a day that would probably be hot before long.

That was enough, and perhaps because that thought had occurred to her, the little girl never forgot that moment. For the rest of her life, she could close her eyes and feel the smooth, white windowsill as she ran her fingers across the painted wood. She could call up the faint, metallic tang of the smell of the screen on the window, and the way the warmer air outside seemed to push against her and against what was left of the coolness of the room where she'd been sleeping. She could hear the birds again. She could even find the anticipation she'd felt then as she'd waited for her mother to call to make sure she was up, and the rest of the day would begin—the part of it in which she was surrounded by people and the things they all had to do.

She did not know, on that summer morning, that the moments alone at the window would be with her for the rest of her life. She would always have the early morning of the day that summer, and the scent of it, and the sounds, and the feel of the smooth sill on her hands. Long after some of the houses she had counted were gone, long after people had built porches or patios, driveways, or gardens full of flowers and vegetables, she would have that morning. And she would have it long after she herself had grown up and left home and born children of her own and watched them grow and move away to lives of their own. She would have it after she had surrendered to a life in a home for people who ate at the same table three times a day and were regarded as fortunate. She would have it as she waited for the only thing there was left to wait for, which would be, she hoped, a quiet cessation of her life in the middle of an otherwise unremarkable and long afternoon, a cessation that didn't much inconvenience anyone, and didn't surprise anyone, least of all the woman who would tap lightly on the door to bring her medication, and who would find her in her chair, quiet as she had been on that summer morning, calling back for the last time the feel and the taste of the beginning of that summer day.

REAL ESTATE LADY

"Yes," Constance Evans said to herself. "I can look at myself in the mirror without cringing, without regret. I did what I had to do. No shame."

She was thinking of the woman from whom she began to learn her new trade. Her mentor, the real estate lady.

The real estate lady knows things. Under the house she has just shown to a young couple, water rises silently. In the basement of the house, the people who had hired her to sell it had hung shirts and jackets on an aluminum rack, demonstrating, they hoped, their faith that the basement was a fine place to hang clothing.

The real estate lady knew the neighborhood, and she knew about the water table. She knew there was water under most of the houses, unless it was under all of them. She knew, as surely as anybody can know anything about water and water tables and houses, that if the young couple buying the house was going to stay in it, they'd have to hire somebody to dig around the periphery of the basement and put in a sump pump.

She mentioned none of this. When she'd first looked at the house, she'd noticed the discoloration low on two of the basement walls. When he'd seen her looking, the owner of the house, a physician, had started to tell her that occasionally they'd had a bit of water. He was going to say it only happened every couple of years, when it rained especially hard, or when warm weather followed a heavy snowfall. But she held her hand up to stop him.

"Don't tell me," she'd said.

Constance Evans understood. "I have no husband. I am living in an apartment with flimsy walls and a stairwell that echoes when you're on the stairs. One day somebody will trip walking down those stairs and grab the metal railing, and whoever it is will pull that railing right out of the crappy, echoing wall," she said to herself. "Maybe I'll be called to testify against the landlord. If I can keep selling houses, I won't be there to see the accident. I'll have moved. They'll have to find me if they want me to say the building should have been condemned, or that it should never have been built, and that whoever built it was a crook, and that whoever inspected it was bribed or drunk. Once I had money, and now I have none, because the husband I used to have lost it back when we had a house that was solid and a staircase that you could walk up and down on without your footsteps bouncing off the cheap-shit walls like they do in the building where I live now."

Constance understood that if nobody mentioned there had been water in the basement, the real estate lady could say nobody had told her about it. She'd learned how liability worked from the women in the office, who'd learned from the women who'd come before them. They were social women. The all rode on a float in the 4th of July Parade. They served on community boards and stood on the side of the road to cheer on the people who ran in a race to fund the search for a cure for Alzheimer's, or bicycled half-way across the state in the exhausting effort to raise money for cancer research.

But they knew their business, and they did it. They helped each other when they could see an advantage in doing so, but they pushed between the inspector and the potential home buyer when the inspector was trying to say something about how the sliders in the basement of the house wouldn't close because the place was gradually sinking and the walls were pulling apart.

"Stand here, close one eye, and look down the length of the back wall," the inspector would say.

"I'm sure it's all right," the agent would say. "The house has been here for years."

Maybe it had been, and maybe it had been built on the back of a payoff so a previous building inspector, preparing to retire to Florida, would look the other way. He would be dead by now, probably, or at the very least hard to find, and what difference did it make? A lawyer would have been expensive. Who knew how long the process might take?

"Maybe the weather. The humidity," the agent might say. "Like the way doors swell in the summer. Anyway, it's the basement, and how often would anybody be going out the back through the basement, anyway? Let's go up and look at that master bedroom again."

Everybody goes upstairs to the master bedroom suite, which is terrific. View of the woods—"conservation land. Nobody can build there, or anywhere adjacent to it. That view's going nowhere . . ." and the sunken tub in the master bath is bigger than a lot of beds.

Sold.

A month later, it rains. Hard. New homeowner heads down the basement stairs to get the laundry he left in the dryer the previous night and he's up to his ankles in water.

"Holy Shit!"

"What is it, dear?"

"Mother of God!"

"What are you doing down there?"

"I'm goddam wading!"

The estimates for a trench, a sump hole, and a pump are reasonable in an unreasonable world, but tough on a couple carrying a mortgage they weren't sure about anyway.

Sometime later, probably on a sunny day when nobody's thinking of books and clothes and soggy cardboard boxes floating in the basement, the guy runs into the real estate lady in the hardware store.

"How's it going?" she says with a practiced smile.

"Not so great," he says. "We had a basement full of water. I thought that basement was dry. They had clothes hanging on racks down there."

"You never can tell, can you?"

But she can. She could have. She just didn't. She's the real estate lady, and she knows her business, the same as she knows it's no good showing fear.

Constance will not go the distance. She will not be a smiling bastard, lying to you everywhere she goes. She can look at herself in the mirror.

This might have puzzled Arthur Baladino, who'd perhaps have said, "Grab a glove and get in the game."

Constance Evans, at the start of her new career, might have been tempted. She'd been married to a man who had never understood that some of the people who trade stocks online are as dumb as some of the people who play the horses, convinced despite evidence to the contrary that they know something nobody else knows. "Horses for courses" and "Weight will stop a train" were exactly as smart and precisely as useless in the long run as the wise sayings and formulas veteran stock traders mumbled to each other over drinks in the paneled club rooms that wouldn't have admitted the horse players, but where Arthur Baladino might have been welcomed, had he ever wanted in.

"We had some money and then we didn't," was how Constance put it when she talked with the real estate lady. "My father made it, and I let my husband fix it with our attorney so he could get at it, and I'll never by god do anything that stupid again, if I live to be one hundred and ten."

But neither would she pretend she did not know there was water under a house, just because nobody had said so. She would not do that.

Constance sometimes found that when she thought of her former husband, she'd talk to herself. "Jesus, what an idiot," she'd say. "What a delusional clown." But she knew even then that Andy

Evans hadn't always been desperate and hateful and dishonest, and when she was with a client, she would try to remember that.

"You're buying a house, you want to feel good. Optimistic," she thought. "This is the place you're going to live for a long time. You're going to make a happy life with the people you love. You don't want to hear about people whose lives have fallen apart, somebody who's lost her house because her husband read some paperback books about trading stocks and checked out some websites and was too dumb to see that the only people likely to make any money were the people who wrote the books and built the websites, people smart enough to ignore the advice they were peddling.

"You're looking for a house, you want to ride with somebody who's as excited about the whole thing as you are—or who can pretend to be. Pretend convincingly, right? You don't want some bitter broad who's driving around in a car full of dog hair. You're in this game, your car's gotta be good, you return your phone messages, and those folks walking into the house with you, they have to believe you're as upbeat about the future as they are."

All this Constance Evans had learned from the real estate lady, and all this she would remember. But she would stop short of treachery. She would do that.

Constance Evans hadn't changed her name after she'd divorced her husband. Maybe she'd get married again, she thought. Who knew? She could change it then, if she felt like it.

Beyond that, once free of the mess Andy Evans had made of their finances and their lives, she was surprised to find that she didn't hate him.

Moving real estate wasn't dependable in the way a salaried job was, but when times were good they were very good, and Constance Evans wasn't stupid. She didn't fool herself into thinking that when two or three good months came along, it meant two or three more good months would come along after them. She'd had the opportunity to think about what her husband had done. She was cautious. She was also sharp enough to adopt some of what the real estate lady had tried to teach her without buying the whole package. She circulated. She listened to people talking about how they might need a bigger house, or a smaller house, or a house that wasn't next to the residence of a sixteen-year-old aspiring pop star whose parents felt they could keep him off drugs by providing him with ever-larger amplifiers and a more complete drum kit. She remembered what she'd heard, and she developed a sense of when the talkers were ready to jump. She called them as if to say hello, listened as they talked about their dissatisfaction with the homes in which they lived, and mentioned that she happened to have just learned of some place that might be perfect.

But she didn't call Katherine Baladino.

"No," she told Emily much later. "She called me."

"What was she like?"

"She was like anybody else thinking about selling a house, or maybe not."

This wasn't entirely true. What Katherine Baladino had said when she'd called was, "You had a husband who was a crook."

Constance had thought it was a pretty strange way to begin a conversation, even for a woman who'd been married to Arthur Baladino.

"I did," Constance had said, "and not an especially good one, as it turned out. Now I don't."

"Right," Katherine Baladino had said. "When can you meet with me?"

"You knew it was about the house, right?" Emily had said.

"I didn't know why else she'd be calling me," Constance had said. "We'd been neighbors, same as you. Maybe I'd seen her drive by and waved. But that would have been back when I still lived here."

Constance had never been in the Baladino house before Arthur Baladino's widow had called, but now she knew houses, and she could have made a good guess about what she'd see there. It was a big, old, hard-to-heat colonial with no family room. It was well-built, but anybody buying it would have been thinking about an addition, or at least rearranging some of the walls. Besides the family room, guests should have their own bathroom, one they could access without going into the hall. That was apparent in all the big houses that were replacing the small houses in the neighborhood. And who could tell how many guests there might be? Maybe an addition out the back.

"It was just me," was what Katherine Baladino was saying.

"Until Arthur Baladino came home to die," Constance thought. What she said was, "It's a lovely house. You've taken good care of it."

"It could use a coat of paint," Katherine Baladino said.

When somebody told her that, Constance sometimes said, "Well, most of us could, right?" It could be a nice ice breaker. A way to say, "You and me, kid. We're in this together, neither of us getting any younger. Let's put something away for the days coming on that are likely to be worse."

She didn't say that to Katherine Baladino. She didn't say anything right away. She smiled and she listened, and she thought about what it would be like if Katherine Baladino moved out of the neighborhood. There would still be a story, of course.

Those who'd lived there for long enough would tell their newer neighbors that the big old house was where a convicted murderer had come home to die.

"Arthur Baladino," they would say. "Of course, he was no danger to anybody by then. He was frail. They brought him in on a gurney. It looked like he didn't weigh much."

They would say that even if they hadn't seen it. They would want people to think they had. And some of them would tell the story enough times so that after a while, they'd believe they HAD seen Arthur Baladino brought lengthwise into the house, maybe trailing the smoke of an expensive cigar.

"What I'd usually do is get you some comps," Constance was saying. "That's if you're interested. That goes into the pricing. Then there's whether you're in a hurry."

She knew the neighborhood well. She didn't need to look up listings. She was saying what she'd learned to say.

"I'm sure you know what you're doing," Katherine Baladino said. "I'm sure you had to learn."

She was thinking about what it must have been like for Constance to learn one day—or, perhaps worse, to learn over a series of days, one after another—that the money you thought you had was gone. It must be a physical sensation, she was thinking. It must be that suddenly you have to sit down. It must be that your stomach hurts.

Constance Evans had learned something about how to work a client. She knew how to become that friend who could get the job done. She knew that selling a home was stressful, and what people wanted was a friend. She knew how to be comfortable assuming that role.

And she knew nothing about Katherine Baladino, this widow of a guy who'd have died in prison were it not for somebody noticing that he might as well be allowed to die in the house where his wife lived, since he wasn't going to murder anybody while he was on his back, breathing with difficulty, pissed because he couldn't make the TV remote work. This woman, this potential client, seemed to know something about the hole out of which Constance had hauled herself—more than some of Constance's friends knew, or seemed to know.

"It wasn't a problem at first," she would tell Katherine Baladino. "Or it didn't seem to be. He bought and sold stocks. Lots of people do. Everybody needs a hobby. He was saving us the commission a broker would have taken, right?"

Constance had learned to be a listener. She'd found she didn't have to pretend she didn't see the water lines in the basement to sell a house, and she didn't have to stop the seller from telling her something she didn't want to hear. She could listen. Lots of times that would do it. Most people weren't aware of how rarely anyone paid attention to them, how thoroughly people were preoccupied with their own problems. Constance Evans had as many problems as most people with enough to eat. She owed her attorney money. She wasn't having much luck with her grown children who wanted to know why she hadn't been more aware of what her husband—their father—was up to. Why hadn't she seen it coming? Was she blind? Couldn't she have done something to stop the hemorrhaging of money that, now, none of them would ever see? She had been part of a couple since she was very young. Now she wasn't. Friends called sometimes, but they rarely invited her to dinner. Dinners were where couples sat around the table and talked. Afterward, wives told their husbands they couldn't believe some of the things those husbands had said. Husbands said they hadn't heard the remarks their wives felt were subtle insults. What would Constance have done at the end of such an evening? Talked to herself, she supposed.

But with Katherine Baladino, she was a talker.

"Then he started spending more time at it," she said. "Which was okay for a while. I'm a reader. When he was sitting in front of the computer, I read. It wasn't so bad, for a while."

"And then it was," Katherine Baladino said.

"Right."

"There's a saying about how you go broke," Katherine said. "It applies to people who have a lot of money, I guess. But maybe also to people who just have enough. People who are comfortable."

"Or think they are," Constance said.

"I guess," Katherine said. "Anyway, 'How do you go broke?' That's the question. And the answer is, 'little by little, and then all at once.'"

Constance didn't say anything then. She was thinking about "all at once." She was thinking about the note from the bank. She was thinking about the first check that had bounced, and then the others. She was thinking about the lies her husband had told her—a mix-up with the account, a clerical error—and how she'd bought that because what else could it have been? She was remembering the day she realized she'd been lying to herself. She remembered her husband's tantrum. He'd cursed the computer programs that bought and sold shares on behalf of investors whose holdings were so vast and grand that the triggering of those programmed moves swamped the humble hopes and pathetic guesses and wispy dreams of chump change clowns like himself. She remembered his rage against the faceless, nameless entities that tirelessly marked every wrinkle or hint in every market in every country advanced enough to host the trading of shares and futures. If you couldn't anticipate what the machinery would do, you were cooked. You'd get left behind. You'd outsmart yourself every time, or, on the rare occasions where you guessed right and caught a wave in the market before it turned everyone behind you upside down and smashed them into the hard sand of a collapse, you came away from the experience with an intoxicating sense of triumph powerful enough to knock haywire whatever judgment might otherwise have remained. After that you were REALLY screwed.

"It's not fucking fair!" he'd wailed, and though she knew it wasn't, she also knew that wasn't the point. She was remembering that she had once considered herself fortunate. Andy Evans was a good-looking guy with a smile for everybody.

"There are lots of places where being able to go along will be plenty," Constance's father had told her. "He'll be fine. People like him. He'll learn what it is they expect him to do, and he'll find a way to enjoy it, or at least to look like he's enjoying it."

"It might have worked out that way, too," Constance told Katherine. "Andy is a likeable guy. Self-deprecating. He'll make fun of himself, say something like, you know, 'I don't know much about cars beyond where you put the nozzle when you get gas.' People eat that sort of thing up, and he knows it. People can think, 'Well, I'm not the only one who doesn't know what I'm looking at when I open the hood,' or 'Maybe I can't tell one side from the other in the war where we've been stuck for the past decade or so, but, hey, I'm not the only one.' He makes them more comfortable with their own ignorance, and everybody's ignorant about something.

"But then he decided he knew something lots of other people didn't know about—how to buy stocks. And in the beginning, playing the market, it WAS play for him. That's the way it looked when it all came out. Because it did come out, and then there was nothing left, and then it was just a matter of what they'd do to him."

"They? The law?"

"We thought so, but no. His employer, though, former employer. And everybody else."

"Your friends."

"My friends," Constance said. "And me."

"You probably wanted to kill him."

"Sometimes," Constance said. "Sometimes it was just that, I don't know . . . I wanted to know what had happened."

"Still," Katherine said, "you must have felt betrayed. You must have . . ."

"It would have been easier if he'd just been a real bastard," Constance said. "You know, if he'd neglected the kids when they were little or had an affair with his secretary."

"He didn't."

"No. And it was funny, too, because there she was, you know? Young, pretty, built great, probably thought Andy was about the smartest guy in the world and let him know it. Nothing to it, though. And with the kids, too. He was their Little League coach. He worked with them all the time. Went out across the street to the hoop on the garage, there, and taught the younger one how to do a lay-up when she was embarrassed because everybody else trying out for the 10-and-under basketball team already knew how to get into a lay-up line and run through the drill. Next practice, she was right there with 'em. He did that. It was years ago, but still. Would have been easier to hate him if he'd been out at a bar instead."

"It's always complicated," Katherine said.

One night sometime later, Constance remembered what Katherine had said. "Complicated." They were together in the house Katherine had said she might want to sell, and Constance found herself thinking about the man who'd paid for it. Her new friend, Katherine, had been married to a man who killed people. Or had them killed. She'd visited him in prison, at least for a time. She'd welcomed him back into her home when he'd been released to die.

"'Complicated' must have been the least of it," Constance thought.

"I know what you're thinking," Katherine said. "How could I have done what I did? Any of the times. Pick your time. But nobody stops being a person because they do something you can't imagine any person would do."

"It sounds like a riddle."

"It's simpler than that," Katherine said. "It's the opposite of a riddle, I think. It's a fact. People remain people. They screw up, or they do things—I don't know, awful things. They find themselves caught up in something, and they look around, and then they try to make the best of what they've found. Or they try to make what they think is the best of it, and maybe they're not seeing all there is to see, maybe they can't from where they are, and if they get tossed around in the system when they're still kids, in and out of it, you know, that will seriously distort how you see things . . ."

"No bad guys?" Constance asked.

"Arthur was out there on the extreme end of it," Katherine said. "I'll give you that. He was what he was, and he never denied it. It would have been a kinder, gentler world if he'd decided to go to school and become a chiropractor. There's a God, Arthur's got a lot to answer for. It'll take a long time, that hearing, though I don't think hell will be part of the plan, all that prison time having done the job about as well as it could be done. But that's just what I think. I saw him there, and I saw a lot of other guys, and heard about them. These guys who were addicts, guys who heard voices nobody else heard, guys who started each day knowing they'd better be careful what they thought, because somebody in a basement somewhere with a receiver would know all about whatever it was they were thinking before they could put pillows over their heads and shout loud enough to drown out the brain waves."

"Jesus."

"And worse," Katherine said. "Arthur told me about a man who'd been in and out of prison since he was eleven. This guy, whatever he heard on the television, they were talking to him. The longest stretch he'd had outside an institution was maybe a year, and that ended when the guy saw something on the news about militants in London, some damn thing. He grabbed a brick and went down to the Goodwill Store, found people waiting to get in, and broke the brick over the head of some guy wearing a turban. A Sikh. No more a militant than he was a man from Mars. It didn't kill him, the brick, but it did a job on his skull, even with the turban.

"Guy defending this guy with the brick said his client thought the Sikh was a threat. Voice in his head said he'd be a hero if he clobbered the terrorist. Guy went back to prison, this time for assault. Arthur told me the psychiatrist who came in once a week was more depressed about it than the guy with the brick. He thought he'd gotten somewhere with the guy, the psychiatrist did."

"He thought he wouldn't be back?"

"Maybe that's what he thought," Katherine said. "Arthur didn't tell me any more of the story than what I've told you."

"He must have told you a lot of stories," Constance said. "It's funny. Maybe like another guy would have brought stories home from work."

"For years," Katherine said. "Not when he came home. He didn't have much to say then. He thanked me for being there. For helping him out. He knew what was happening. At least he had that."

They sat together with what they had, and Katherine wondered if the return of her husband and the short time she'd had to feed him and sit with him had created the possibility that Constance Evans had become.

"I might have died one night, and nobody would have known," she thought. "I WILL die some night, and now someone WILL know. Constance will know. I will not be at the mercy of whatever kindness a police officer might have mustered while doing his unpleasant duty. I'll have an advocate. Or she will. Constance will."

"That was important," Katherine said. "I think it was. I think it mattered that he knew he'd come here. I suppose nothing had changed . . . nothing about what was going to happen, anyway, and nothing about when it would happen. But he knew he wasn't locked up. I don't know. He knew he was with me. I had stayed. It was such a long time ago, but here I was. To me it felt like that should have been important. Being here. For him, but for myself, too. For who I was such a long time ago, and who I am. Mercy, I mean. I don't know how Arthur felt about it."

"You were with him," Constance said.

"I was," Katherine said. "He was quiet toward the end. Maybe he was sleeping. Then one morning I was sitting beside him, and then he was gone."

"What did you feel?"

"No surprise, certainly," Katherine said. "Loss, of course. Relief, I suppose, though he hadn't been suffering at the end. I don't think he had. Responsibility. There were things I had to do. Arrangements. Then the same quiet there had been in this house before they brought him home."

She turned to Constance and stroked her bare shoulder. "And then you," she said. "Then there was you. Now there is you."

.   .   .

When it began to get dark, they stayed where they were. The traffic outside the house eased. The lights came on in the house across the street. Katherine found that if she rolled on to her side and looked out the window, she could see the evening's first stars. Constance rolled over and curled up against her.

"Are you hungry?" Constance asked. "I could make an omelet. We wouldn't have to go out. We wouldn't have to go anywhere."

"That would be nice," Katherine said.

A few minutes later they were asleep.

MICHAEL

"It's not your fault," Audrey said.

"I know it's not," I said. I knew it was.

We had buried Michael two days earlier. We had not gone into his room yet.

"I heard the same thing from so many people," Audrey said. "At least he didn't suffer. That's what they said."

"No," I said. "I suppose that's right, and I suppose one way of looking at it is that it's a good thing he didn't."

"Doesn't help much, does it?"

"Doesn't help at all," I said. "Maybe it helps the people who said it."

Michael had died of a broken neck. He'd fallen out of the tree house that we had built together, which meant that I'd built it. It was not an elaborate tree house, featuring a trap door and a deck and a rain-proof roof and electricity. It was a collection of found boards that I'd nailed to convenient branches. Michael got on it by climbing ten or twelve feet up the branches of the apple tree in the backyard, and then pulling himself on his belly along the slanted platform we'd established as the floor. I'd made that floor out of a pallet that had been left over after a delivery of shingles to the house being built down the street. We'd covered part of it with a sheet of beaverboard, which I'd nailed to the pallet. The beaverboard warped in the weather almost immediately, and when it got wet, it was slippery. I told Michael not to climb up to the tree house in the rain. I didn't tell him to stay out of it until well after the rain had stopped.

"It was a perfectly good tree house," Audrey said. "He loved it."

"It was what a clumsy father could do," I said. "I should have asked for help. Somebody who knew what he was doing could have helped."

"What would he have added? Safety bumpers?"

I was tired of the conversation. Talking about it felt like work. I was going to blame myself for a while. Maybe I would forever. Maybe I would. The lessons I thought I'd learned about forgiving oneself as well as others seemed, at best, irrelevant to the circumstances. How could I rely on them? How could I rely on anything I said? My son was dead.

An umbrella is a fine thing when you get caught in a summer shower. In a winter hurricane, it's worse than useless. Try holding onto it, the wind will tear it out of your hands and send it sailing down the street, where, likely as not, it'll stab some poor bastard in the leg while he's trying to open his car door with a key he's trying to jam into the frozen lock.

"So, this is a hurricane?" Audrey said.

"No," I said. "A void."

Sometimes we could stop talking about what had happened. That was a relief. I knew I couldn't sit alone with the pain forever, but that was what I wanted to do. I remembered situations where people in pain—not similar pain, because there could be no pain like this—but people in pain had sometimes been comforted by the contention that though the pain would never go away, it would gradually become something with which they could live. It would become a thing of great but diminishing weight among more and more other things.

I thought this should be true of Michael's death, and even as I thought it, I didn't believe it. He was a bright, glorious, inquisitive, loving child who was dead from a broken neck. He didn't suffer? Maybe not. I'd suffer for him. I'd suffer for everybody. I'd lie in bed with my eyes open, my dry eyes, and I'd will myself to stay awake because of how guilty I knew I'd feel if I slept. Sleep? I didn't think so. He was dead.

When Audrey had to talk again, she said, "You wanted him to be an athlete."

I couldn't hear that as a neutral statement, a statement of fact. I heard it as an accusation.

"You think that's why he liked to climb trees?"

I knew it was a stupid and cruel thing to say. I said it, anyway.

"I'm sorry," I said. "That was stupid."

"Yes, it was," Audrey said.

"What do you want? For him, I mean."

"I wanted him to be happy," she said.

I didn't say anything. If I had, I might have said, "It's more likely he'd have been an athlete." I'm glad I didn't say it. I only nodded.

Then I said, "I think he would have been. I think he was."

"He was loved," Audrey said.

"Yes, he was," I said.

We could have gone on like that, reassuring ourselves of the obvious, until one of us threw a glass against the wall or started to cry again.

A little later in the day, I walked into the backyard. Next to the house, daffodils and tulips bloomed idiotically. Birds sang. A breeze fluttered the leaves in the apple tree, which hadn't produced apples of any size for years. What grew on it fell to the ground and became food for bees. Later in the summer, the yard around the tree would smell of fallen, half-rotten apples.

I looked up into the tree at the place from where Michael had fallen. Later I would climb up and take that goddam tree house apart. I would haul its parts to the dump.

I would do my best to pretend it had never been there.

I would fail.

People who lose a child sometimes move to another town, or to a new neighborhood. Maybe it's because there are too many memories associated with the house and the room where the child slept. Maybe it's because the parents know that even when they've moved a little beyond the paralyzing grief, people around them—people they've known well and people they don't know at all—will speak of them as the couple that lost a child. In the place where it happened, they'll never be able to be anything else. That's the way they feel.

They're wrong. Other people have their own worries, disappointments, even tragedies. They aren't so obsessively concerned with what's going on around them, who's doing what to whom. They can't be. Not for long. Not after the initial horror of a boy falling out of a tree house and breaking his neck and dying there, lying twisted and broken, among the hard green apples. Not after the days of delivering casseroles and pies to the grieving parents, who will be "the couple that lost a child . . . what was it? five years ago? Six?"

From time to time, the subject will come up, maybe when another child is injured. But they move. They make new friends, and for a long time they don't tell those friends about the child they lost. Then one night they do. Maybe one of them has had too much to drink. Maybe one of them is overwhelmed by the need to talk about what is no more. Maybe one of them is angry that the other one seems to be able to get beyond the pain, or more able, anyway, more the person he or she was before the child fell and broke his neck and was no more.

They both do what they can to resume their lives. But those lives carry the grief forward. It may occupy a different space on one day than it does another. It may recede when she is laughing at something in a movie. It may come rushing back when he drives past a park where a boy is running with a dog.

They talk about it with each other, but one of them needs to talk more than the other one can listen, and the one who can't listen anymore needs silence.

Audrey and I stayed where we were.

We turned his room into a den. We gave his clothes and toys to Goodwill, and we gave his books to a group that was teaching at-risk kids how to run a business by helping them to collect, organize, and sell used books.

We put a television in the den for the nights when Audrey wanted to watch something I didn't want to see. I had never fallen asleep in front of the television before, but I began doing it when I was alone downstairs. When I woke up, I'd go upstairs and find Audrey had fallen asleep in front of the other TV.

We did not often see the people who had become our friends because their children had been Michael's friends. At first they tried to include us in their dinners, their group trips to the movies. Somebody would call, sometimes, to see if Audrey or I wanted to go to a basketball game or a baseball game involving the team for which Michael had played. I went to a couple of games. It was as hard as I thought it would be, and I didn't talk about it when I got home. I just said I thought I wouldn't do that again, and Audrey nodded. She'd known enough to say, "No, thanks," when the invitation had come. She knew enough not to push me, and she knew I'd talk about what I'd seen and what I'd felt on some night when we were lying together in bed, each of us knowing that neither of us was about to go to sleep.

I remember the night Michael was born. It was late in the evening, maybe 10:30 or so when he arrived. I held him for a while. I'd asked beforehand if I could stay in the room with Audrey and Michael overnight, but the hospital didn't allow it. So, early the next morning I left them. It was raining and it was November, so the rain was cold. I'd left my coat in the car when we'd driven to the hospital, so by the time I got back I was wet. I was shivering as I started the car, and I remember thinking, "How can it be so cold and damp and miserable? My son was just born!"

The world went on its way that morning, and the morning after that.

After Michael died, the world kept going on its way. Audrey and I were not the same within it, that was all. But we were still there. We were still in it. We might sometimes have wished it were otherwise, but we were still in it.

We held each other. I learned to listen more carefully when she needed to talk, and she learned to do that for me, too. We both learned not to say things like, "How can you say that?" and "How can you feel that way?" We said what we said and felt what we felt and cried about it sometimes, and we got up the next morning in the world that kept going on its way.

On one of those mornings, when we were both awake early, we decided to go for a walk before doing anything else. It was early April, and it was still cold, though on that morning there was no wind. The sky was clear. I don't know why it is that the sky seems clearer where there's no wind, but that's the way it seems. That's the way it seemed that morning.

We walked toward town, where there would be hot coffee. We were walking toward the sunrise. Walk at a time like that, and you may find yourself wondering why you don't get up early each morning, just to see the sky change colors. Audrey said something like that.

"I remember when you would groan at the sunrise," I said. "When you were going to feed Michael at night, the morning would always come too quickly. You'd be awake, and he'd be fast asleep, full of milk."

"And I'd groan?" Audrey said.

"You would. All you wanted was to go back to sleep. It was crazy how long you and that baby operated on—I don't know—different cycles? Was that it? When he was awake, you were half-asleep. When he was asleep, you were wide awake. That's the way it seemed to me."

"I don't even remember."

"No," I said. "That's how people go on to have more kids. They don't remember. Or moms don't. I don't know why I do. Your memory's better than mine."

"Different," she said. "It's just different."

"Better," I said. "Think about all the times you remember a dinner with friends, and so-and-so said such-and-such, and we had salmon and a sauce you'd found in that cookbook you got out of your mother's kitchen when you were cleaning out her house, and I don't even remember who was at the table. I nod and say something. I know I don't fool you. You remember things like that."

"But not movies," she said. "How many times have I picked a movie, and you've had to say, 'We saw that. That's the one about the guy who meets the girl in the office, and they hate each other because they're in line for the same promotion, but then they get locked in the storeroom together, and . . .' And then I say, 'Oh, yeah.' But half the time I still don't remember it."

"This is good," I said. "This is promising. We've changed the subject."

Audrey looked at me and smiled. "I guess so," she said. "I guess we have. Do you think it means we're forgetting him?"

"No," I said, "I don't think it means that. No."

"It means we're still alive," Audrey said.

"Simple as that," I said.

"I'm glad we're together," she said. "I'm glad it's both of us here, now. Today. And we can talk about him. And then we don't."

The sky was lighter then. There was a pale blue line where there had been red and orange. In a house a little further down the block, a first-floor light went on.

"Somebody else is up," Audrey said.

"Too late," I said. "They missed the best part."

The time came when we could appreciate moments less grand than the glory of a sunrise. I remember the perfect biscuit. Or perfect biscuits, really. All of them were that good. Audrey made them early one morning when she hadn't been able to sleep as long as she'd have liked. I came down to the kitchen, into the smell of baking, and just as I arrived, she was pulling the pan out of the oven.

"They look perfect," I said.

Moments later we ate some of them with butter and blackberry jam. They tasted as good as they looked, and Audrey said so.

"Perfect," she said.

It was the first time I'd heard her say that about something she'd cooked. No matter how much I liked her casseroles or her gumbo, no matter how crispy her hash brown potatoes or how savory her chicken, she would say, "bland." Or she might say, "Is this cooked all the way through?" or maybe "Next time I'm going to make sure we have enough tomato sauce and lemon before I start putting this together."

But not this time.

"Perfect," she said.

And they were, those biscuits, and we ate them happily. Neither of us said, "Michael would have loved these," though both of us might have been thinking it. Perhaps each of us was being considerate of the other, wanting to stay, if even just for a moment, in the "perfect."

On other days our loss hung on us like a weight. It felt hard to stand up straight. And sometimes I wished I was alone. Sometimes it seemed that the guilt I felt would have been more bearable if nobody had been looking at me from across the room when I looked up from whatever I was reading. But it wasn't true. Without Audrey, the weight of the grief would have crushed me, or I'd have worn myself out trying to prevent that from happening, trying to distract myself from the death of the boy at the foot of the tree where I'd knocked together the crappy tree house.

We could bear it together. It came down to that. And one day, I could say to Audrey, "Do you remember how I told you Michael had asked me what happens when you die?"

And she could say, "Yes."

"I hadn't thought about what happens to us," I said.

Audrey looked at me. "Not the sort of thing you think about, is it?" she said.

"No," I said. "I'm thankful for that." And then I said, "Do you think it mattered? What I said."

"You loved him," Audrey said. "He knew that. And he loved you. That's what mattered. All the rest is . . . I don't know. Words. Fumbling. Trying your best to say something true. He was a child, but he knew that, too."

And then I could say, "I love you."

And she could say, "I love you, too."

THE FIRE

By the time her house burned down, Katherine Baladino had been spending half her nights in Constance Evans's apartment.

This was fortunate because the fire was thorough. The house had been solid, but it was old, and it was mostly wood. Katherine Baladino had told the fire fighters she'd thought she'd smelled smoke when she woke up, though she didn't know if that was what had woken her. The smell seemed stronger when she went downstairs, and when she opened the door to the cellar, the heat rushed up. Then she could hear the crackling of everything burning below. The open door created a chimney within the house, and smoke and flames roared up the stairs. Katherine turned and found her way to the back door. The open door created another draft. In the yard, after she'd gone down the steps, she could still feel the heat at her back.

By the time she made her way around to the front of the house, she could see the fire dancing behind the windows of the first floor. Flames climbed the stairs and the walls toward the bedrooms. Somebody across the street was shouting at her to get away from the house.

Katherine told the fire fighters that as she'd stood in the yard she'd thought about what would be lost, but she'd never considered trying to re-enter the house.

The fire would have been investigated, even if the owner of the house hadn't been the widow of a man who'd recently died there after spending much of his life in various state and federal prisons. It didn't take the fire inspector long to establish that, if the fire had been set, it hadn't been set by an amateur.

Arthur Baladino's enemies? The list was long and impressive. There were the men and women whose family members Baladino had killed or ruined so thoroughly that in the early morning hours when they were staring at the ceiling, they might have wished he'd finished the job. There were former associates who felt Baladino had shortchanged them after good and faithful service. That would have been back in the days when he was still getting out of prison from time to time, bargaining through attorneys with various officials and agencies. There were people who blamed Arthur Baladino for things he'd never done, and though the men who'd fought Baladino for territory were dead or close enough, babbling into their soup, they had sons and grandsons in the family business.

But the investigation of the fire turned up nothing.

"I couldn't tell them anything," Katherine Baladino said to Constance Evans.

"Maybe you wouldn't have, even if you could have," Constance said.

"Ratted?" said Katherine. Then she laughed.

"That's not what I mean," Constance said.

They were on the sofa in her living room. Katherine's feet were in Constance's lap. She was rubbing them.

"Did I sound like him? Saying 'ratted'?" Katherine said. "You wouldn't know, of course. You never met him. Anyway, I don't."

"Don't what?"

"Don't sound like him," she said. She leaned forward to grab a cushion to put behind her back. After she'd shifted her hips to get more comfortable, she said, "That's probably the end of it. What Arthur had built is gone. What he did. Who'd feel the need to hurt him now? No more gang wars when all the gangsters are dead, and their widows are old."

"Not so old," Catherine said.

"You're sweet."

"But if there was somebody . . . I mean, my place isn't exactly secure," Constance said. "Anybody could get in. Push all the buttons in the hallway, somebody would hit the buzzer for them. My name's on the mailbox."

"It's over," Katherine said. "Really, it's been over for a long time. Don't worry about it."

Constance didn't say anything more, but she couldn't help thinking about whether she'd even hear somebody coming up the narrow stairway. Not if he was quiet, probably. Careful. Not if he knew what he was doing, even though everybody's footsteps bounced around in the hall. The building echoed, as tinny buildings will. Constance knew what her neighbors watched on TV. She knew which of them had dogs. She wondered if maybe she should get one, too, in case somebody coming in knew how to be careful.

"I hadn't visited him in a long time," Katherine was saying.

"I wouldn't have," Constance said. She was thinking about her husband. She didn't think she'd have visited him, either, if the company had decided that he should go to jail. Time had passed. She was glad for him that whoever was making the decisions had figured it would be better to cut him loose quietly and let it go at that.

"Sometimes it wasn't so bad," Katherine said.

"I'll have to take your word for it," Constance said.

"You've never been in a prison. Of course, you haven't."

"I'm not sure I even know anybody who's been in prison."

"You do, though," Katherine said. She nudged Constance with her foot. "That feels good. Don't stop. Anyhow, you probably do."

"Because they're out there, you mean?"

"Don't make it sound so scary," Katherine said. "A lot of people who go to prison young, they come out old enough to know better. They're building houses. They're delivering your packages. Whatever. Arthur met a guy in there who was so good at helping other prisoners with their court appearances and appeals that when he got out, he found a job with an attorney. He never went to law school, but he could help the guy who helped guys. He could talk to them. They trusted him. They knew he got it. Understood."

Constance looked up from Katherine's feet and smiled. "That's why you called me," she said. "You knew I'd understand."

"I didn't know," Katherine said. "I hoped you would. It was worth a try, right?"

They had talked about betrayal. They had talked about how each of them had been married to a man for whom one thing led to another, as the men themselves, much later, might have put it with a shrug.

"You figured out what you had to do, and you did it," Katherine said. "I liked that."

Constance hadn't understood when Katherine had called. What was she getting at? This woman was the widow of a man who'd spent most of his life in prison. He'd been convicted of awful crimes. He'd have been convicted of more of them if the state had felt there was any point in piling on.

"Sure," Constance had thought. "My husband was a crook. He stole from his employer and he stole from me. He was so bad at it that he lost everything he stole and got caught. Then he got lucky. He avoided prison by promising to go away quietly. But he never shot anybody."

"You loved a guy who turned out to be unworthy of what you were providing," Katherine was saying.

Constance looked at her and nodded. It was good to stop thinking about people getting shot.

"You know what's occurred to me," she said, "you'll have to shop for a new wardrobe. It'll be fun."

"I think it will be," Katherine said. "You'll come with me, of course. I'll step out of the dressing room, and you'll tell me 'yes' or 'no.'"

"I wouldn't presume to do that."

"You'll have to," Katherine said. "I would be lost without you."

She was kidding, and she wasn't. Katherine Baladino had lived by herself for a long time. When her husband came home, it was only to die. He'd been slow enough about that to irritate a probation officer, but in fairly short order he'd done what he'd been sent home to do, and Katherine had been alone again.

"It wasn't so bad," she'd have said, had anybody asked. But looking back, she felt as if it should have been intolerable to be alone for so long. Now she was looking forward. She and Connie would eat in a nice restaurant after they'd finished their shopping. On some evening weeks later, they'd return to the same restaurant to see if it was as good as they'd remembered. They'd laugh about the clothes Katherine had returned.

"I knew I'd never wear that," she'd say about an unlikely pair of hip-hugging jeans. "But you were so enthusiastic about them."

"They looked great on you," Constance would say. "Everything looked great on you. You should have kept the jeans."

"Your closet—" Katherine would start to say. "I don't think so. It's good discipline living with you. Only the essentials."

"I hope it's not just 'good discipline,'" Constance would say.

Then neither of them would say anything while they waited for their coffee. Katherine thought it was comfortable, not having to say anything.

Both of them could imagine how people were talking. They didn't say anything about that, either.

Which of them was more surprised at what they had become to each other? The rookie real estate lady who'd discovered she had a knack for the trade when she had to figure out how to make a living? Or the widow of the old man who'd been in and out of prison since he was a kid? And how, some of those who talked about Katherine and Constance wondered, how had Katherine become the wife of a crime boss? Was she sixteen when he was thirty-five? Was she one of those deluded women who married a guy who was incarcerated? Did she foolishly assume she could change him?

If anyone had asked her, she'd probably have said, "you wouldn't understand."

.　.　.

Though Katherine knew that property values had risen spectacularly since her husband had bought the house, she'd been surprised by what Constance told her she could get for the property if she made up her mind to sell it. After the fire, nothing much had changed.

"They didn't wait until it was out," she told Constance. "The phone calls from the developers, you wouldn't believe. They were bidding against each other."

"Same as when the people in the little houses, the ranches, die or move away, you know, into a home or something. Maybe to live closer to their children," Constance said. "Big market for big houses."

"Big market for lots," Katherine said.

"And not a lot of lots, but business is good, anyway, thank you very much."

The rubble that had been home until it burned had been full of paintings and pottery, dishware, furniture that hadn't been moved in decades, linen, and stereo equipment. Katherine had let it all go. No matter that her husband had died in the house, and there had been photographs of her children.

"Dead children well enough mourned," she'd thought. "And a dead husband, too. A husband who died in the house he'd provided, if that still mattered to him."

She turned away from the ashes of the house and walked the rest of the way into another life she'd already begun making.

"Maybe it was what I needed," she told Constance.

"You'd be here, anyway."

"If you think about it, it's kind of poetic. Like a phoenix. A new life rises out of the ashes."

"I like it," Constance had said. "No tragedy unless you let it be a tragedy, right?"

"No tragedy," Katherine said.

It was, however, a new story for the neighborhood. As the fire burned, Libby had watched from her window. She'd never seen anything like it, of course. The flames, multi-colored, seemed to breathe. Even from down the block, she could hear the wood crackling, and once the crash of a beam collapsing into the center of the blaze. When the fire trucks arrived with flashing lights and sirens, all the dogs in the neighborhood had begun barking. People had rushed from their homes, driven by concern, of course, and by excitement, certainly. Even a child could see that.

Libby remembered a winter storm that had also brought people into the street. Ice had coated the branches of the trees that hung over the power lines, and when some of the heavy branches fell, the neighborhood had lost electricity. A few older children were ice-skating in the street, and Libby remembered wishing she could join them. The adults looked at the dangling wires and asked each other how long they thought it might be until the crews arrived to restore the power. Libby was in no hurry for that to happen. She loved being out in the dark and the cold with everybody else.

She remembered that night while she watched the fire with the rest of the people on the street.

Even at her age, Libby knew enough not to say she thought the fire was beautiful. She took her cue from her parents and the other grown-ups. The fire was a terrible thing. The poor woman had lost her house. Besides that, what if it had been windier that night? Whose house might have gone up next? And what if the fire department hadn't arrived as quickly? And what if there hadn't been a hydrant so close to the Baladino place? They couldn't save the house—who knows why it had gone up so fast?—but the neighborhood would be all right.

Though she wouldn't be able to say it, Libby sensed that the fire gave everybody in the street the opportunity to feel fortunate.

"My house is okay," they could say to themselves. "It may be smaller than I'd like, and the kitchen needs updating, but it's there. It's all in one piece."

Libby was not old enough to sense some of the other things the people around her were feeling. She couldn't have seen in her mother's expression the suspicion that maybe Mrs. Baladino hadn't bothered with smoke alarms.

The fire department was efficient and thorough. Within a short time the fire was out, but not before it had done its job. The charred ruins of what had been the house beams were leaning across piles of unrecognizable debris. Everything dripped dirty water. Muddy streams ran down the street and the dirty water had pooled in a couple of the adjacent yards.

In high, black boots, the firemen were winding yellow plastic tape from the trees that remained in the Baladino yard. "Caution" the letters on the tape said, and "Cuidado," perhaps for the women who cleaned some of the houses in the neighborhood, though none of them would have thought about stepping into the filthy yard.

Katherine Baladino did not return to the charred shell of the house that had been her home the next day. She'd never hidden anything in the place, and neither had her husband. She knew what had burned, and she knew what the insurance company would pay her.

Though she had long ago become accustomed to living by herself in the big house, she was pleased to find that she could be content in Connie's apartment, at least for a time. She would embrace her lover's kindness and she would be grateful.

There were, of course, things to do. She'd lost her passport and all sorts of papers that would be irritating to replace. She'd made sure of that.

"You were giggling," Constance said.

They'd been asleep in the apartment. It was still dark.

"Giggling."

Each of them was lying on her back, looking at the shadows sliding across the ceiling as cars drove by.

"There was no mistaking it. It was lovely."

"Better than grinding my teeth," Katherine said, although she had never, to her knowledge, done that.

"Or swinging your arms around. Or farting."

"Have I done that? Swung my arms around?"

Constance rolled on to her side and put her arm around Katherine's shoulder. Katherine shifted under the weight and Constance's hand slipped to her breast, where Katherine allowed it to rest.

"That's nice," she said.

"Only once, I think," Constance said.

"Once what?"

"The arm-swinging. I caught your wrist just before you'd have hit me in the nose."

"It must have been a nightmare," Katherine said. "I'm sorry."

"But no nightmare this time, right? You were giggling. That's what it was. Unmistakable."

Katherine suddenly remembered what she'd been dreaming about.

"It was a house," she said. "It was a beautiful new house. It was full of sunlight."

In the silence of the bedroom, both women considered the dream. Then there was a loud, metallic sound, and some intermittent ticking. The heat was coming on in the apartment, which was never full of sunlight, even on the brightest days.

"It sounds great," Constance said.

"It will be great," Katherine said.

"Come again?"

"They can probably use the same foundation," Katherine said. "Or most of it, anyway. They'll maybe have to dig a new hole for the sunroom."

"What are you talking about?"

"Our new house," Katherine said. "It'll be great. We can plan it together. You'll have whatever you need. An office, of course. You can sell houses from there as easily as you can from anywhere else, right?"

"Wow," Constance said. "All this from a dream, huh?"

"You like the idea?"

"What's not to like? It's got an office and a sunroom."

Constance pulled Katherine toward her. In the dark, she couldn't see her lover's eyes. She leaned over and kissed Katherine between her breasts.

"You would do that?"

"We'll need a guest room," Katherine said. "Maybe two, because what if both of your kids want to visit at the same time? Christmas, or something like that."

"I don't know what to say."

"Or a sleeping porch!" Katherine said. "It could be like one of those summer houses on a lake, you know? With—I don't know—half a dozen beds. Cots, probably. But winterized, so we could use it all the time. Kids would love it. Grandkids."

"You're serious."

"It'll be great," Katherine said. "The hard part's taken care of. We've got the place to put the house. Get a couple of bulldozers in there, couple of dumpsters, and we're down to the foundation and the dirt, ready to begin again. You know all about permits, right? You could take care of that."

"I don't think you need a permit to build a sleeping porch."

Katherine laughed.

"You're like a little girl," Constance said.

By then they were in each other's arms.

"What do you think?" Katherine asked.

"I think it would be amazing," Constance said. She pulled away from their embrace and propped herself up on an elbow. "But it would be a big deal."

"It wouldn't have to be that big. The house, I mean," Katherine said. "Besides, we've got to live somewhere."

"That's the part I'm talking about. The 'we'. I mean, this has been wonderful. Terrific. But building a house, planning it together, that would be something else, wouldn't it?"

"Something better," Katherine said. "That's what I think. I'd hoped you . . ."

"I wouldn't be able to bring as much to it is all I'm saying."

"Hey," Katherine said. "You bring you. I'll bring me. That's what's worked here in this shitbox of an apartment, right? Why shouldn't it work in our new house? Especially a house built so you could have some space of your own when you need that. Tell me you're not worried about the money, please."

Constance looked at her lover and smiled. "People who have it don't have to worry about it," she said. "People who've lost it, it's different. And we didn't have much to begin with, which is maybe what made my husband think he had to become a hotshot stock trader."

"Not your fault," Katherine said.

"No," Constance said. "Maybe I didn't complain any more than lots of people complain. But maybe he took it more seriously than lots of husbands take it. I don't know."

Katherine shook her head and said, "Not how it happens."

"Really," Constance said.

"Really not," Katherine said. "And in any case, it's over."

"That much is certain," Constance said.

"So now is now, and as I said, we're going to have to live somewhere. You weren't planning on staying in this place until it was time to find a retirement home, were you?"

"No!"

"Not that we won't be able to find a perfectly good one when the time comes," Katherine said. "When we're leaning on each other to get from the bed to the bathroom, I mean. When one of us is waking up in the middle of the night to make sure the other one hasn't died in her sleep."

"Jesus!"

"So, for now, a nice house, I think. And the more I think about a sleeping porch, the better I like the idea. It'll be on the other end of the house from our bedroom. We won't be able to hear what's going on there, and nobody will know what we're up to, either."

Constance rolled onto her back. Katherine was still talking about the house and how it would be decorated, how they would go about ensuring that there would be no clutter. It would be all clean lines and, again, lots of light.

Constance was thinking about the security she'd thought she had before she'd discovered that her husband was losing their money, and that the kind of gambling he was doing was as crazy as betting every day on cards or dice with money you didn't have.

Her life had been what she'd anticipated it would be. Her children had gone through school and left home on schedule. One of them kept in touch, the other she had to call. No grandchildren yet, which had been fine with Constance. What she wanted to do before she and Andy got too old was to travel.

"Maybe China," she'd thought. "Something completely different. Some place where I couldn't read the signs."

She looked forward to feeling like a kid, but a kid who knew that after her adventures, she'd be flying back to a sold home and money in the bank. Maybe even flying business class. They'd saved money for that, hadn't they?

"What's the matter?" Katherine asked her.

"It's nothing. Go on."

Katherine looked at her. Constance had rolled onto her side again, and their noses were almost touching. Katherine waited.

"Okay," Constance said. "It's what you're suggesting. It's—"

"Scary?"

"Not scary, exactly. I don't know. Maybe."

"You've got something going," Katherine said. "You've built something. You got a lousy deal, and you found a way out of it. Of course, you feel good about that. And the last thing I'd ever want to do is take that away from you, make it so you weren't doing what you want to do."

"It's not that I'm in love with showing people houses," Constance said. "Sometimes I feel like—when I've got somebody in the car, and I know they're just looking, and they're going to look until their feet are tired, and then they're going to go home and put those feet up and look around and decide to stay where they are . . . I'd like to grab them by the ankles and turn them upside down until the money fell out of their pockets. Or their pocketbooks. Whatever. It's not my dream job, you know?"

"YOUR job, though." Katherine said. "You made it. You had to do it, and you did."

"You think I'm tough?"

"You're you. You found out what you could do when you weren't sure you could do anything about a mess you didn't make. Exceptional."

Constance shifted in the bed and kissed Katherine's lips.

"Thank you," she said.

"For what?"

"Sometimes I don't feel so noble," Constance said. "Sometimes I don't even feel . . . I don't know. Sometimes I don't feel as if I know what I'm doing."

"Not so unusual," Katherine said.

"But I do, with you," Constance said. "You make me feel better. Thank you."

"You, too."

"You know what I feel like?" Constance said. "I feel like that part of Romeo and Juliet where they're in bed, and it's morning, or almost morning, and they feel like there's no place else and nothing else but who they are and where they are."

"Romeo and Juliet? Really?"

"Not them. Not like them. Like that part in the play. But I haven't read it in a long time. Not since school. Maybe I'm not remembering it accurately."

"I like the way you remember it," Katherine said. "Now I'm going to have to read it."

"You never—"

"I left school early. And I didn't read a lot while I was there. I got married when I was sixteen. I told 'em I was a year older."

"Arthur?"

"Arthur," Katherine said.

"He must have been a lot older."

"He was older," Katherine said. "Also, he was terrific. You should have seen him. Big, strong guy. Had all the confidence in the world. Nice suits. Beautiful. Nobody pushed him around. I thought he was the top of the line."

Constance looked across the pillow at Katherine. Without her contacts, the image was blurry. "I know this woman as well as I know anyone on the planet," she thought. "And I don't know anything."

"So you were, I don't know . . . 'snowed?' Isn't that what we used to say?"

"It sounds corny," Katherine said. She propped herself up on the headboard. "But here's the thing. You know how they say now, like they've just figured it out, that boys' brains are still developing when they're teenagers. Even longer, I guess. Into their twenties?"

"I'd read that," Constance said. "I think they're off by several decades."

"But seriously," Katherine said, "I think maybe it's no different with girls. Or some of them, anyway. What I knew when I was sixteen was that I didn't want to be in the house where I'd grown up, with all kinds of nonsense going on, and me right in the middle of it. I was ready for something else. Anything else, is the way I was thinking. Which is why I'm not sure you want to call it 'thinking.'"

"You made a bad decision?" Constance said. "How soon did you realize that?"

"No, it's not that simple, is it? It was a decision, all right, but was I making it just by going along? And then, how bad was it? Arthur was a good provider. He never tried to force me to do anything, you know, anywhere. Not socially, I mean. Not in bed, either. He was considerate. I think you'd have to say he was."

"He wasn't violent?"

Katherine smiled. "You mean how could he be doing what he was doing and not be hitting me when he came home? No. He never hit me. He never hit the kids. I think he probably honestly wished that he could have been around for them, at least until Teddy got older. They didn't like each other much. But it was his life. He made it, I accepted it, and then after they began to figure out what he was up to, they kept him locked up a lot of the time, or out on various conditions, parole, you know, which is not so different from being locked up when they're following you around because they're sure they'll get something else on you. Which they did. And then he'd be back in prison."

Katherine stretched her arms over her head and pulled her knees up to her chest.

"I visited lots of prisons," she said.

"But over time you must have felt . . . I mean, you were on your own, right?"

"Like you wouldn't believe," Katherine said.

"I wasn't. Ever," Constance said.

"I don't understand."

"Big family, small house," Constance said. "Parents who hovered over all of us. Older brothers and sisters who did it, too. When I finally got out of the house and went away to school, not much changed. Somebody from the family was always calling. Could I do this? Didn't I want to come home on the weekend and do that? Mom's birthday, Fathers' Day, all the holidays, of course. Everybody came home for all of them. I don't remember anybody ever saying we had to do it. It's just how it was."

"What would have happened if you'd said, 'No?'"

"I don't know," Constance said. "It never occurred to me to do that."

"Then you got married."

"Then I got married," Constance said. "Then his family was in it, too. They had a little summer place up on the lake. That's where we went for our vacations. Always. I don't think we ever talked about going somewhere else. The cottage was there. Then the kids came, and that was the place they knew, too. That was it. You'd have to be an idiot to spend money on a vacation when you had the cottage right there for free, right? That's how his mother and father saw it. His father, especially. After they died, the cottage was ours."

Constance shook her head at the memory of scrubbing mildew off the dirty white walls each spring.

"Goddam place," she said.

"One of those mixed blessings," Katherine said.

"No," Constance said. "Nothing 'mixed' about it, as far as I was concerned, and nothing blessed. Then he lost it. Now I'll bet it's been knocked down and somebody's put up an eight bedroom 'retreat' on the property. Or a 'camp.' Isn't that what they call it, no matter how big it is?"

"Okay for them," Katherine said. "Someday we'll drive up there and see, just for the hell of it."

Constance smiled. "With you, it would be fun," she said. "I would do it with you. Sure."

It would be another way to bury what had been, she thought. Wouldn't it be something to hold her lover's hand, walk past the grand replacement for the cottage that had been and laugh?

"I would not be laughing maliciously," she said to herself, or perhaps to her former husband, or to his father, who had always insisted that they use the cottage. "I would not mean any harm. Not now."

No, she thought. It would be the laughter of somebody freed from the past. The laughter of a woman who'd received a gift— though debt, embarrassment, shame, and desperation hadn't felt like gifts when they'd arrived. She remembered feeling sick to her stomach. She remembered having no idea what to do next. She didn't call friends. She didn't know how she could talk to them. She could imagine what they were saying about her, and about what her husband had done, and about what her part in his apparent desperation must have been, and, of course, about what she would do next. Maybe she'd disappear.

"It's obvious she can't stay in that house."

Certainly they'd be saying that. Maybe some of them would even call friends who lived elsewhere to tell them about the house down the street that was bound to be on the market soon.

Maybe that was where the idea to sell houses had come from, though she hadn't been aware of it until later, when she could focus a little and begin to remember what she knew about people, which was that they had enough problems of their own and wouldn't spend all their time gloating over hers.

She thought, then, that she'd have liked to have sold the cottage, too, but she found it was already gone.

"Too bad," she thought. "How the old man would have squealed at my doing it. But all right. I'll walk past the spot where it was, whether or not there's a new house there or a concrete foundation or nothing but vines and ground cover that have crept in to occupy the lot."

"We'll do it," Katherine said.

"And what about you?" Constance asked. "Where do we go to revisit your past? If we're going to share my shame and cast it off, where do we go to even it up? You must have a neighborhood."

"Gone," Katherine said. "Long gone and hard to find. Impossible to find, as it happens. Well, I mean, the city's still there, but there's nothing of what I knew. It was just apartment buildings, and most of the people living in those apartments had lived there for a long time, unless that's just the way it seems to a kid growing up anywhere. Maybe it does. Anyway, the buildings—the ones that are left—they're unrecognizable. It's condos now, little lawns and little mailboxes and little parking spaces drawn on the lots in front. They're all built so you can see at least a little slice of the bay."

"Water view!" said Constance. "I know how that works."

"Used to be it was a good apartment because it was close to work if the guy worked on the docks, unloaded cargo on the trucks, went out to fish, something like that. Now, as you say, it's a 'water view.' Put another zero on the number."

"You could argue that I'm part of the problem," Constance said. "My job to sell as fast as the developers can build, right?"

"I forgive you," Katherine said. "Now, forgive yourself."

Constance looked at her and wondered how seriously to take what she'd heard.

"Really," Katherine said. "Start there. Hey, someday you may even be able to forgive your husband. Sorry. The guy who used to be your husband."

"You took your husband back when he was dying," Constance said. "You didn't have to do that."

"It wasn't because I needed the company," Katherine said. "I was as comfortable by myself as anyone by herself is likely to be."

"You forgave him? I mean, for leaving you alone, living the way he did, spending all those years locked up. He'd provided for you. I mean, in his way . . ."

"That didn't have much to do with it," Katherine said. "In a way . . . well, I loved him. That's about it."

"So, it wasn't about forgiveness?"

"It was. There was. Forgiveness, I mean. That's how you get free."

"Free?"

"Sure," Katherine said. "Out from under the weight. Holding what he'd done, whatever I'd had against him . . . how was that going to hurt him? He was what he was. I learned that, and I never stopped knowing it. I never wanted to hurt him, anyway, and I certainly didn't want to hurt myself."

Constance believed what she was hearing. She wondered if it was because she loved Katherine. She could not imagine anything for which she'd ever have to forgive her.

"Is there anything, I wonder . . . anything for which you couldn't have forgiven him?"

Katherine put her hands on Constance's shoulders and gently pulled her down until Constance was lying on top of her.

"That's nice," she said. "You're so light. It's nice to feel you there."

Constance kissed Katherine's chin and said, "That's a sweet thing to say to a lady."

"Lady, eh?"

"What? Gal pal? Broad?"

"Lover," Katherine said.

Constance sighed, shook her hair off her face, and said, "You're an amazing person."

"You think so? Maybe one of the reasons I like you so much. You think that of me."

"I mean it. I've never met anyone like you."

"I'm glad," Katherine said. "If you had, maybe you wouldn't have been there for me."

Later, sitting at her desk after she'd gone back to the office, Constance would replay the conversation. What if it hadn't happened the way it did? What if I hadn't lost my house? What if my kids hadn't been old enough to pretty much take care of themselves? Then I wouldn't have what I have now. Whatever it is, and whatever it's going to be, I wouldn't have it.

She realized that since Katherine had moved in with her, she'd been looking at her watch more often and scheduling fewer appointments in the late afternoon. She found she was looking forward to stopping at the grocery store to pick up something for dinner, or to calling Katherine to see if she'd already started making something.

"It's fun," Katherine had said. "I didn't do much cooking for myself all the time I was alone. And when Arthur got out, he couldn't eat much of anything. It's nice to look through cookbooks and find things to try. It's even better to remember what I used to make years ago. I like sharing that with you. Who I was, I mean. What I did."

Constance realized she was anticipating Katherine's voice, hearing it when she opened the door to the apartment. At first living alone had felt strange, though at the same time, it was a relief. Fairly quickly, she had adjusted to the quiet of her evenings. Most of the time, she'd enjoyed the phone calls with the kids. She told herself she had not been aware of the empty place in her life that Katherine had arrived to fill.

"People make all sorts of lives in all sorts of circumstances," she thought. "I was married, then I wasn't. I was alone for a while, now I'm not. Keep your eyes open, you're likely to see all sorts of things."

"And your imagination," Katherine said. "Keep that open, too."

"Not your heart?"

"That's for a greeting card," Katherine said. "That's for kids. When you've been around for a while, it's the imagination you need."

Constance thought about that. It was imagination that had led her to think she could sell houses. Not a lot of imagination, maybe. She hadn't decided to apply to medical school. Still, she'd been dependent all her life on somebody else's ability to make a living, and she'd learned pretty quickly that she could do what she had to do.

"I guess you're right," she said. "How are you gonna do anything if you can't imagine yourself doing it."

"It's that, sure," Katherine said. "But it's also, you know, you and I, we're not first-timers. We've both got some miles on us."

"You mean you have to imagine I'm attractive?"

"I have to imagine—maybe 'understand' is a better word, keep in mind, whatever—that what we see all around us for sale is nonsense. It's nothing. I have to understand and imagine that what we have here, together, is everything. And I have to imagine we can hold on to it . . . that you won't quit on it, and I won't either, and that we'll be honest with each other. Something like that."

"Sometimes I just like to enjoy it," Constance said.

"Imagine that," Katherine said.

. . .

The next morning, before it was light, Constance was jerked into consciousness by the remnant of what she thought was a bad dream. In the act of waking, she gasped.

Katherine woke.

"Are you all right?"

"Yes," Constance said. "Yes. But I have to tell you something."

"I'll make coffee," Katherine said.

"Stay," Constance said. "If we get out of bed, I might lose my nerve."

Katherine pulled her pillow up against the headboard and leaned against it. She smiled at Constance. Then she shrugged as if to say, "You're on."

"I had a dream about something I did a long time ago," Constance said. "Only maybe it wasn't exactly a dream. More like a memory, because I did do it. I did it. Maybe it was a memory. Because when you have a bad dream, or when I do, I wake up relieved, you know? I'm so glad what I've been dreaming about didn't happen. I didn't wreck the car, or fall out of a hot air balloon, whatever. But this DID happen. I did it."

Katherine adjusted the pillow so she could turn comfortably toward Constance. "Tell me," she said.

"I was just a kid. Fifteen, maybe. Sixteen? I was out with some friends and we were drinking. No big deal, you know. Nobody was sick or anything. Just kids on a weekend. I guess it must have been a weekend."

"So far I'm not impressed," Katherine said. Right away she was sorry she'd said anything, but Constance acted like she hadn't heard it.

"I needed a ride home," Constance said. "This girl I didn't know—maybe I'd just met her that night. I don't know. Anyway, she gave me a ride. We drove halfway across town, and when we got to my house—my parents' house—the lights were still on. We could tell my parents were up. And the girl who gave me the ride—I don't even remember her name . . . Lynn, maybe. I'm not sure. But she said she really had to use the bathroom. She asked me if she could come into the house with me to, you know . . . she really had to pee. And I said, no."

"You wouldn't let her come into the house."

"I figured I could sneak in, get past my parents all right. They were probably downstairs watching television. It would be no problem getting upstairs, if I was careful. Quiet. But if this other girl came in with me, they were sure to hear her in the bathroom. And then they'd want to know who she was. And they'd see we'd been drinking."

"So, you told her she couldn't come in."

"I did. And I told her if she turned left at the end of my street and went a mile or so down that road, there was a place open late, and she could use the restroom there."

"But there wasn't."

"There was an ice cream place. It would have been closed for hours."

Katherine turned again and leaned back against the headboard. "What a lousy thing to do," she said.

"She probably pissed herself," Constance said.

"Sounds like she probably did. Or maybe she got out of the car and squatted behind some bushes."

"Oh. Yeah, maybe so. That wouldn't be so bad."

"Or she didn't, and when she got home she was wet, and her car seat was stained and stinky."

"Stop. You'll make me feel worse."

"Hard to imagine I could do that," Katherine said. "You're doing the job about as well as it can be done, I think. Can I put the coffee on now?"

"That would be good," Constance said. "Yes, please."

Katherine got up and took a couple of steps toward the kitchen. With her back to Constance, she said, "Really, though. Do you feel better, now that you've told me about that girl. Lynn, or whatever her name was."

"Lynn. Right," Constance said. "I think that was it."

"Well, maybe her family was rich, and her father bought her a new car," Katherine said. "You could imagine that, if it helps."

"It was such a long time ago," Constance said.

"And that doesn't matter, does it? Doesn't matter a bit. You still feel bad about it."

"Awful."

"You feel sick when you think about it."

"I do. You're right. But maybe it won't be so bad, now that you know about it. Nobody else does."

"Lynn does," Katherine said. "Lynn knows."

Constance picked up the pillow that had been on Katherine's side of the bed and threw it across the room at her.

"Why would you say that?" She was laughing when she said it.

"There," Katherine said. "You'll never take that night so seriously again. You've laughed at it. First you told me about it, and then you laughed at it, and I'm laughing with you. And what do I think? I think you were a child capable of cruelty in the service of saving your own ass. Let's see . . . puts you in the same boat as about everybody else, I'm thinking. But you remember it, and you feel bad about it, and it's a big enough deal so you haven't let yourself off the hook, ever, for something you did when you were—What did you say? Sixteen—and now I invite you to do that. I invite you to think of that poor girl, who probably wasn't as helpless as you've thought she was, and who probably stopped the car the first time she saw a place where she could get behind something a little bit and squat down and piss . . . cursing you the whole time, certainly . . . I'll grant you that . . . and who may have left her panties in the road, for all you know, and it may not have been the first time she came home without them. How's that?"

Constance shook her head. She was coughing and laughing at the same time.

"Okay," she said. "Yeah. Maybe it was like that. I was sneaking upstairs as quietly as I could, and Lynn, if that was her name, was peeing in the bushes a couple of blocks away. She was doing what she had to do, right? And by the time she got back in her car, with or without her panties, and found a good song on the radio, she'd probably have forgotten my name, too."

"Didn't know who to blame," Katherine said. "Wouldn't have done her any good, anyway. Maybe she already knew that."

"Maybe," Constance said. "She was older."

"And it's doing you no good to rerun the story and blame yourself," Katherine said. "Though looked at one way, it's a pretty funny story."

"I'm going to hold on to that image of her peeing in the grass and peeling off her panties. She looks at them. They're a little wet. How could they not be? She decides, 'Hey, I got nicer ones at home.' She drops them. Maybe they're still there. Maybe hanging on a bush beside the road where I used to live."

"We could go there," Katherine said. "We could look."

"Another road trip," Constance said. "But I don't think so. It's better to have the story. I think maybe the story's all I need."

"Done and done," Katherine said.

"One day you'll have to tell me about something you wish you hadn't done," Constance said.

As soon as she said it, she felt foolish. Katherine had been married to Arthur Baladino.

"Maybe one day I will," Katherine said. "Or maybe I should tell you about something I'm glad I did."

"What would be the fun in that? The whole point of telling my story was to see if you'd hate me when you heard it."

"Okay," Katherine said. "Now I'll tell you about something I did that you might hate. But I'm glad I did it."

Constance looked at Katherine, who was smiling.

"It's the smile of a risk-taker," Constance thought. "She's going to tell me something she thinks will shock me. Something she thinks might change the way I feel about her."

"It has to do with my house," Katherine said.

"What about it?"

"I'd had it with the house. It had served its purpose. When Arthur got out, he had somewhere to land. Then he died, and it was more empty than it had been before he got out. Full of stuff, but empty."

"I didn't know."

"You did, I think," Katherine said. "You knew, somehow."

"No."

"You knew to invite me to stay with you."

"And it scared me to death," Constance said. "I was afraid you'd think I was pathetic, living in an apartment where you could hear whoever was coming up the stairs, the car alarms going off at all hours, the temperature different in all the rooms. Jesus. I was afraid you'd be disgusted."

"You'd made it yours," Katherine said. "Just by being here, you'd done that. And then it was ours."

"But you digress," Constance said.

"Right," Katherine said. "Okay. Here it is. I had some guys set the fire. I knew them from some work they'd done for Arthur. I knew how to reach them, anyway. I knew who to reach."

"The fire. You mean the fire that—"

"That burned down the house. My house. Yes."

"And these guys who did it. They did . . . what? The same thing for Arthur? One of the times he was out?"

"In or out. I don't know. He had them do some things. Arthur could do that. But the point is, I had these two guys burn the house down. So that's it."

Katherine was looking at her feet, which were bare. When she looked up at Constance, she was relieved to see her smiling. Then she was laughing.

"What's so funny?"

"It's nervous laughter," Constance said. "Just . . . you really did that? Weren't you afraid you'd get caught? I mean, that's a serious crime. Arson. Insurance fraud. And what about the other houses in the neighborhood? What if somebody else's house had caught fire?"

"I trusted the guys Arthur used," Katherine said. "And I was right. They knew what they were doing. They checked the house first, you know, to make sure there were no code violations. No wires going around the corner from one room to another, where somebody could shut a door on the wire. No piles of oily rags in the basement. Nothing plugged into the wrong kind of socket. They said they'd rig it so it looked like an electrical fire. Something that could have happened to anybody. Bad luck, is all."

"But why?" Constance said. "You could have sold the house and used the money to build somewhere else."

"I like it here."

"You could have had the house knocked down. People do it all the time. Look around. Usually it's so they can build a bigger place, okay, but you could have done it and built a smaller one, if that's what you wanted."

"It was cheaper this way."

"Sure," Constance said. "Besides, Arthur's guys probably needed the work, him dead and all. Arsonists have to eat, too."

"You're kidding," Katherine said. "That's good, right? You're still going to live with me in the house I build because it's going to be terrific."

. . .

Gibby didn't talk about his work. Never had. Francis was similarly inclined. Had he been asked, he'd have said that as often as not, or more likely more often, guys who get pinched for doing something are guys who talk about it.

"Besides that," Gibby might have added, "what was it but a job?"

Together they had been doing that sort of job for some time. They had made a fire in a liquor store look like it started when somebody flipped a cigarette butt into the leaves that had blown up against the door. They had made a fire in a dry cleaning shop look like the kid hired to handle things while the owner was on holiday must have left something on in the back. Maybe a coffee pot. Some of what was left back there looked like it might have once been a coffee pot.

They were good at what they did, which is why they didn't lack for work, and why they were unsurprised to hear from Katherine Baladino after their previous employer had passed away quietly in his home, which was the same home Mrs. Baladino wanted them to burn down.

It was a job Gibby would not forget.

"It was her," he'd said to Francis after the first time they'd driven past Katherine Baladino's house to give the job a look.

"Who?"

"The girl on the beach," Gibby said.

At first Francis had no idea what he was talking about. When the hell had Gibby been to the beach?

"When I was a kid," Gibby said. "I told you about it. A hungover kid, lying in the sand, sand up my nose, my head like a brick. I told you."

"The woman who saved you."

"The girl," Gibby said. "She was just a girl. I was a kid. But, yeah."

"How'd you know? I mean, 'a long time' doesn't begin to say it, does it? Jesus, it had to be thirty years ago."

"It was her," Gibby said.

"Well, I hope to hell she didn't recognize you," Francis said.

Gibby didn't have to look in the rearview mirror to see how unlikely that would have been. "I was skinny then," he said.

"And you had more hair," Francis said. "But what about her? What are you telling me? She looked the same?"

"Not the same," Gibby said. "But good, you know? Enough the same. Like she takes care of herself."

He thought about that while Francis drove. How the years were more kind to some than they were to others. How the girl on the beach had gone one way, and how there she was, looking good. Unless it wasn't her. But it looked like it really could have been her. Should have been. And he remembered that one of her friends had called her Annie. "Annie, what are you doin' with that guy?" He wondered what would have happened if he'd remembered the name while they were driving by the woman, and if he'd said, "Stop!" And what if Francis had done that, stopped, and Gibby had called out.

"Annie!"

"What would have happened is she calls the cops."

Gibby could hear Francis saying it.

"He would have been right," Gibby thought. "You don't stop to talk to somebody when you're looking over a job, even if it's Annie."

It was strange being reminded of her, strange suddenly remembering her name . . . the sound of the friend yelling "Annie!" down the beach. Maybe the friend was worried about what she was doing. Gibby knew he hadn't looked good.

He thought about what might have brought her here—Annie. He didn't know anything more about her than that she'd hauled him into the surf and that then he was wet, dripping wet, and his headache was gone.

"Maybe she'd been headed to this neighborhood all along," he thought. "You see somebody on the beach, you don't know. Lotta people on the beach."

Then he thought about where he'd gone after the beach, and where he'd been.

"It's . . . I don't know," Francis said. "But she didn't recognize you, it's okay, whatever you think you saw. You don't want that, you know?"

"We go by in the car is all. She wasn't looking at the cars. Just walking along."

"So," Francis thought, "what you did was, you recognized her from the back." But he didn't say anything more until he said, "This place, I don't see any problem. Old house. Wood shingles. Gonna be a basement, prob'ly unfinished. Nobody's been down there in years, I bet. Steep steps. Who needs that? No light, or not much. Maybe a hanging bulb down the bottom. Who's checked the wiring for that? Lotta stuff lyin' around, nobody checked for mice, long as they stayed down the basement. Might be they came in, ate through somethin'. Lotta stuff can happen, you don't keep up with it."

Gibby was looking out the window.

"So no problem, right?"

"Right," Gibby said. He still wasn't looking at Francis.

"What you don't want to do, though, even if there's nothin' to worry about, you don't want to get distracted from what you're there for. You don't . . . the thing is, you want your mind on what you gotta do, even if it's somethin' you done lots of times before. You with me?"

"Right," Gibby said. "Sure."

Now he WAS looking at Francis, but he was still thinking about the beach. He was remembering the surprising strength of the girl who'd grabbed him by the arm and pulled him toward the water. He was remembering how he'd gone with her, coming up off the sand because she was hurting him, hurting his arm where it joined his shoulder, which had been dislocated more than once—coming up off the sand hurt. The world spun in the heat of the day and he thought he might puke. Then the girl was propelling him toward the foam that the small, quiet waves left on the beach, and he understood what she was doing, and he went along with it as well as his stumbling feet could. He half-ran over the foam and into the knee-deep surf, colder than he'd expected, and then he was down, pushed by her hand in the middle of his back, down under the shallow, lapping water, and then up again, shaking his head, which no longer hurt.

"And that was what she did," he said quietly. "What she gave me."

"What?"

"Nothing," Gibby said. "Nothing. You're right. Should be easy."

. . .

It was not only easy, it worked out better than they'd planned. Because the way they'd planned it, nobody was supposed to be home. Both Francis and Gibby were definite about that, always. Once they'd burned down a little sweatshop up a flight of stairs from a storefront where two brothers sold vegetables and fruit.

"Nobody up there at night, right?" Francis had said to the guy who wanted the building gone.

"Right," the guy had said.

"I see anybody up there, hear anybody, footsteps, anything like that, I walk away with the money you paid me already," Francis said.

"Nobody up there. The seamstresses, they clean up after themselves before they leave. Sweep up, empty the trash, whatever. Nobody cleaning up after hours. Place'll be empty."

If it hadn't been, Francis would have walked. And he and Gibby would have walked if they'd known Katherine Baladino had been upstairs on the night they burned down her house. But all the lights had been off. There hadn't been a sound in the place. The back door had been open, as she'd said it would be, and there had been no reason to suppose the boss's widow hadn't gone off somewhere, just as she'd said she'd do.

Afterward, though he'd been angry at himself at first for not making sure the house was empty, Francis had realized that it was only that Katherine Baladino was smarter than he was. Of course she'd stayed home. Who could have suspected her of burning down her house if she was in it, asleep in her nightgown, when the fire started?

"She's out of town somewhere, somebody might wonder how it happened to be that way," Francis said to himself. "Might be somebody asked that question, and then might be it got asked again, and who knows? She prob'ly figured, 'the hell with that. I'll be there. I won't tell Arthur's guys, because then they won't do the job. And I'll lose all sorts of things in the fire, stuff nobody'd want to lose.'"

Like Francis, Gibby felt it was a very good idea to stop short of killing people, though he'd sometimes nodded agreeably when people who didn't feel that way had told him about various people they had killed and explained why it was necessary.

"I didn't always agree with them," Gibby told Francis when the subject had come up one day. "It wasn't like that. But, you know, you're listening to a guy tell you why he did that, you're probably not gonna argue with him. I mean, knowing what you know about what he's done already, right?"

"Just so we're in agreement about this," Francis had said. He'd said that lots of times, beginning when he and Gibby started hiring out together, having discovered not only that their skills in the arson line complemented each other, but that neither of them wanted to be responsible for killing anybody who, either by design or bad luck, or for lack of a better place to sleep, happened to be curled up somewhere in a corner of a building Francis and Gibby had been employed to burn down.

"Imagine it," Francis had said. "Guy comes in out of the rain, needs some place to get his thoughts together, falls asleep in a pile of newspapers, maybe a floor above the one with the pile of newspapers we found when we were looking through the building the day before. Guy didn't crawl in there to die, did he? I don't want to have that happen, even if he's some old bastard past doing anybody any good, as far as anybody can tell. Who knows? Maybe he rallies?"

"But not if we kill him," Gibby sometimes said. "I'm with you."

Of such shared convictions are lasting partnerships made, or so it seemed to both of them.

"Also, there is the practical side, which any businessman must consider," Francis sometimes said. "Arthur Baladino was a businessman, certainly, and what we did was only a small part of his business, but it was a business, just the same."

"So he would agree . . ."

"What he would say, if he were here to say it, is that a fire in which somebody is fried, or a collection of somebodies, whether they're persons of some renown or guys nobody could identify as anything other than unlucky, a fire like that will draw attention. Sometimes a lot of attention, if somebody burns up and leaves around a curious relative or friend. And what Arthur knew, what he learned a long time ago, is that when you burn down a building, or do a lot of other things he was likely to do, it's better if there is less to investigate. When the building is the point, that's what you burn down, isn't it? Or we do. That's what they pay us for. Get people mixed up in it because they're in the building when we do what we're paid to do, that's the last thing Arthur or any businessman wants."

"Did you call him Arthur?"

"I did not."

"You called him Mr. Baladino."

"When I called him anything, yes."

"That's what I thought," Gibby said.

"Or sometimes, 'Sir,'" Francis said. "Now you know."

"Ah, it's all right," Gibby said. "You and me, we're still here, right?"

. . .

Now they sat, side by side, in the car Francis had had for too long, neither of them knowing what would be next, both of them wondering about it, each of them unlikely to say anything about how much they appreciated each other.

Then Gibby suddenly did say, "It's good you didn't laugh at me."

"When was that?" Francis asked. "I laughed at you lots of times, seems to me."

"But not when I told you about the beach," Gibby said. "I never told anybody else about it. About getting saved."

"Saved," Francis thought, but he didn't say anything. "I don't know from 'saved.'"

But he didn't say that. He didn't say anything. And he didn't laugh.

"Because," he thought, "I have laughed at him. I have laughed at him over and over, and he knows it as well as I do, and here he is, still. Because I did something right when he told me about the girl on the beach, which is something he can't leave alone, or it can't leave him alone, which, they are maybe the same thing, and it must have been a wonderful thing at that. That's what it will remain, until somebody laughs in his face and tells him he's an idiot, and who does he have could do that to him but me?"

Francis knew the answer to that was nobody. Nobody else could do it, because there was nobody else connected to Gibby by time and proximity and shared experience by which either of them could have put the other one in prison for a long time.

"It seems like forever," Francis thought, though it wasn't. Francis had not known Gibby when Gibby was a skinny kid on the beach who'd been included in the trip to the shore to somebody's parents' place that was empty. Maybe they'd taken Gibby along for a joke. Maybe they were all jocks and they were going to kick sand in his face when they got to the beach, and he beat them to it with that hangover that had him head down in the sand and hoping to die.

"Because that's what he must have been," Francis thought. "The kind of pimply guy nobody wanted along unless it was to laugh at him to remind themselves of what they were and what he wasn't.

"And when, half-asleep, or maybe all the way, Gibby, skinny and sick, had told one of the bigger, stronger boys to fuck off, there had been that. And then there had been the rescue by the girl on the beach who'd assumed, in the years that followed, wings and a halo, though Gibby hadn't actually mentioned them.

"And I didn't laugh when he told me about her the first time, about what she did. And I haven't laughed since. Haven't told him to stop. I've been a friend, I guess. I haven't fouled that up. Maybe I won't."

TIME'S GIFT

It was the house Katherine had promised it would be. She'd directed the developer to cut down the fir trees that had shaded the old house from the sun. Sometimes the old house had looked as if somebody was hiding in it. The house Katherine and Constance had built welcomed the light.

The neighbors commented on that, of course. They also commented on the size of the place. It was smaller than the house that had burned down. Given the opportunity to build, who went with something smaller?

That was one of the things that struck Gibby when he drove by the house, which he had not told Francis he was going to do when he asked if he could borrow the car, because certainly Francis would have told him that what you don't want to do after you burn down a house is to go back to see what's been built on the lot that was a heap of smoking rubble, last you knew about it.

"They call it 'returning to the scene of the crime,'" is what Francis would have said, "and you don't do that unless you are in a TV show about a criminal so dumb that he does that so he can get caught."

Gibby figured that since nobody had established that there had BEEN a crime on the premises, he was maybe not returning to the scene of one, even if he knew he was.

"That is only because we are good at what we do," Francis would have said if Gibby had offered him that argument. "But probably we're not perfect, and why there's nobody still sniffing around that burned down house is for several reasons, and only one of them is that the house isn't there anymore. Another is that we're good at what we do, like I said, and then there's the matter of life going on, and it no doubt provides the police and all those connected with them with lots of other things to worry about and to try and figure out, so that whatever they might think about that house that isn't there anymore, it's something that's becoming less important to them every time somebody knocks over a liquor store or shoots his neighbor or drops a suitcase full of drugs off the carousel in the airport, and it pops open to scatter medications all over the floor. But that is no reason for you to get a flat tire or a dead battery across the street from the house that now stands where the other once stood, because you would likely be asked by somebody who are you and what are you doing there, and from those questions it's a short road to your known associates, which, one of them, is me."

But Gibby asked for the car anyway, and Francis let him have it, and though Gibby was impressed by the new house and thought it must be a fine place to live, especially if you liked glass and a lot of sunshine in your home, he was not in the neighborhood to admire the place where Katherine and Constance were now living, and out of which Constance was conducting more business than she could have imagined.

"I think I've become something of a celebrity," she said to Katherine one night as they were eating dinner.

"How so?" Katherine asked, although she knew.

"I'm getting more clients than I can handle."

"That's good, right?"

"Sure. But maybe 'clients' isn't the right word. Some of them—the people who call—it's like they just want to see me. Or see this place, is more like it. They come here, and they're looking at what you've built—"

"You and I," Katherine said.

"Okay," Constance said, "but maybe they're thinking about selling a house or maybe they're not. Anyway, they're looking around this one. Some of them, that's maybe all they're doing."

"Can't blame them," Katherine said. "It's a nice house, isn't it? Tell them it's not for sale."

None of that was Gibby's business. He was in the neighborhood because he had been thinking about what he'd seen there when he and Francis had driven through it in order to look at the house that had stood on the same land that the new house now occupied, land that became available because Francis and Gibby had made it available.

"It was her," Gibby had said that day, and though at first Francis hadn't known what Gibby was talking about, he'd soon learned. He had made the obvious objection. That day on the beach in New Jersey, Gibby had been a skinny, hungover kid squinting into the summer sun. Probably had sand in his eyes, too. How did he know what he'd seen? Then there was time. Time beat the hell out of everybody.

"You go to a funeral for a guy who was eighty-five when he died. They got a photograph on the casket, picture of him when he was in the army, he was twenty-two. Looks great in uniform. You get it?"

Gibby drove slowly along the streets nearest to the one where stood the house Katherine Baladino had built. It was a warm enough day so that Annie Blake, who had been Annie Gonzales, might have been out on the porch in front of one of the houses. Or she might have been walking with a friend.

He might have had the opportunity to see her again.

"Then what?" he thought.

The insolent "beep" of the horn of the silver SUV behind him startled Gibby. He pulled over to the curb of the narrow road and stopped. The SUV, full of kids, slid by him. A large, red rubber raft tied to the top of the car bumped up and down under its ropes. A little boy leaned from his window and stuck his tongue out at Gibby.

For a moment more he stayed where he was, realizing quietly that where he was was not where he had been.

Libby saw the car pull slowly away from the curb. She'd been watching it since she'd overheard her mother ask her father what he thought the guy in the car was doing just sitting out there.

"I think I've seen that car in the neighborhood before," Libby's mother had said.

"It's not familiar to me," her father had said.

"You're not here all day," her mother had said.

"No," her father had said. "There's that for which to be thankful."

"But what do you suppose he's doing, just sitting out there?" her mother had said.

"Nothing," Libby said to herself, as Gibby drove slowly away.

She stayed at the window. After a while, Corkie and her owner came around the corner. Dog and man both walked with their heads down. They'd covered the same ground thousands of times, but it looked to Libby as if Corkie was still finding fascinating new things to smell. The dog snuffled and shook her head, then plunged her nose back into whatever it was she'd discovered. The man stood patiently by. He didn't look as if he had anywhere special to go.

Suddenly Corkie rolled over and began stretching and rubbing her back against the grass. She kicked her legs in all directions as she rocked from one side to the other, groaning happily.

Libby laughed loudly enough to attract the attention of the man walking Corkie. He smiled up at her, looked down at the happily writhing dog, then up again at Libby.

"World's oldest puppy," he said.

"She looks happy," Libby said.

"She does, doesn't she?" the man said. He was still smiling. "What about you?" he said. "Are you happy? I hope so."

Libby shrugged.

The dog jumped up, like she knew she'd done her job. She started trotting purposefully across the street, the man at her heels.

"Have a good day," Libby shouted.

"That's what I'll try to do," the man said. "You, too."

Now, as he followed the sniffing dog, the man's head was down. Again he was looking at the ground. But for a moment he'd looked up.

About the Author

For 25 years, Bill Littlefield hosted and wrote for NPR's weekly sports magazine program, *Only A Game*, which he helped to create in 1993. His commentaries enlivened *Morning Edition* and appeared in *The Boston Globe* and various other papers and magazines. Littlefield is the author of seven books, including two novels, *Prospect* (Houghton Mifflin) and *The Circus in the Woods* (Houghton Mifflin.) He was a professor in the English Department at Curry College for 39 years. He is currently working with the Emerson Prison Initiative to help incarcerated men earn college degrees.

Note from the Author

Word-of-mouth is crucial for any author to succeed. If you enjoyed *Mercy*, please leave a review online—anywhere you are able. Even if it's just a sentence or two. It would make all the difference and would be very much appreciated.

Thanks!
Bill Littlefield

We hope you enjoyed reading this title from:

www.blackrosewriting.com

Subscribe to our mailing list – *The Rosevine* – and receive **FREE** books, daily deals, and stay current with news about upcoming releases and our hottest authors.
Scan the QR code below to sign up.

Already a subscriber? Please accept a sincere thank you for being a fan of Black Rose Writing authors.

View other Black Rose Writing titles at www.blackrosewriting.com/books and use promo code **PRINT** to receive a **20% discount** when purchasing.

Made in the USA
Monee, IL
04 August 2022